Praise for
The Tension of a Coming Storm

"The glimpses of the worlds Ludens' characters inhabit have an extra dimension to them beyond many I have seen in contemporary horror fiction. It's like standing in front of a mirror. You see yourself and what's behind you if you stand directly in front of the glass. If you move in closer and look to each side or up or down, you see the rest of the room even though it is *not* in front of the glass. It's that extra dimension, the peripheral world in which the narrative at hand exists, that Ludens so skillfully implies, that sets these tales apart...

"*The Tension of a Coming Storm* deserves its place on the bookshelves of any true lover of weird fiction. The writing is sensual and tactile, and stylistically brilliant. The characters are complex and extremely well-drawn. Do not miss this book and make sure to not miss future volumes inscribed: *By Adrian Ludens.*"

- John S. McFarland,
Author of the dark stories from Ste. Odile, including *The Dark Walk Forward*, *The Black Garden*, and *The Mother of Centuries*

"One of the great triumphs of this book is how it explores non-traditional monsters. Yes, the human beast is still the most terrifying creature of all, but Mr. Ludens succeeds in reaching outside of the established tropes and expectations to conjure up some truly original beasties.

"Of course, horror stories largely serve to both magnify and evaluate the human condition in a frequently gory fashion. That holds true here as well, but the ways in which he goes about it are novel and refreshing. Plus, I honestly cannot recall reading another single-author collection featuring this much diversity. Third-person POV, first-person, speculative tales, revenge thrillers, run-ins with historical figures, and even transcripts from an ill-fated Apollo moon landing... *The Tension of a Coming Storm* is a veritable smorgasbord of options and offerings."

~ Jack Wells,
Reviewer and Author of *Monochrome Noir*

"'The worst monsters are people' is a phrase that gets thrown around a lot. It's not one I can fully agree with. Bring that phrase back around when you find a person with a face full of tentacles and the ability to drive someone to madness by invading their dreams. The reality is that people can be their own special class of awful, without relying on the absolving title of 'monster.' Monsters are who they are because that's how they were created, while people have choices.

"Coincidentally, that brings us along to a review of *The Tension of a Coming Storm* by Adrian Ludens. It's a collection of horror short stories, mainly about people. Although there are some monsters thrown in too...

"All of these are horror stories, but they demonstrate that, at their core, they're about people. I find a lot of the Brothers Grimm reflected in them. This is a book that could be taken camping, and brought out around the fire to read out loud while the s'mores digest, eyeing the other people around the camp fire, suspiciously."

~ Carl R. Jennings, Reviewer for *Phantasmagoria Magazine* and Author of *Just About Anyone*

"Adrian Ludens' *The Tension of A Coming Storm* is a smorgasbord of dark delights. The stories in this collection cover the entire spectrum of speculative fiction: from Poe-esque pastiche to space horror. You will travel to far-off places and meet some unique characters, from a would-be killer ending up in a very strange jail to a girl who could move mountains. You will visit a circus and a spaceship. You will peek into the household of a very dysfunctional family. But most of all, you will be totally enchanted. Ludens' collection is a must for every horror fan. Beautifully written and highly imaginative, it is a celebration of the art of storytelling not to be missed."

~ Elana Gomel, Author of *The Hungry Ones* and *The Cryptids*

THE TENSION OF A COMING STORM

A Strange and Speculative Collection by

ADRIAN LUDENS

From

Dark Owl Publishing, LLC

Arizona

ISBN 978-1-951716-27-1

Cover art by Greg Chapman
dark-designs.com

Author photographs by
Russ Hadden

Visit us on our website at:
www.darkowlpublishing.com

ALSO FROM DARK OWL PUBLISHING

Collections

The Dark Walk Forward
A harrowing collection of frightful stories from John S. McFarland

The Last Star Warden:
Tales of Adventure and Mystery from Frontier Space, Volume I
Sci-fi pulp fiction at its finest by Jason J. McCuiston

The Last Star Warden Volume II:
The Un Quan Saga
More chronicles of the Warden by Jason J. McCuiston

No Lesser Angels, No Greater Devils
Beautiful and haunting stories from Laura J. Campbell

Anthologies

A Celebration of Storytelling
The anthological festival of tales

Something Wicked This Way Rides
Where genre fiction meets the Wild West

Novels

The Keeper of Tales
An epic fantasy adventure by Jonathon Mast

Just About Anyone
High fantasy comedy from the twisted mind of Carl R. Jennings

The Black Garden
The beginning of the dark mysteries within the town of Ste. Odile
by John S. McFarland

The Mother of Centuries
The continuation of the dark gothic story that began in
The Black Garden by John S. McFarland
Coming October 2022

The Malakiad
A hilarious mythological misadventure by Gustavo Bondoni

Carnivore Keepers
Sci-fi adventure where humans and dinosaurs collide
by Kevin M. Folliard

The Wicked Twisted Road
A gritty grindhouse sci-fi thriller
by D.S. Hamilton

Young Readers
Annette: A Big Hairy Mom
A touching story of a boy and his motherly friend, a Sasquatch
Written and illustrated by John S. McFarland
Coming October 2022

Grayson North, Frost-Keeper of the Windy City
A totally cool urban fantasy adventure by Kevin M. Folliard

Shivers, Scares, and Goosebumps
Short tales to chill you to your bones
Written and illustrated by Vonnie Winslow Crist

Available on Vella
The Last Star Warden: The Phantom World
Eight episodes of nail-biting sci-fi action from Jason J. McCuiston

Buy the books for Kindle and in paperback
www.darkowlpublishing.com

More titles are planned for 2022 and beyond!

For Lizzy, with love.

TABLE OF CONTENTS

Inside a Refrigerator 1

Calliope 12

Reynolds' Tale 27

Aiding and Abetting 36

The Value of a Dollar 46

The Monster's Leather Apron 57

Blind Faith 70

Wendigo, Going, Gone 86

Animate Objects 94

Behind His Smile 105

A Frozen Moment 114

N.O.A.H.'s Voyage (A Future Fable) 123

Try to Remember 129

Pest Control for Dummies 139

The Masks You Wear.. 155

Pitchover 158

Hollow.. 167

Time to Say Goodbye..171

The Trunk in the Junk Room...180

The Runner, Stranded...184

About the Author 202

INSIDE A REFRIGERATOR

I am ashamed of what I have done. I am remorseful for the actions I have taken. It is important to convey that upfront. Sitting here now and reflecting, I wish I could hit a cosmic reset. That kid, Darren, did not deserve what happened—what I did. He was innocent. But then again, that was why I chose him.

I'm not a horrible person. I work hard. I do my best. I live paycheck to paycheck, and I guess what happened pushed me into doing something I would have never considered under normal circumstances.

Darren's dad and I were colleagues, even friends. Or so I thought. We said we'd stand together in solidarity against the out-of-state company who'd bought our newspaper. Jeff and I raised our glasses and toasted the merits of independent reporting and journalistic integrity. In less than a month, Jeff had a new office and a promotion. My friend became my editor and supervisor. A paltry two weeks later, he fired me. Jeff offered a strained smile and a few empty platitudes, but I knew he'd barely hesitated before sacrificing me to the corporate gods of downsizing.

I packed the personal items scattered around my cubicle into a cardboard box and relocated the carton to the back seat of my salt-rusted sedan. I drove out of the Employees Only parking lot with bitter bile roiling like magma in my throat. I stifled the eruption and aimed my vehicle toward the suburb where Jeff and his family lived.

I'd been there before in happier, more optimistic times. We'd hung out, cracked open a few beers, played an amateurish game of pool, and commiserated. Funny how the events of four months ago now seem like ancient history.

When I slid my car up to the curb, fortune smiled upon me. I found both of Jeff's kids bundled up and playing in the snow-covered front yard. Looked like a scene from one of those feel-good holiday movies you find on cable. I vowed to scar this family, make Christmas a time of mourning.

Darren's sister, a pale, elfin girl named Lily, recognized me first. "Uncle Brian!"

I let myself in the front gate and grinned at each of the kids in turn. "Hi guys! Your dad wanted me to tell you to get ready to go out for pizza as soon as he gets home from work." The kids' faces lit with excitement. "Lily, run inside and tell your mom, okay?" Lily didn't think twice. She raced into the house.

A voice in my brain screamed at me to get in my car and drive away. I ignored it. Instead, I scooped up Darren and loaded him into the back seat.

We chased the headlights out of the city while the lies tumbled from my mouth.

***

We arrived at the abandoned structure just after dusk. It hid from view behind a stand of overgrown trees just off the highway, fifteen miles north of the suburb we'd left behind us. I'd been here before and explored the building several times, in fact. What had once been a roadside tourist attraction had also served as a residence for the onsite caretaker. When the business failed, he'd moved on to parts unknown, abandoning what possessions he couldn't load. Pickers had taken the best items, and vandals had destroyed the rest, but something I remembered seeing in the cellar during my last visit drew me onward.

Snow had begun to fall, and a breeze swirled the moonlit flakes around the towering evergreens like fairy dust. I parked and pawed through the personal items in the box in the back seat until I found an item I could use to my advantage.

"Darren, remember when I first picked you up, I said I was taking you to meet Santa?"

The boy nodded, but I could see in his eyes that the unexpected drive had rattled him. He still had not decided between fear or trust.

"It was a long car ride, wasn't it? But we're here. We are at Santa's Workshop at the North Pole."

Darren knelt on the seat and gazed at the shambling, darkened structure before us. "It doesn't look like Santa's Workshop."

"Of course not! It's disguised by magic, so people won't know." I twitched a photograph I'd removed from the box between two fingers, attracting the boy's notice. "Aren't you curious why you get to meet Santa early?"

He nodded, still wavering between curiosity and mistrust.

"It's because me and your dad both work for Santa." I flipped over the photograph, and Darren's mouth fell open in guileless amazement. I knew I had him. The snapshot, taken at last year's staff Christmas party, showed Jeff and I decked out in ridiculous red and green elf hats, complete with plastic pointed ears glued to the sides. To a four-year-old kid, it was indisputable proof. His father and I both grinned for the camera, our drinks just out of frame.

"Lily didn't get to come because she hasn't been as good as you have," I confided. "That's why it had to be a secret surprise."

Darren nodded. He'd composed his features to match the solemn honor of the occasion, but his eyes danced with excitement.

"Santa has lots of secrets. The elves are making all kinds of new toys for good boys and girls, but you don't get to see any of those, okay? You only get to meet Santa and tell him what you'd like for Christmas."

I got out from behind the wheel, walked around the rear of my car, and unlocked the trunk. I rummaged around until I found a cheap plastic flashlight that was part of my half-assed survival kit. I pressed the thumb switch and found the beam of light serviceable. I slammed the trunk and approached Darren's passenger-side door. I paused, contemplating the desolate road over the roof of my car. I could still walk away. I could return the boy to his home, use the journey back to fabricate an excuse for taking him.

The bitter wind hissed its derision at my indecisiveness, and the snow-laden branches of the trees shook with laughter at my weakness. I pressed my lips together and threw open the car door. "Since there are certain things inside Santa's Workshop that you aren't allowed to see, we're going to do something silly, okay buddy?"

Darren's lips upturned in a shy smile.

"We're going to take your coat off super quick and put it right back on again backwards!"

"Why?"

"Because your coat has a hood. We'll put your hood up as a blindfold so I can carry you in past all the elves until we get to Santa's special meeting room."

Darren let me unzip his puffy parka, and I had it reversed and his face covered in all of fifteen seconds. I lifted him into my arms, and we crunched through the freshly fallen snow toward the back of the old house, where I knew a busted door would allow us entrance.

***

I don't understand Jeff's betrayal. It felt so spiteful and unnecessary. Sitting here now, stiff and uncomfortable, I keep pondering his actions, turning them over in my mind. I keep examining the situation from all angles, trying to find the reason. Professional jealousy? Did he fear accusations of nepotism? Am I a slipshod journalist?

Jeff wasn't content with the promotion and the raise. He'd climbed a rung or two up the ladder and still felt the need to stomp on my fingers, to kick me off the ladder entirely. It was so damned sudden, so malicious.

Two could play that game. I would show him "sudden." I would show him "malicious." That's what I thought at the beginning of all this.

Now, I'm not sure what I did or didn't do.

***

Carrying Darren in my arms, we made our way through the accumulating snow toward the back of the ramshackle structure. Each footstep caused a muffled crunch as I eased around the edge of the house. I could hear the wind blowing through the trees; unknown animal tracks zigzagged across the snow. I stumbled in a deep drift left over from a previous storm.

At last, we reached the rear entrance. My breath came in ragged gasps. The rotting wooden door hung from one hinge. Ice melt and drifted snow turned the three descending steps into an invitation to break a leg. I lowered Darren down, took his hand, and led the way. "Watch your step, buddy," I cautioned. I turned on the flashlight app on my phone. I had other plans for the flashlight.

I ignored the stairs that led to the main level and guided the boy left, past a rusting washing machine, dryer, and two deep basin sinks. I pushed open the creaking door below the stairwell into what had once been a workshop and storage area. I shone the light along the floor, now covered in a thick carpet of scattered pinecone scales—the nest of something I hoped was deep in slumber. I noticed an old-fashioned grade school desk. Rusty tools used by the long-departed caretaker hung like bloody crucifixes on the concrete walls of the foundation. Wooden shelves leaned beneath the weight of gift shop fossils, petrified wood, minerals, and faux gemstones. A machine used for sharpening blades sat on an oblong countertop; the rusted blades hung like macabre trophies above it on the wall.

Among the jumbled detritus, I saw several straight-backed wooden chairs encased in cobwebs, leaning stacks of dust-covered boxes, bundles of moldering newspapers, and a high wooden cabinet. Coffee cans and glass jars filled with nails, screws, washers, and other workshop miscellanea filled the shelves.

Beside me, Darren's breathing came fast. Whether from walking or excitement, I couldn't say. Maybe it was just hard to breathe through the backward-facing hood.

We took another left, ducking through a door beside the wooden cabinet, and moved deeper beneath the building into a sunken, T-shaped root cellar. We passed burlap bags of rotten potatoes and onions. Jars of seeds and of homemade canned vegetables lined dust-caked shelves. I saw beets, asparagus, and other produce I could not identify floating in cloudy yellow fluid.

The path was so narrow I had to steer the boy ahead of me. We passed canned goods, a dark brown pelt that may have come from a bear, and a cardboard box, white and rotten with mold. I shined my phone's light and relayed verbal warnings. We stepped over broken jars of stewed tomatoes—now black and desiccated—dried hawthorn, and a spilled profusion of empty prescription pill bottles.

Someone had stacked chopped wood on a second set of stairs at the end of the walkway, completely blocking that egress. Rather than proceed farther, we turned right, into the heart of the cellar's maze. Here I would wall in my Fortunato-by-proxy. No catacombs or stones this time. The boy and I stood before a 1960s vintage Tru-Cold refrigerator.

"Step back, okay?" I steered Darren a few feet out of my way. "Santa has a special area where he will meet you, kind of like in the mall, but the one in the mall is just pretend." I raised my voice while I worked. I had opened the door and removed the wire shelving, placing it on the scat-covered concrete floor.

"Remember, don't make a peep." I guided Darren toward the refrigerator. "Climb up one step." He did so, hands outstretched, feeling the sides of the interior.

"Okay, buddy, now sit down." The boy sat with his legs crossed.

"When do I get to meet Santa?" He hadn't spoken for so long his muffled words startled me.

"Soon," I said. "Here, hang onto this." I placed the bulky flashlight from my trunk into the boy's hand. The air felt dank and oppressive. Using the light from my phone, I tore the Christmas party photo in half and pressed the piece containing his father's image into Darren's other hand. I noticed my own face in the other half of the photograph. My image seemed to be imploring me to stop this madness. But, I realized, that was the old me, a previous, inferior incarnation—his knowledge of the situation was incomplete by default.

I knelt beside the shivering child. "This is a magic portal. I need to close the door, but don't be scared. When the door opens, you'll be able to meet Santa, okay?"

"Okay." The hand holding the picture of Jeff shook. I rose and closed the refrigerator door. The old-fashioned handle latched.

Darren lasted ten seconds—the time it took for him to put his hood down and turn on the flashlight—before he started yelling.

The boy pounded on the inside of the fridge. "Let me *out*!" he screamed.

"Darren!" I shouted. "*Darren!*"

The noise stopped for the moment.

"If you feel scared, just look at the photo of your dad. Okay, buddy? If you be good, he'll be there to open the door for you."

I felt a cruel thrill at providing him with false hope. I wondered how soon before his hope crumbled, how soon until he panicked, and claustrophobia had him screaming again. I speculated over how long he could last in there without air circulation. Perhaps I could adjust the fridge just enough to crack the door and allow a little airflow; then I could string him along and torment him into tears. I'd build him up again with reassurances, rekindle his hope, and douse it. Maybe he'd wet his pants when he couldn't hold his bladder any longer, and I would scold him for it. My mind raced with the possibilities.

I could just leave him, alone and afraid, until he suffocated. If I gave him some air, perhaps he'd die of dehydration. Undoubtedly, the ordeal would drive the boy insane first. Part of me relished the idea, wanted to be there for every moment of the boy's suffering. Another part of me wanted nothing more of this, wanted to flee as if waking from a nightmare.

Perhaps some fresh air and a chance to collect my thoughts

would help me decide my course of action. I rose and crunched through broken glass and discarded pill bottles. Inside the refrigerator, Darren started to sob, then to scream.

I moved along the passage and turned left. Jars of peaches and beets lined one shelf. A dark brown pelt sat on another. This seemed like familiar territory, but at the end of the passage, shelves barred my path. Before me, jars of seeds, dried hawthorn, and pickled asparagus lined the shelves. I looked over my shoulder. At the far end of the walkway, split logs were piled up on the steps. This had to be the right way.

I reached out, shoved the jars aside. A bottle of stewed tomatoes fell to the concrete and exploded like a shot. I jumped back a step. The light from my phone caught the mess of shattered glass and blackened vegetables while behind me, Darren had started pounding on the confines of his makeshift tomb. I looked again at the shelves in front of me and at the wall behind them. I reached out, rapped on the surface. I expected wood, a closed door, perhaps, but the wall behind the shelves was solid concrete. I'd turned myself around. I just needed to go back to the refrigerator and get my bearings.

I spun around and followed the light from my phone's flashlight to the piles of stacked firewood. In an attempt to expose the second door, I grabbed three chunks of wood and tossed them over my shoulder one by one. My phone's light diminished markedly. I paused to check the battery and saw I'd hit fifteen percent. A quick glance showed me I was not in cell tower range. I shoved the phone into a gap in the firewood and squinted. I was confronted by another concrete foundation wall.

I muttered a few curses, turned and retraced my steps, then my breath hitched in my throat: two pieces of firewood lay ahead of me. *Two*, I realized, not three. I did my best to ignore Darren's terrified cries as I passed the refrigerator and tried to rationalize the missing piece of wood. I used my flashlight to examine my surroundings. More jars of canned vegetables sat on the shelves to my left, definitely no longer safe to eat. As I watched, something in one of the jars shifted. I flinched before realizing it had to be dust motes floating in the air in front of the jar, causing the illusion.

The flashlight app on my phone shut down. I slid my thumb on the screen, and it illuminated, albeit dimly. My battery sat at eight percent.

I turned again, glancing at a cardboard box covered in frostlike white mold that should have been around the corner, ten feet away. My phone's screen faded, leaving me in darkness. I stood still, trying to get my bearings. That's when I noticed the silence.

"Darren?" My blood seemed to pound against my eardrums with each heartbeat. I strained my eyes to no avail; no light penetrated the bowels of the basement. I needed the flashlight.

"Hey, buddy? Knock on the side so I can hear you."

A tapping came in response, ahead and to my left. My feet crunched broken glass as I shuffled forward. The sound stopped. "Keep knocking. I'll open the door and let you out of there."

The tapping resumed. I realized I'd overshot my mark. The tapping now came from behind me—and to the right. I started to turn but stopped. I forced myself to remain calm and use logic to solve my predicament. "Darren, I need you to holler, okay? If you keep calling my name and knocking on the wall of your special room, I'll come let you out, okay?"

"I'm here, Uncle Brian!"

The voice and the tapping overlapped and echoed from every direction in the concrete maze. I reached out with both hands and felt my way along the passage, doing my best to ignore how my skin crawled every time my fingers encountered something unsavory or unexpected. After what seemed like much longer than it should have taken, I relocated the refrigerator. At my touch, the cries and tapping fell silent.

I'd decided if the boy had fainted, I would take the flashlight, close the door, and be on my way. I had no desire to remain any longer.

I opened the door, and something rolled out and fell onto my foot. I fought the impulse to kick it. If it was the flashlight, I didn't like my chances of finding the damned thing in the dark. I crouched and felt the hard plastic casing. With a relieved sigh, I stood and clicked the flashlight's switch. A bright beam of light stabbed the darkness, and I recoiled, blinded for a moment. I pointed the beam at the floor and let my eyes adjust. The shadowy interior of the refrigerator arrested my attention. I lifted the beam.

Darren wasn't inside.

For half a minute, I just stood there staring into the boy's would-be tomb, now miraculously vacant.

I took a deep breath and held it. Nothing changed. I kept silent, hoping he would make a sound, betray his location. I stepped around the appliance and shined my light down all three walkways. No sign of the boy. I returned to the refrigerator, knelt, and felt the interior with my fingers, tapping and shining the flashlight's beam. Could there have been a false back, some Houdini-like explanation for the boy's seeming disappearance? I found none. Rising, I aimed my light down all four passageways.

My hand shook. There should have been three corridors. I looked again down four passageways, at four dead ends. Now, even the woodpile was gone. My mind was playing tricks. I decided my own guilty conscience had caused my confusion. The way out had to be right in front of me.

I explored this idea further, following the thread of logic to see where it led. Darren was not here. Maybe he never had been. What did I have as evidence to prove his physical presence? Perhaps I'd left him in the car, or maybe I hadn't abducted him at all. Possibly I'd just imagined it, had a psychotic break that allowed me to release my pent-up rage. With this realization came a liberating sense of relief.

If my theory was true, it seemed only rational that I should also now be able to find the door and make my escape. As I turned, the flickering beam of my flashlight fell on the torn photograph taken at the Christmas party. It had dropped out of the fridge and lay face down under the toe of my shoe. I crouched, picked it up, and turned it over.

The fading light revealed Jeff's grinning face. He seemed to be laughing at me. My flashlight's beam faded to nothing.

The blackness disoriented me. I couldn't even detect the motion of my own hand in front of my face. Something touched my back, and I instinctively recoiled, arching forward and away. My fingertips found the bottom of the now-empty refrigerator. I felt reapplied pressure on my back; a small pair of hands shoved me forward. As I floundered against the force of this push into the unyielding confines of the antique appliance, something hard struck the back of my head. False bursts of light illuminated my vision, and throbbing pain followed. My arms and legs felt numb and heavy. Hands shoved me forward into the painted steel interior of the antique appliance.

Before I could protest or react, the hands fell away, and I heard the door of the Tru-Cold's old-fashioned handle latch close with a subdued, yet horrible, click.

***

Now I am inside what I had intended to be Darren's tomb. My knees are shoved up under my chin, and my tailbone aches, but I refuse to give up hope.

I do not pretend to understand what happened. How much of this have I imagined? Is Darren in the basement, waiting for me to beg for my release? Did I leave him upstairs in the car, freezing but unharmed? Is he still safe at home?

Or did Jeff follow my car to his house and then pursue me to the abandoned basement?

Tiny bursts of light sparkle across my field of vision. My pulse is racing, and it's hard to breathe. I feel dizzy. I want to take it back, to behave differently. I am not a killer, nor do I deserve to die. If Darren got out of here, maybe I can too.

But what if I can't?

I am inside a refrigerator in the cellar of an abandoned building fifteen miles from town. My flashlight battery is dead, and it is so very dark. I will not give up hope. Someone will find me.

Eventually.

CALLIOPE

While scoping out another in an endless procession of small Midwestern cities and posting bills announcing the upcoming show, Calli encountered a kindred spirit. She glanced at his misshapen, claw-like hands as they clutched at the air.

"It's all gone wrong," he said.

"What has?"

"Everything." His eyes held a sorrowful, faraway look.

He had gone all out, she observed; part Lobster Boy, part Wolf Man, part Tattooed Lady. It seems to her too much—and yet, somehow, not enough.

"Not finding work?" she asked.

"Of course not." He made another snatch at the air, perhaps trying to pluck memories of happier times. "Half want to prevent anyone from seeing the likes of us and the other half don't care to see us in the first place."

Calli tipped her head back, gazing skyward, in a modified sword-swallowing pose. "It's the politically-correct versus the ambivalent. Two warring factions and neither want us to exist."

The tattooed lobster wolf nodded. "And we're the innocent casualties."

Calli looked down, assessed him again. His visible tattoos all seemed to be admirable copies of notable pre-Raphaelite paintings. He had filed his canine incisors in a successful attempt at appearing more wolf-like. His spilling cleavage drew her attention next and she wondered what hormone cocktail he took to grow both facial hair and breasts.

She flashed one of the show bills like a badge. "We're setting up now. Would you like to come back to the lot with me? See if the Baron will hire you?"

He examined his glittering platform boots for a moment, shook his head, and then turned to leave.

"Hey, what do you call yourself?" Calli asked.

His gleaming eyes peered at her from behind stray locks of his scruffy mane. Misshapen hands plucked another memory from the air. Perhaps he wanted to save their brief interaction for future consideration. He spun on a sparkling heel and threw the words over his shoulder:

"I'm Average Joe."

Calli stood alone.

By ones and twos, her classmates had piled into waiting cars and disappeared down the sleepy town's residential streets until none remained but her. Her parents had forgotten her. Again. She waited, though in her heart Calli knew she'd have to walk if she wanted to be home before dark. She scuffed the toe of her one-size-too-small black Mary Jane into the gravel and gazed around the empty playground. No breeze ruffled her hair; even nature itself had forgotten Calli, had left her alone. She counted to twenty, then fifty, then one hundred. She sighed and began to trudge across the playground in the direction of home. As she passed the vacant swings, an idea came, and she altered her course.

Calli returned to her living quarters, a private trailer parked in a field near the outskirts of town with the rest of the Baron Backroad's Freewheeling Circus of Wonders entourage. The Baron, she knew, had left to visit the city administration building to fill out paperwork for the right to perform. This was, in her opinion, yet another nondescript city, bereft of joy and imagination, another stagnant pool of sameness, where even the red tape was gray.

The condition seemed to be catching, infecting her circus brethren. Her husband, Daredevil Dave, lay sprawled, silent, and immobile. Comatose without the added feature of hospital equipment chirping a notification for every one hundred dollars spent. *Dead, but not dressed for the occasion, she realized.* He hadn't spoken or eaten in days.

Calli perched on the edge of the bed and considered her husband, curled in a sweaty tangle beneath a dirty sheet. His skin had turned, like that of so many others, to gray. A drowned rat rolled in flour. Perhaps his thoughts were gray as well. He had lost his sense of wonder. It pained her to see him reduced in this way. He was supposed to be the strong one, the rock. Instead, she felt weary and drained after a few minutes in his presence.

"Calli." Her husband's vocal cords were dried cornhusks, hinting at the word rather than speaking it.

She bent closer. "You're awake."

Dave said nothing.

"I posted all the bills I had with me, even got a few shops to put posters in their display windows. I'll go back with more later tonight. I just wanted to check on you." In truth, the need to leave the gray city and return to the reassuring comfort of the colorful entourage had become unbearable.

An idea came to her. "You won't believe how excited everyone is for the show! You should see all the lot lice standing around, watching the tent go up! No need to paper the house this time; ticket sales will be through the roof!"

All lies, but she watched a small degree of color seep into her husband's cheeks.

"Feel better soon, hon." She patted his leg. "The circus needs you and misses you. I need you and miss you."

That time she'd spoken the truth.

"Calliope Jean Jenkins! Get over here!"

No apology, no explanation, only annoyance expressed that her daughter had inconvenienced her by not walking home. Calliope tracked her mother's progress across the playground from the giddy arc of her swing. She'd enticed the wind to return; it playfully whipped at her hair with each forward and backward flight. Never before had she reached such heights.

"Calliope, get down from there! You hear me?" Her mother, hands on hips to express her irritation, loomed and receded. Calliope's mother turned her head to check on the rusty family sedan still running at the curb, as if worried someone would take it for a joyride while her back was turned. Calliope let her head drop back and pointed her toes at the sky.

"I won't say it again!" her mother's voice cut the air. "Get... down... NOW."

Calliope let go of the chains. For one heart-stopping moment, she soared. Before gravity reasserted its authority, Calliope glimpsed her mother. Her jaw had dropped open in amazement, arms clutching the air, eyes riveted on the spectacle unfolding.

Then Calliope plunged. The shock of impact and the grinding pain rose up and tore through her broken ankle and shinbone. She didn't mind. Her mother had finally given Calliope her undivided attention.

Calli allowed her mounting frustration to get the better of her and she threatened a cab driver.

The Baron had sent her back into town with more bills to post and even a few hole-punched tickets to pass out to the right people. She kept a sharp lookout for the leaders, the influencers. If the Queen Bee got in free, then all her worker-bees came along and shelled out alfalfa for tickets of their own.

She'd ended up on the opposite end of town, and not wanting to walk all the way back, hailed a cab. She had no cash for the fare, but the cabbie didn't know that. They passed motionless pedestrians, most of them existing in varying shades of gray.

"When's the show?" he asked, when he saw the last of her not-yet-posted bills.

"Tomorrow night. Seven o'clock."

"Oh." He already seemed to have lost interest and she felt

disappointment pinch her heart. "Too bad; I already have plans."

An idea came to her and she instructed the driver to pull over three blocks short of her destination. When they had stopped, Calli withdrew the dagger she kept concealed in her boot and held it against his throat. "Get out of the cab."

"You want my cash? Take it." The man's hazel eyes pleaded with hers in the rearview mirror's reflection. "Just take it and go. I've already forgotten your face."

"That's what I'm afraid of," she muttered. "Get out."

He fumbled with his seat belt and then pushed open his door. Calli slid from the back seat at the same time, contemplating his eyes. They'd been hazel—not gray.

She motioned with the dagger. "Take the keys out of the ignition."

With something akin to a groan escaping his lips, he did as she'd instructed. He held the keys out to her, but she shook her head. "Toss them in the grass."

He threw his keys. They landed with a muted jingle about ten yards away. Not as far as she'd hoped, but she decided it would have to do.

"Now," Calli said. "You need to give me your full attention."

The cab driver swallowed hard and nodded. She lifted the dagger, clasping it so the twelve-inch blade swayed over her head. She swung it like a pendulum for effect. She tipped her head back, readying herself for The Big Swallow.

The tip of the blade was too dull to cut, but the cabbie didn't know that. Her gag reflex being a ghostly relic of the past, Calli poked the upper glottis muscle until it opened up and gave her access to her throat. She eased the blade down until the crossguards rested on either side of her open mouth. She extended her arms out, held her pose for a moment, and then withdrew the blade. She bowed with a flourish and slid the dagger back into its scabbard.

"Sweet baby Jesus, lady," the cabbie said. "Do you have a flyer for your circus?" He held out a hand that, she noted, looked healthy. Calli withdrew her last freebie ticket and handed it to him. Excitement had mottled his cheeks with pink patches. His eyes sparkled.

"I hope you'll come see the show."

"I will, and I'll bring my buddies too!" The cabbie looked enthused. He stuffed the ticket into the front pocket of his jeans as Calli turned and strode away.

She glanced back once. The man had located his keys; the cab receded in the opposite direction. Calli grinned. *He forgot about the fare*, she thought. *Two birds with one stone.*

She returned to find the Baron giving a speech in the Back Yard.

"I blame the Inter-webs," he said. She couldn't tell if he truly thought that's what people called it or if he meant to be ironic. "People can see just about anything you can imagine with a few keystrokes."

"Funny you should use the word 'strokes'," Flexy Lexi said. "The men aren't as interested in my contortionist act as they used to be. What do I have to do? Incorporate props to jump start their dirty imaginations?"

A few performers snickered or murmured agreement—with her sentiment, at least—but their leader raised his arms to silence everyone. He frowned. "I'm sure we will never have to stoop to that. I pride myself on running a classy show that instructs while it entertains. What we need is more interaction with potential patrons on a diverse array of social media platforms."

Calli shuddered and tried to elbow her way through the assemblage but couldn't make any headway. She dreaded where this conversation might lead. She vowed to pull up stakes and quit before falling in with the white noise blizzard of social media.

The Baron drew a deep breath and continued. "Remember when Gonzo the elephant sat on poor Jerry while he was relaxing and having a smoke?"

"Oh, Lord, yes," Murray, one of the roustabouts, murmured.

"I warned him those cigarettes would kill him," Bunko the Clown said.

The Baron let the scattered laughter fade and then spoke. "I believe we missed an opportunity there." He rubbed his hands together, as if warming himself before a fire rather than warming up to an idea. "Instead of hushing the whole thing up, we should have posted his picture online. 'In Memoriam,' you see. We should have made a bigger deal out of it. Dedicated the next several shows to him and milked the sympathies of the crowds in each town."

"Feh." Bunko spat in the dirt. "The only surefire way to get people's attention these days woulda been to post a picture of his head smashed open like a melon."

The Baron, ever the showman, raised his arms again. "Let us not be morbid. If we each took it upon ourselves to promote the shows via our own—"

Calli withdrew her dagger and poked Bunko's backside with the dull tip. "Comin' through!" He lurched out of the way. Performers and roustabouts alike parted before her outthrust dagger and Calli hurried to her trailer to check on her husband.

Calli sat beside Dave's bed and thumbed through an old photo album. For her, there was no substitute for four by six matte prints. She came across one of her husband in full Daredevil regalia, post cannon-shot, helmet off, hair mussed, posing with a trio of kids. They were all blond, missing baby teeth, and grinning from ear to ear. She held it up to show her husband, but he didn't respond. Calli paused at a picture she had snapped ten years ago of the big top after a blowdown. No serious injuries reported, but they couldn't do a show that night because of that storm. A couple pages later another shot made her grin. Dave, her, Roscoe the boss hostler, and whole group of kids all mugging for the camera. The colors seemed vibrant, more real than the reality around her.

Calli realized several of her fellow Cirkies had been missing during the Baron's speech. She wondered if they too had fallen into lethargy. Daredevil Dave, the larger-than-life persona, had ceased to exist. Her loving husband was fading into oblivion in seeming acceptance. Had her missing colleagues also lost their passion for performing, and by extension, for life? She considered Dave. How much longer could he, or would he, cling to life? If he died, could she find the strength to go on without him?

She had a momentary flash then, a vivid vision, of swallowing her dagger in front of a packed house. She saw a crimson haze, followed by an eruption of vibrant colors beneath the big top.

A muffled pounding against the trailer door brought Calli back to reality and she started, dropping the photo album onto the linoleum floor.

"Calli! The Baron needs some help!" The speaker, roustabout Murray, sounded angry—or scared.

She rose, hurried to the door, and pushed it open. "What's wrong?"

Murray's face looked pinched, anxious. "It's Milo, the Strongman."

Calli felt her guts tighten, a constricting boa. "What about him?"

"We need everyone's help moving him," Murray said. "He's turned to stone."

Still flesh, of course, but Milo had turned a shade of gray akin to granite. Someone could have carved him from stone, for as heavy as he seemed.

"Maybe we cart him out front," someone said. "Our own Petrified Man."

"Don't you mean the Cardiff Giant?"

"Shut up, the both of you!" The Baron's voice sliced the air like a dagger, silencing the chatter.

"The Baron's right," Calli said. "We need to work together to move Milo somewhere safe, like when we moved Dave..." she let the sentence drop.

In all, it took six of them to haul Milo the Strongman across the lot and into the trailer that he shared with Alfredo and Alberto, the aerialists. *We look like pallbearers*, she thought. *Another one bites the gray, gray dust.*

They avoided making eye contact with one another as they shuffled away, all seeming to flee in separate directions. Calli found herself wondering if the dwindling, apathetic crowds triggered this blight amongst her brethren, like mold fulfilling its manifest destiny across the surface of a rotting peach, or if the performers themselves were somehow to blame.

The sun fled and night took the stage.

Tomorrow they would open the souvenir and concession stands outside the big top hours before the performance. The Baron might even decide to place an exhibit wagon downtown to drum up ticket sales. Calli knew she'd be expected to help with a dozen or more tasks, and yet she grew restless and could not sleep. She couldn't bear lying next to Dave. It seemed every moment he slipped further away from her. At last, she rose, and found herself wandering the city streets alone.

Occasional headlights from passing vehicles illuminated her as she walked. Each time, she resisted the urge to pose as if reveling in the glow of the big top's spotlight. Calli encountered few people. Most of them shuffled along as if in a daze. Some didn't move at all. She wondered if they would stand immobile all night, or if they had someone who cared enough to track them down and ensure they got home safe.

Calli rounded a corner and the garish lights, neon and blazing against the night sky, took her by surprise. She had encountered so many gray-hued citizens in this municipality of darkness that she'd almost forgotten color existed at all.

A nightclub stood before her. Music emanated from inside the building. Calli took a deep breath and pulled open the door. A thick-necked bouncer stamped her hand without bothering to ask for I.D. The club was resplendent in garish colors. A near-deafening dubstep song throbbed from the speakers. Calli let the strains guide her to the middle of the dance floor where just over a dozen revelers alternately danced or pogoed as the song progressed.

A motley assemblage of men and women cavorted around her, pressing against her from all sides. The mingling of perfumes and colognes created the olfactory equivalent of a mat shot. Attempts at maintaining personal space became futile, the dance floor a fully clothed orgy.

A square-jawed kid in a numbered sports jersey grinned and made eye contact as Calli turned. His features were still natural with no touch of gray present as far as she could see in the strobe light.

Calli touched his shoulder and shouted over the pulsing music. "Hey, what's your name?"

The sports fan leaned in and yelled into her ear. "Yeah! I love this music, too."

Calli nodded, letting their miscommunication go. Everyone whirled around them. Now that they'd stopped moving, the effect was dizzying.

"I get such a rush from this!" Calli detected the piney scent of gin on his breath when he spoke. She found she didn't mind, rather liked it in fact. His breath on her neck elicited goose bumps despite the oppressive body heat permeating the room. "I haven't seen you here before."

Calli craved attention, wanted badly to perform. "How dirty is the floor?" she shouted.

He just stared, his features blank. "The floor?"

She clutched herself against him, poured her words into his ear. "The dance floor, how dirty is it?"

He scrunched his features in a mock grimace of exaggerated disgust. "It's filthy!"

"Good. Lie down."

Calli drew back as the strains of the dubstep song gave way to an industrial-tinged bump and grind. She guided him to a prone position, making sure he kept his hands at his sides. The crowd parted around them, eager for a spectacle. She straddled his waist and pinned his arms to the grimy floor with her knees. She let the music flow through her, gyrating to the beat. Her partner's features had glazed over, but not like the gray populace; a vibrant *joie de vivre* seemed to flow through him. Calli felt the physical manifestation of his mounting excitement as she bore down on him.

Then, with the eyes of everyone in the club clinging to them like glitter on wet skin, she slipped a hand into her boot and withdrew the dagger. She swept it up over her head. The gleaming blade caught the flashing lights and even over the music, Calli heard a collective gasp from those surrounding her. She swept the blade down with a theatrical flourish toward his throat and he let loose a bellow of primal terror. The crowd pressed in on them, but no one made an effort to stop her.

Calli tilted her head back and focused on swallowing the dagger. If someone were to jostle her, she'd need an ambulance. She focused on the fear, welcomed it, and then overcame it. Calli gave the swaying throng what they wanted: The Big Swallow. They shouted their approval.

Calli withdrew the dagger, slid it into its scabbard, and rose. She thought the guy on the dance floor would need a change of underwear when he got home—but in a good way. Hands clutched at her hair and clothing; fingers stroked her skin. Everyone wanted in on the action, wanted to be associated with something exciting.

Inspiration hit and she withdrew a sheaf of folded show bills from a pocket and threw them into the air. They rained like enormous confetti on the avid, upturned faces.

Calli used the distraction to hurry out the door and into the cooling arms of the night. She hoped their enthusiasm would remain kindled and that they'd turn out in droves and pack the house.

By the time she returned to the lot and the silent, looming big top, dawn was sending exploratory fingers of pink light up over the horizon. The light spoke of rebirth.

She reached her trailer and stepped inside, pulling the door closed. An odor both foreign and unwelcome greeted her. Near palpable silence reigned. An immediate sense of guilt guided her to the bedside. She perched on the edge of the mattress and took her husband's hand. It felt cool. She leaned in and kissed his forehead only to find it cool and dry.

"Dave?"

He didn't respond.

"Dave!"

She shook his gray arm, pinched his colorless cheek. "Wake up! The show's about to start."

Calli clasped her hands around his and, sick at heart, she sobbed. Had he died while she danced at the club? Guilt stole her breath like hands crushing her windpipe. She tipped her head back, tried to catch her breath.

What were his final words to her? A blizzard of random thoughts created so much white noise in her brain that she could not remember. What had she last said to him? When had they last kissed or held hands? When had they last walked together under the night sky or laughed over a joke one of them had made? Calli cursed her faulty memory.

Dawn had broken and so had her heart. Calli spent the morning sitting beside her husband's empty husk. She stroked his skin, ruffled his hair, and held each of his hands in turn. Calli ignored the buzz of activity outside the trailer. Instead, she reminisced, recalled good times and bad. She laughed, sobbed, and even dozed.

She dreamed of Dave, fired from his cannon, soaring through the air, and landing with practiced grace in her outstretched arms. He didn't feel heavy to her at all. In fact, though she fought to keep hold of him, her husband floated out of her grasp, up and far beyond her reach.

Calli jolted to wakefulness. An invisible wad of cotton seemed stuffed into her mouth. Tears polluted by despair stung her eyes and spilled down her cheeks. She sat in stubborn silence until the sounds of activity coming from the lot grew too loud to ignore. Then she rose, drew the sheet over her husband's face, and departed the trailer.

The saying was true: the show *must* go on.

Calli told no one about Dave. The Baron took her aside about an hour before show time. "Calliope, I wonder if you might be interested in taking on a larger role." He eyed her as if he expected her to feel flattered, but she only felt empty.

"I don't think so, Baron."

"I believe you'd thrive in the spotlight," he pressed. "And I'm not the young man I once was. I'd like you to share ringmaster duties with me."

Calli's mind slid back to her husband, his performance concluded. *All out, all over*, as the circus saying went. She thought about the epidemic of gray, immobile citizens infesting every new city and the dwindling attendance at each performance.

"I appreciate the offer," she said. "Let me consider it during tonight's show."

"All right," the Baron said. "But I worry about you, Calliope; you're looking peaked." He appraised her with one final glance and hurried away to make final preparations.

She pondered many things in the minutes leading up to show time. Her husband's death seemed to have hollowed her heart. Calli tried to take solace in the throng of circus-goers perched on the bleachers. She thought the house looked closer to full than any show they'd performed in at least a year, perhaps longer. The tent was a cacophony of excited murmurs. Why were they here? What spectacle did they hope to witness?

She inspected each face in turn. This motley assemblage invited comparisons to the bloodthirsty, unwashed masses that once filled the Roman coliseums, roaring their approval every time a criminal or wild animal lost their life. Calli stood in the shadows, searching for faces that held some color, indicating a vestige of innocence, some sense of wonder retained. She felt as if she were scanning for survivors in the waters of a storm-tossed gray sea. She found a few: the cab driver, surrounded by a trio of healthy-skinned friends; the young guy from the club sat with a small group. Her gaze found Average Joe sitting alone and her lips quirked into a half smile.

Stick around, she thought. *The Baron might offer you a spot after the show.*

The faces of the vast majority were ashen. Not yet entirely lost, these souls might yet find rejuvenation. Calli felt sure that an extraordinary occurrence tonight would embed a thread of enduring exhilaration within their collective subconscious. Like the filament in a light bulb, the people at tonight's performance would come alive every time someone threw the switch. The conduit for the current—in the form of circuses, carnivals, rodeos, monster truck shows, and more—could revitalize them, staving off the gray pall, rejuvenating their souls, and allowing them to return to their everyday lives revived. Their excitement could spread like a contagion, leading to resurgence in the public's enjoyment of shows like Baron Backroad's Freewheeling Circus of Wonders.

This much she hoped.

The Cirkies around her hurried to their places. Calli turned and caught sight of her reflection in a lighted mirror Bunko and the other clowns used when touching up their makeup. For a long moment, she forgot to breathe.

She had turned gray.

Grief, she felt sure, had brought about the sudden change. She'd lost her husband, and with him, her zest for life and her desire to perform, all in one fell swoop. Life had served her a poisoned platter of heartache and she could not leave the table until she devoured every bite.

Calli waited for her cue and then stepped to the center ring. First, she would test the waters, would give them a taste, hoping for proof that her plan stood a chance. She gave the dagger a twist, and let a sharpened edge split her lower lip. Blood coated the edge of the blade. She withdrew it and lashed it, whip-like, in the audience's direction. Inky droplets arced through the air and spattered a gray-skinned man and woman slouched in the nearest row.

A murmur of surprise rippled through the crowd, followed by—did she dare hope?—signs of avid interest. Calli grinned, and felt more blood trickle from her lip and down her chin.

The makeshift baptism yielded thrilling results; the couple regained their color. Many of the spectators nearest them regained their natural hues as well. Calli could see it would not be enough;

she had to do more.

The dagger's blade slid into her mouth and down her throat. Calli pushed it, working it forward, forearm muscles flexed with the effort. She arched her back, snarling against the eruption of pain. Moments later, the tip of the blade emerged from her solar plexus, the head of a metallic serpent reintroducing humanity to feelings they had forgotten.

Calli fell to her knees the same moment the audience rose to their feet. Jaws dropped open in amazement, arms hung in slack surprise, all sets of eyes opened wide, fixed and fascinated, on HER. She hoped they'd never forget this moment, would never forget her. Amid shouts, screams, and thunderous ovation, their faces loomed and receded. She realized they now shone in a plenitude of flesh-colored tones. Their vibrant features looked glorious as Calliope Jean drifted away, torso awash in crimson, vision fading to black.

All out, all over.

REYNOLDS' TALE

I t has been written that there are secrets which should never be shared. I am in partial agreement with this assessment. Men and women toss and turn in their beds at night, and wring their hands throughout the day, guilt gnawing away at their resolve to live. The thread of their long-kept secret steadfastly unravels the fabric of their mortal coil until they no longer have a tether to this earthly realm. Up these thoughts must drift into the endless inverted abyss. But what if the dreaded secret were revealed at a time not inopportune? Could one's conscience be eased and death staved off? Perhaps. I have two secrets. I shall endeavor to share one of them, lightening the burden that I bear and thus extending—I fervently hope—my life. I only ask that you hear my tale and judge me not.

Call me Reynolds. A few years ago, on the second of October, 1849, to be precise, I sat at a large bow-window of a coffee house in Baltimore. For some weeks I had been in ill health. My body endured the challenges associated with an extended illness, while my mind underwent certain changes. But now I found my strength returning in unprecedented abundance. So also, *joie de vivre* enveloped me. A happy and inquisitive mood fell upon me. I rushed headlong into each new day with an alacrity and curiosity heretofore unknown to my personality.

With a newspaper still folded on my knee and a fine cigar hanging idly from my lips, I found myself happily distracted by those who bustled along the dirty street below the window. The street, being one of Baltimore's principal thoroughfares, was crowded with humanity. As the lengthening shadows assimilated into the growing darkness that comes with the retreat of the sun, the tumultuous sea of faces below filled my mind with a hundred flights of fancy. I gave up completely on my paper and cigar. My coffee grew cold. I became absorbed in the contemplation of the ever-changing scene below me.

At first my observations were random in nature. My eyes would fall upon a face, or perhaps only a single feature—a woman's nose, for instance—and with a preternatural clarity, I could know everything I cared to about that person. I noted at a glance the birds of a feather. I mentally sequestered groups of merchants, tradesmen, clerks, gamblers, lunatics, pick-pockets, drunkards, murderers, clergymen, noblemen, and lawyers; each aforementioned grouping more capable of misdeeds than the last. Deeper and darker character studies presented themselves for my speculation.

As the night deepened, so also my interest in the ebb and flow of humanity below me deepened. The character of the crowd altered, growing more sinister and more decadent. Ruffians seethed and searched for violence by swaggering down the center of the thoroughfare. Heavily painted women of the night kept to the shadows and attempted to seduce and beguile with toothless, slack-jawed smiles. The rays of the gas lamps spotlighted many interesting visages. The sight of a legless man rolling himself along on a small, wheeled cart brought forth in me a smile so broad that I felt my dry bottom lip split. I relished the discomfort.

Then a pick-pocket misjudged his mark and the intended victim clamped down on the miscreant's wrist and drew him in close. The mark used a grimy thumb to gouge the shifty fellow's right eye out. The pick-pocket howled and the throng parted around them, but never stopped moving. The intended victim's lips moved and I interpreted his words clearly. "How'd ya like it? Me taking sumthin' from you? Now ya know how it feels!" The pick-pocket scurried up the street, his hand cupped over his empty socket. The angry man held a pose reminiscent of Jack Horner for a few moments. Then, apparently realizing this "plum" on his thumb could lead to unwanted attention, he shook it loose and hastened away in the opposite direction.

I stifled a titter and, taken aback, wondered why the events I had witnessed caused this reaction within me. My eyes skipped over the throng when there came into my view a countenance so forlorn—so *haunted*—that I lost interest in all else. His presence among the throng was like that of an exotic fish among a school of carp. I pressed my brow to the glass and scrutinized the object of my instant fascination.

The man was short in stature, and quite thin. A shock of hair the color of raven's feathers contrasted with his waxy-white face. A mustache perched atop lips twisted in a petulant frown. A broad forehead and prominent nose lent strength to his features. Conversely, the deep hollows beneath and the furrowed brows above the stranger's eyes revealed a profoundly troubled heart. But his eyes held the most damning evidence. From only the briefest of glances, I felt as if I experienced firsthand his vast mental capability, his excessive terror, his fervent desire to love and be loved, his avarice, his hopefulness, his overwhelming guilt, and his supreme despair. He disappeared for a moment, lost in the waves of filthy, ragged humanity. I readjusted my gaze and found my own reflection in the glass. An overwhelming interest in the stranger pressed me into motion. I threw a few coins on the table, put on my overcoat, and seized my hat and cane. I made my way onto the street and pushed through the crowd in the direction I'd seen the haunted-looking man take. With only slight difficulty, I found him among the throng and fell in about twenty paces back.

A thick fog, refracting the rays of the gas lamps, illuminated the scene with a garish luster. I followed my quarry and gradually closed the distance between us. His clothes were shabby. He hunched his shoulders against the clamminess of the night. Never once did he turn his head to look back. By and by he passed an alley, and I seized the opportunity to speak with him in a semi-private environment.

I lunged forward, grasped his right arm just above the elbow, and pulled him into the alley. My quarry thrashed and struggled to break free. "Unhand me!"

I spun him so that we faced each other. "I shall, but do not flee. I have friendly intentions and wish only for a moment of intelligent conversation." Our eyes locked and after a moment's hesitation, the stranger gave me a brief nod. I released his arm and he waited with countenance guarded and mistrustful.

"Who are you and what business would you have with me?" he asked.

"Call me Reynolds. When I saw you on the street, I first mistook you for a long-lost friend." The lie would do him no harm. "I drew close enough that my error became apparent. I realized that I would not rekindle an old friendship on this night after all, but thought perhaps I could forge a new one instead." I lifted my inflection and turned the statement into a question.

The despair so prevalent in his deep brown eyes gave way to a spark of hope. I fanned the flame with an encouraging smile. He tentatively responded with one of his own. "Do tell me," I invited. "What your name is, good sir, and what is your trade?"

A giddy, mad gleam came into his eyes. "I am Poe. I am a writer." This time he seized *my* arm and steered me deeper into the alley. We strode between tall, worm-eaten tenements that leaned over us as if they would topple at any moment. Our path wound in random directions and my new friend spoke rapidly and with vehemence as we maneuvered along the crooked paving stones and around rank brown puddles.

"I write, but I must censor myself at every turn. It is my most fervent desire to write about love. But—" he broke off and shuddered. "The love I feel—the love I believe in—cannot be discussed rationally or with intelligence in general company without threat of persecution. I am a *vox clamantis in deserto*, a voice crying in the wilderness. Inside my chest beats the heart of a romantic. I laugh, I cry, I love with reckless abandon."

I nodded my encouragement and Poe continued.

"For instance, some years ago I had intended to write a love story about an old man and his live-in companion. I had the first line of the story written: 'I loved the old man.' Yet I knew such a tale would never sell, would only ruin me. My own inner fears preyed upon me and twisted my original intentions into an abomination. What started as a story about love devolved into one of murder, guilt, and madness.

"In another tale, I intended one character, Valdemar by name, to reveal his love for a colleague while under the influence of hypnosis. I included in the first draft a scene of passionate lovemaking between Valdemar and my narrator. My body and soul were alight with desire as I wrote, but upon completion I took the pages and hid them away."

Poe's voice cracked with emotion at this revelation. I put one arm around his shoulder in a gesture of consolation. We did our best to ignore the filth that festered around the dammed-up gutters. The overall atmosphere around me, including the author himself, conveyed nothing but desolation.

"Every story or poem I have ever written started out vastly different. But always the evil creeps back into my heart and into my work. My corrupt revisions are of death, sorrow, loneliness, and madness! Why must it be that way? I have become my own worst enemy. My works, upon my re-reading of them, rear up and spit in my face!

"The treasure-seeker and his servant in 'The Gold Bug' were meant to be lovers! Another of my characters, Roderick Usher, buried his sister alive in the published version of his tale. My original draft pitted Roderick and his sister in a precocious battle for the affections of the unnamed narrator. Oh, the adventures in lovemaking they shared!"

Poe's mind seemed far away for a moment, placing himself in the story, perhaps. Then his shoulders sagged, and his eyes once again took on their defeated, yet defiant cast. "That manuscript and so many others molder in a locked box somewhere. I couldn't bear to burn them, nor could I allow them to be discovered by prying, judgmental eyes."

Our pace had slowed. We turned a corner and a blaze of light burst upon our view. We stood before a temple erected for the purpose of whiskey and gin worship. A tattered sign next to the entrance advertised upstairs rooms for rent, *by hour or by night.*

Poe spun to face me. "Do you know that in my original version of 'The Cask of Amontillado,' the hole left in the wall was not at eye-level but instead was positioned parallel with Fortunato's waist? Montresor forgave him, you see. Only wanted to tease him, ply him with drink, and then tear down the wall between them so that they might abandon themselves to their desires in privacy. But my practical side got the better of me, and the story now is one of cruel revenge."

He stepped forward and seized the lapels of my overcoat. "William Wilson only ran from his own desires! The revelers in what became 'The Mask of the Red Death' were meant to indulge in a night of freedom and self-discovery. I changed the stories only because I needed money for food and lodging!"

A clock struck eleven. The author gazed into my eyes imploringly. "Is it too late? Can I repent of past mistakes and seize salvation at this both literal and figurative eleventh hour?"

I looked down into Poe's eyes and could find no fault in him. His wants, needs, and desires, so long-buried and hidden, could still be tended to, fertilized, and brought to fruition. Though I had no particular attraction to men in general, I felt I could help this unfortunate fellow achieve some small measure of happiness. Thus, I navigated the creaking, rotten stairs to the entrance and once inside inquired about securing a room.

Poe visibly trembled as we ascended the stairs. With the door closed and the begrimed key turned in the lock, my companion fell upon me with fervent kisses. Never before had I felt so *needed* by anyone. We removed our garments rather ceremoniously and stood before a grimy looking-glass. I nuzzled his neck and cupped one hand on his heart, which beat like that of a frightened captive bird. Of the haunted look that had dominated his visage there was no trace. At length, we fell together onto the bed.

The bookish fellow proved to be an attentive lover. I did my best to impress upon him my appreciation and repay him for his efforts. Poe's kisses left on my lips a pine-needle flavor; evidence of time spent in the gin mills. I kissed and licked my way down his spine, eliciting shivers quite unlike those he brought about in his readers. But when I caressed his buttocks with my erect manhood, Poe cast an anxious look over his shoulder. The brooding, tortured soul had returned, and I decided instantly not to welcome it. Instead, I bounded across the room and removed the grimy looking-glass from its place. I tossed it on the mattress and maneuvered Poe into position over the mirror. His physical arousal still evident, I knew I had only to contend with his mental reservations. Using my own saliva to facilitate our congress, I pressed myself forward until we were one. Then, as I caressed his shoulders, neck, and back with my fingertips, I exhorted him, saying: "Cast aside the shackles that bind you! Look inside yourself. Love yourself!" He groaned and rocked in a rhythm that complimented mine. Tentatively at first, and then increasing in passion and intensity, we moved until I felt my own climax approaching. I let one hand slide across his hip, intending to pleasure his member, but stopped short. I confess I gasped at the serendipitous event I witnessed. Poe was weeping, not with sorrow, but with joy, as if the rusted chains that choked his soul had been shattered. As his tears pattered onto the glass, he bent, and tasted them with the tip of his tongue. I watched Poe press his lips to the glass; his reflection returned the kiss. It was the most beautiful thing I'd ever witnessed.

In the end, we lay exhausted and tangled in the dingy sheets. As the pale gray of dawn crept upon the city, Poe began to twitch and show signs of growing unease. I inquired what troubled him.

"It cannot be this way. I cannot allow it." He sat up pulled a sheet to his waist, as if suddenly ashamed. Feelings of confusion and frustration welled up within me. I could not fathom why one would deny happiness and forsake love, instead choosing to turn and rush headlong into despair and loneliness. I told him as much.

"You can't begin to understand! Have you no fear of discovery? No fear of derision, loathing, and ruin?"

I did not, and I admitted as much. It was then, in my attempt to soothe his misgivings, that I made my most horrific mistake. It was an error of judgment I deeply regret to this day. But how could

I guess the outcome? My illness and accompanying fever had changed me, as I have already indicated. And, not knowing what result my words would have, I told the tormented little author my secret.

"Last year, I spent several weeks among an ostracized tribe from one of the Greater Antillean islands," I revealed. "While living with the tribe, they introduced me to an act of depravity so taboo I dare not say it aloud. Yet the desire to perform the act has sunk hooks of addiction into me. I am a slave to it in body and mind. You needn't feel guilt, my friend. There is no comparison. For my most pleasurable experiences were…"

I cupped one hand to Poe's ear and revealed my most cherished act. His eyes widened and then glazed over as I described the process. I stopped speaking, realizing I had said too much.

Poe rolled from the bed, crashed to the floor, and grabbed a pair of trousers. "Villain!" He hurled this accusation as he hurriedly dressed. The author ignored my entreaties, would not speak to me again. My attempts to placate him had no discernible effect. When I reached out to him, he recoiled violently from my touch.

Poe's disheveled silhouette ahead of the slamming door was the last I ever saw of him.

In his hurry to flee my company, he'd dressed himself in my clothes. Thinking he might realize his mistake, I waited for a time, but he did not return. Finally, I rose and dressed, struggling into his smaller articles of clothing and mulling the morning's dramatic chain of events. I faced the looking glass alone, with a curious lump of sorrow lodged in my throat.

***

A few days later, I found myself seated before the same bow-window in the same coffee house along the same thoroughfare in Baltimore. Once again, the coffee grew cold. My cigar remained unlit and forgotten. But this time I ignored the endless throng of passers-by on the street below. My attention focused instead on a write-up in the newspaper. Poe, to my astonishment, had died. The paper indicated the same morning he had left my company, my author friend had encountered one Joseph Walker, who believed him to be "in great distress, and in need of immediate assistance." Poe had been taken to the Washington College Hospital. Had I known of his whereabouts, I would have tried to shed some light on the situation or assisted in some way. According to the article, he even called my name, though no one present knew who I was or how to contact me. And how could they? Our meeting came about by chance. Whether Poe desired my company or if he cursed my name for preying upon his sanity with revelations of my wickedness, I know not. I sat there reading and rereading the tragic news as hot tears burned my cheeks.

Thus, my story comes to an end. I fear I am utterly lost. Life and death are equally cruel jests. I have shared one dark secret in the faint hope of easing my conscience. But I say again, there are some secrets which should never be told. I made a colossal blunder once before and a troubled genius paid for it with his sanity and his life. Guilt over my depraved desires pushes me to the cusp of madness, but what those interests may be must remain a secret. The burden must be mine to bear alone.

AIDING AND ABETTING

Between convulsive sobs, Chesil Ach du Lieber managed to tell her doctor that her husband, Depp, had traveled into the city to attend a business conference. Dr. Obadiah Gee used the distraught woman's cell phone to telephone the man.

The phone rang three times, then: "Hiya sugar britches, how you doing?"

Dr. Gee cleared his throat. "Excuse me, this is Dr. Gee calling."

"Oh, my mistake! I thought this was my wife. She used to have this number."

"Mister..." *Ach du Lieber, or just Lieber?* Gee didn't know. "Sir, she *still* has this number."

Five seconds of silence passed. "I don't follow."

"I'm calling you from her phone."

"Did she lose it?"

"Good heavens, no. I'm here with her now. I made a house call."

"But you didn't call my house, you called my cell."

"Mr. Ach du Lieber, please stop joking around. Your wife is greatly distressed, and I believe she could benefit from your presence."

"I've been in meetings all day and haven't had time to buy her any presents," the man complained. "What's wrong with her? Spell it out for me, Doc."

"She's suffering a bout of..." He caught himself, unsure of how to best proceed. *Everything is under such scrutiny*, he thought. "Do you remember the title of the rock band Def Leppard's best-selling record? The one that came out in 1987."

"Oh my God! She's burned down a building?"

"No. No. You're thinking of 1983's *Pyromania*. I'm referring to the next record, *Hysteria*."

"What does she think is so damned funny?"

"That would be the word 'hysterical.' I assure you this is far more serious."

"So you're saying she needs a hysterectomy?"

"No," Dr. Gee mentally added, *you hair-brained nincompoop.* "She is hysterical and suffering a bout of hysteria. She's convinced your baby is a danger to her. I've tried to get her to take a sedative, but she refuses. I'd advise you to get here as soon as you can."

***

"Oh God," Chesil Ach du Lieber lamented. "I hear someone coming!"

Dr. Gee listened to the heavy tread of dress shoes bounding up the stairs. "I believe you are right."

"Do you think it's the baby?" Chesil looked fearful.

"No, ma'am." Gee frowned. "I'd say that your husband has arrived." At his words, Depp Ach du Lieber entered his wife's bedroom. He crossed the floor to the bed, leaned over, and embraced her. "Darling, are you all right?"

"Yes, I'm fine now. I just get so stressed and fearful." She sighed and dabbed at her eyes with a frilly hanky.

Depp's brow furrowed as he scanned the room. He turned to his wife. "Where's the kid?"

Dr. Gee spoke up, hoping to ease the man's mind. "Your son is resting peacefully in his crib in the next room. I checked on him only minutes before you arrived."

"'Resting peacefully,' he says." Chesil's voice quavered. "Scheming and planning our deaths is what that would-be assassin is really doing in there."

Gee frowned at his patient.

Depp had fixed his attention on the doctor. "I bought my wife an emotional support animal, but it isn't here." He gave his wife a searching look. "Well?"

"I hardly think it fell down the well, darling," Chesil said. "As far as I know, we don't even have one!"

Depp forced an icy smile. "Where is the goat that I bought for you?"

"I don't know. And that darned goat is not a good companion at all. Every time something goes wrong, and I feel the need to cry, when I reach for it, the goat just goes all stiff and falls over. He's really no comfort to me at all." She dabbed her eyes again with her hanky.

Depp looked at Dr. Gee. "How do you like that? I went to great lengths to have a special myopic goat flown in from Tennessee, and she doesn't appreciate or use it."

Dr. Gee felt rising discomfort. "I believe you mean to say you've purchased a myotonic goat," he said. "Some people call them fainting goats. They have a hereditary condition which causes them to stiffen or fall over when startled. Frankly, I'm hard-pressed to think of an animal less suited for emotional companionship."

Depp lifted his chin. His eyes blazed. "How about a South African scorpion?" he challenged.

"Point taken. Be that as it may," Gee said, "I feel as if I should be on my way. There's not much more I can do here."

Chesil yelped. Depp's face contorted with fear. Dr. Gee turned to see what had disturbed them. Their cherubic tot stood unsteadily, staring wide-eyed at the room's occupants. He took an awkward step, lost his balance, and ended up on his rear end.

Gee clapped his hands together. "Why hello there, little chap! How in the world did you get out of your crib?" He crossed the room and scooped up the youngster in his arms.

Depp stared at the baby with obvious misgivings. "Doctor, meet our son. Lucifer Anton Damien Aleister ach du Lieber. But we call him Chucky, for short."

The doctor gazed into the little boy's innocent blue eyes. He could find nothing at all wrong with the child, nothing that would help explain his parents' unusual paranoia.

He returned the tot to his crib, patted the boy's head, and reentered the bedroom. The fainting goat had wandered into the room while he'd been gone. It bleated once, defecated on the rug, and began nibbling on the end of the bed's comforter.

Chesil started to weep. Depp's haughtiness fell away like a discarded candy bar wrapper. "Doc, please! What can I do for my wife? Better yet, what can *you* do for her?"

"For now, she just needs some rest."

"Just name it and I'll take care of it."

"As I said, she'll benefit just from you spending more time at home."

"Money is no object."

"If you help out with the baby..."

"...is there somewhere we can send her? Perhaps a retreat?"

"Pitch in with the cooking and the household chores..."

"...an expensive medication you can prescribe?"

"Most of her problems will be solved if you pay..."

"My checkbook is ready. Let me find a pen."

"...more time with your wife and your son."

"Stop beating around the bush, Doc! Just tell me in plain English!"

"You need to help her..."

"...a medical procedure, perhaps?"

"Feed and change the baby. She's overwhelmed."

"...a frontal lobotomy?"

"*What?*"

"...what?"

Chesil shrieked so loud it made Dr. Gee's ears ring. The goat stiffened and toppled onto the floor.

"Good heavens!" Gee exclaimed "What's wrong?"

The woman raised a trembling hand and pointed at the doorway. "He's here," she intoned. "*Spying.*"

In the doorway, Chucky lifted his arms and gazed imploringly at Dr. Gee. He lifted the baby and carried him back to his room. "I am so sorry, my little friend." He whispered. "Between you and me? You seem to have a wig in a hatbox for a mother and a spittoon filled with tobacco juice for a father."

"Uck," the baby replied.

"I concur wholeheartedly." Gee lay the baby in his crib and returned to the next room.

He addressed Depp. "As I was saying: bedrest for her," he indicated the woman with a nod, "Mr. Ach du Lieber. And for—"

The man raised a hand to stop him. "That," he said, pointing at his wife. "Is *Mrs.* Ach du Lieber. *I*," he poked his index finger into his chest, "am Mr. Ach du Lieber."

For the first time, it occurred to Dr. Gee that he might be the victim of an elaborate television prank show. "I know that, of course. I only meant—"

"Perhaps it would help if we all introduced ourselves using our first names," the bedridden woman suggested. "For instance, I'm Chesil."

"I'm Depp." The man's finger remained pointing at his chest.

Dr. Gee sighed. "I'm Obadiah, Obie for short."

"Nice to meet you, Obie," Chesil smiled. "I'm Chesil."

Dr. Gee watched her, hoping she'd laugh to show she was kidding. She didn't.

After an awkward silence, Dr. Gee cleared his throat. "I'll just be on my way."

Depp frowned. "Hang on a moment, Doctor."

"What's the matter now?"

"Something's bothering me, something from earlier." The man looked perplexed. Gee imagined a three-legged hamster trying to run on the wheel that powered the man's brain.

"You said goats did not make great—or even good—emotional support animals. Well, why are certain sports stars, like Michael Jordman, Tom Grady, and Waylon Gretzky, referred to as 'the GOAT?' Why do people call them that if goats are not, in fact, the best?"

Dr. Gee wished he'd called in sick this morning and hit the golf course instead. "I believe you mean Michael Jordan, Tom Brady, and Wayne Gretzky."

Depp shrugged. "I don't know who any of *those* guys are, but the question remains."

"In this instance, GOAT is an acronym. It stands for Greatest of All Time."

Chesil frowned. "Where does the goat come in?"

Gee bit down on his lip and counted to five before he responded. "With an acronym, you take the first letter from each word and then pronounce it like a new word. Greatest of All Time becomes GOAT. Acronyms should not be confused with another form of abbreviation called initialism. An example of that would be vee, eye, pee which stands for 'very important person.' See the difference? We say, VIP, not vip."

Depp blushed, and he gazed down at the carpet.

Dr. Gee pretended not to notice the other man's embarrassment and turned toward the bedridden woman. "Contractions are probably the most common form of abbreviations. I'm Dr. Gee, but of course I don't spell 'doctor' out every time. The acceptable shortened version is simply dee, are, and a period."

"Oh, thank goodness," Chesil murmured, apparently to herself. "I've been spelling the entire word out in my head every time."

Gee scanned the room, looking for an intelligent adult who would commiserate with him. He didn't find one. The closest he came was a glimpse of the baby, who peeked into the room one moment and was gone the next. Chesil sniffled and wiped her reddened eyes.

Convinced more than ever that someone was having an elaborate laugh at his expense, Dr. Gee bounded across the room and threw open the closet door. Finding no hidden camera operator inside, he dropped to his knees and lifted the bed comforter. Only a gleaming pair of eyes belonging to the diminutive goat stared back at him. He stood.

The couple stared at him as if he were mad.

The temptation to contribute to the inane conversation became too much. "My name could be considered an acronym," the doctor announced. "My name is Obadiah Gee, shortened to Obie Gee to sound less formal. I am a doctor specializing in obstetrics and gynecology. Thus, Obie Gee—or OBG—is both my name and my job."

The couple gave him blank looks. Depp caught his wife's eye. She frowned. He shrugged.

The doctor decided to leave. Again.

"I'll be on my way," he said.

"Doctor! Wait!" Chesil pleaded.

Gee paused. "Yes?"

"We don't feel safe here." Depp said. He darted his eyes in an exaggerated sidelong gaze toward their son's room. "Alone. With the baby."

"Why on earth not?"

"He's trying to kill us." Chesil's voice quavered.

"That's absurd."

"Is it?" Depp stepped closer his voice low. "His face is always red. As if he'd been crying."

"Well, he probably *has* been crying," Gee said. *I would cry too if I were stuck here with you two numbskulls.*

"Ah, but that's just what he wants us to think." Depp both hissed and whispered his words. Gee idly wondered if *hisspered* might be a real but underutilized word as his host went on. "Chesil and I both know the truth. Chucky's face is always red, not because he's been crying, but because he's been eavesdropping."

"Lurking, creeping around, skulking about, prowling, spying, lying in wait..." Gee glanced up and glimpsed Chesil shoving what looked like a well-thumbed thesaurus beneath the comforter.

"I'm not sure I follow," the doctor said.

"Well, *he* certainly does!" Depp grimaced. "Follows us from room to room! That baby isn't natural."

"I recommend an experienced psychiatrist."

"How will that help?" Chesil asked. "He can't even talk yet."

Gee closed his eyes and massaged his temples. He felt a thunderstorm-sized headache coming for him.

"Just suppose," Depp clasped his arms around himself as if terrified. "I get up in the middle of the night and I put on my slippers and robe with the intention of going downstairs for some warm milk. At the top of the stairs, suppose my foot slips on something. Suppose I nearly plunge headlong down the stairs, but I catch the railing."

Depp's cheeks had turned a hectic pink. "Now suppose—and this is all purely hypothetical, you understand—but suppose I reach out, with the intention of identifying the object. And suppose I touch it, but in the act of touching it, I inadvertently brush it away. Suppose it tumbles down a couple of the steps. Suppose I recognize it as a cloth patchwork doll I purchased for the baby. At that moment, I'll *know*. I'll know, and I won't even be surprised! The baby placed it there, deliberately, in hopes of killing one of us!"

"Well, now, that's quite a stretch..."

"And suppose, the next day, Depp comes home from work to find me dead." Chesil added.

"Dead?" Gee asked.

"Yes. Lying at the foot of the stairs," Chesil's eyes swam with tears. "My neck broken, after slipping on the doll."

"You think you'll slip on the same doll? In broad daylight?" Gee looked first at Mrs. Ach du Lieber, and then at her husband. "Why didn't you pick up the doll on your way back upstairs after getting your warm milk? Why leave it there if you were so concerned and so shaken? —hypothetically, of course."

Depp flushed and then paled. "The unmitigated gall! You should be helping us, Doctor, not pointing the finger of blame!"

Dr. Gee felt his own cheeks burning. "I'll be on my way," he said again.

"Wait!" Depp grasped Dr. Gee's sleeve. "Suppose after the funeral, I am so distraught I take something to help me sleep. And suppose the baby's bloodlust is not yet satisfied. Suppose you were to stop here only to discover me in my bed—dead!"

I don't ever intend to set foot in this house again, Dr. Gee thought. *The inmates clearly run* this *asylum.*

"He'll have had his revenge on us both!"

"How do you figure?"

"Well, he..." Depp cast his eyes about the room. "He turned on the gas."

"Wouldn't your baby succumb to carbon monoxide poisoning too?"

Depp frowned. "Well..."

"These scenarios are asinine." Dr. Gee scowled first at Depp and then at his wife. "You two ought to be ashamed. What I see before me, are two very spoiled and entitled people who barely have time for each other, much less time for another human being—one who is dependent on them for his own survival."

Mrs. Ach du Lieber paled. Her lower lip trembled. Her husband wrung his hands together and stared at the floor, appearing suitably chastised.

"I ought to call Child Protective Services." Dr. Gee paused for effect. "But I won't. Stop with the insane speculation. Your baby loves you. He needs you. Start loving him, and caring for him, before it's too late."

The couple nodded. Tears streamed down their cheeks. Dr. Gee clapped Depp on the shoulder and bowed in Chesil's direction. He picked up his old-fashioned medical bag and strode from the room.

He tramped heavily down the hall.

After ten feet, Dr. Gee glanced back, slipped out of his shoes, and padded in silence back to the baby's room. He slipped inside, hardly daring to breathe. At the far end of the room, something rustled.

Dr. Gee took half a dozen purposeful steps until he stood at the side of the crib. The baby waited, hands on the rail, staring up at him with wide, intelligent blue eyes.

Imagine being raised by those two imbeciles. Poor little chap.

As the silence spun out, an understanding passed between them, without either of them speaking a word.

Dr. Gee reached a decision. He put a hand into his medical bag. Mostly an ostentatious affectation, it still contained a few useful items. He found what he wanted and withdrew it. Knowing that babies learn by mimicry, he demonstrated the object with a few flicks of his wrist.

"See, baby! Here's something *useful*."

A scalpel.

Author's note: "Depp" is a German word for a clumsy or inept person. Chesil is a feminine biblical name meaning "foolishiness."

THE VALUE OF A DOLLAR

Cedric Williams woke up knowing he had to earn some quick cash. He knew who to see about it, and he knew what kind of work he'd have to do. He had already decided what he intended to buy with the money he earned. Cedric liked to have a plan and he liked to keep his plans simple. Simple meant no surprises. Cedric didn't like surprises.

He shuffled down the hallway toward the kitchen. Gran had left coffee on the warmer and had saved him half of a store-bought pastry. Cedric grabbed a mug from the cupboard and poured himself some of the sludgy brown brew.

His grandmother was ancient—pushing sixty—but knew better than to treat him like a kid. He took a swallow and grimaced. He wished coffee tasted half as good as it smelled, but he drank a cup every morning, anyway. He was the man of the house. Lung cancer had stolen his grandfather, and he'd never met his father.

Two years ago, at thirteen, the state awarded custody of Cedric to his grandmother. His mother was serving five years in Lowell Correctional for voting while on probation. Cedric didn't know why his mother had been on probation in the first place. He did know he wasn't going to vote, even after he turned eighteen. His vote wouldn't change anything anyway. He'd learned that from Fat Leon one afternoon. Leon was sharp. He knew how the world worked.

Cedric planned to hoof it over to Fat Leon's right after breakfast. The man always had work. A local jack-of-all-trades, he owned a beat-up panel truck and sometimes made pick-ups and deliveries. He always had odd jobs for Cedric, and best of all, Leon always paid him in cash.

***

Cedric's grandmother met him in the back yard. What she had to say gave him a serious case of heartburn.

"I seen them no-good thugs again, Cedric." She stared as if she had x-ray vision and could see through her house to the street. "Always comin' 'round here, selling drugs. They think folks don't know, but I *do* know! I recognize 'em. And if I see 'em again, I'm gonna march right over and tell 'em I'm callin' the cops!"

This was sounding worse and worse.

"Gran, don't!" Cedric said. "I know Ernesto. I'll talk to him, okay?"

His grandmother put her hands on her hips and stared up at him. "What's the difference if you talk to him or if I talk to him?"

"You don't want to cross him, believe me. I think he has gang connections. I don't know what they do to snitches, but you can bet it ain't good."

"Well..."

Cedric held up both hands. "I'm dead serious, Gran. If they come around, you just keep yourself to yourself."

His grandmother pursed her lips and finally nodded. She gestured toward a pyramid of bricks loaded in a wheelbarrow. "You gonna help me put in a walkway between the buttercups and periwinkles this morning, like I asked?"

Cedric groaned. He'd forgotten. And just looking at the bricks made his back ache. "I can't. I'm helping Fat Leon today."

"That man who does odd jobs? I don't trust him much more than I trust that Ernesto character. His property looks like he's trying to grow his own junk yard."

"I already told him I'd help him move some stuff," Cedric said. He thought for a moment and then continued. "I got a real good work ethic. And *you* taught me the value of a hard-earned dollar. I can't back out now, it wouldn't be professional."

"Listen to you." Gran rolled her eyes. "Lay it on much thicker an' you'll need a butter knife."

"I'll be back before dark and I'll lay the bricks into a path wherever you tell me, okay?"

"Before dark?"

"Yes."

"All right, but I don't much like the idea of sitting around idle all day…"

"Read a book. Watch TV." An image of his grandmother staring out the front window popped into his mind's eye. "No snooping, no confrontations, no cops. Just let me get my work done for Leon and then I'll be home to help you with the bricks, okay? And I'll talk to Ernesto."

Cedric didn't intend to "talk to" Ernesto, except to buy a quarter gram of crystal from him. He *would* help with the backyard project. He could do that much, at least. The paying job took priority, though. Gran's project would have to wait.

"Just make sure you're back with enough time to get the job done right."

"Don't worry." Cedric turned on his heel and called back over his shoulder. "I'm just trying to help pay the bills. Love you, Gran."

His grandmother said something in reply, but Cedric didn't hear. He was already jogging down the lane in the direction of Fat Leon's.

***

He kept his plans simple. Most days he walked down and worked for Fat Leon. Grunt work. No-brainer stuff.

He always brought most of the money home to Gran, as a sign of good faith. It helped pay for groceries. He was family, yes, but nobody could ever accuse him of being lazy. He'd hand the money over, all smiles, but he'd hold enough back to buy some crystal from Ernesto. Most of the meth in Florida came from Mexico, and Ernesto had quality product.

Cedric got a rush of confidence and energy when he used. It

helped him power through whatever tasks Leon lined up for him. Cedric never felt hungry on crystal, either. Paying around thirty bucks for all those benefits was a steal. A quick snort and you were good to go for the entire day.

***

The light from the single naked bulb showed Fat Leon's cot, an overturned peach crate, and little else. Cedric scuffed across the concrete floor and stood with his hands clasped behind his back. The older man leaned over the crate and folded up what Cedric thought was a detailed map of the swampland surrounding them.

Leon straightened. The lines on his weathered face made Cedric think again of the map. He felt restless, resisted the desire to scratch his arms. If Leon found out he used, he wouldn't give him work anymore. The older man had warned him point blank the day they'd met.

"Busy day," Leon said now. "Let's get to it."

Outside the shack, he descended a flight of stairs leading to his outbuildings. Cedric followed him down the spongy wooden planks and wiped sweat from his brow. He glanced up through the cypress trees at the blazing sun. It seemed to bleach the blue out of the sky. Cedric thought of his grandmother, and hoped she'd kept her promise not to work on the brick walk until he returned home.

He followed Leon past the outbuildings and down a path overgrown with encroaching ferns. He knew they'd check the older man's traps placed at various spots along the water's edge. "Coons, possums, beavers, we can use," Leon had once said. "Minks and muskrats we have to release. State law." He'd winked as he spoke, and Cedric understood.

Leon always carried a .22. A shot in the eye or ear of the captive animal usually did the trick. Then, back at the shack, they'd skin and field dress their game. Leon had showed Cedric how to do both, though the teen found it easier to do if he let his mind wander during the grislier tasks.

One of his most persistent daydreams was one he and Fat Leon had discussed before.

"What if the creator of the universe made everything by committing suicide?" Cedric had asked one day. "Like, God is everywhere. Because all the planets and stars and stuff—it's all him, scattered across creation as we know it." He'd been trying to get a rise out of Leon by being a smart ass, but the older man had frowned, seeming to give the question serious consideration. "When the other beings discover his remains, the cleanup of the scene will prove to be catastrophic beyond our wildest comprehension." Leon said. "Thankfully, time must pass slower for them than for us."

The older man's serious response had messed with Cedric's mind that day—and many subsequent days. In fact, he sometimes wondered if he used crystal more often because of the cosmic dread Leon had planted in his thoughts.

Cedric scanned the sky through the trees again. He took a deep breath of the warm, soupy air. He looked back down and saw that Leon had stopped on the trail and had turned to face him.

"Remember when—" Cedric broke off as his companion raised his .22 and pointed it at his chest. Cedric froze. "What the hell, man?" His mind raced. He tried to think of what he'd done to anger Leon but came up blank.

"You deaf or just daydreaming?" Leon bared his teeth in a terse smile.

Cedric raised his hands. "Whatever this is about, it's a misunderstanding."

"Daydreaming." Leon nodded as if a puzzle had been solved to his satisfaction. "Look down at the path between us."

Cedric followed the older man's gaze. There, in the middle of the path, a thick snake lay coiled.

"Cottonmouth," Leon said. "If you get bit, we got trouble."

Cedric wiped sweating palms on his shirt and slid a step backward. "What should I do?"

Leon lowered the .22. "Just walk around it. He wants nothing to do with you."

Cedric stepped off the path but stayed close to it. As he passed the snake, it tipped its head back and opened its jaws. Cedric got a good look at the white inner flesh that gave the snake its name. He felt his arms erupt in goosebumps and once again resisted the urge to scratch.

The cottonmouth's head twitched but it did not strike. True to Leon's assurance, the snake apparently would defend itself, but would not attack unless provoked.

Leon resumed walking and Cedric rejoined him on the path. "Thanks for the warning."

"Don't mention it," Leon said. "I didn't want to have to tell your poor old granny you up and died from a bad case of inattentiveness."

***

They were back at Fat Leon's shack.

After finding the traps empty, Leon had directed Cedric to help him move crates. They piled them onto wooden pallets placed along the fence bordering the southern edge of the property. As the task neared completion, Cedric, soaked with sweat and feeling edgy, said, "Y'know, renting a skid loader would make this job go a hell of a lot faster."

"You better check your attitude." Leon said. His blue eyes flashed. Cedric let the smirk fall from his face.

"You aren't half as smart as you think you are." Leon lifted a crate and stacked it atop the others. "You don't even know what you *don't know*."

Cedric's cheeks burned as if from a slap, but he held his tongue.

"You," Leon hefted the final crate and mopped his brow. "Don't even know my name."

Cedric scowled. "Yes, I do."

"But you're saying it wrong."

"What do you mean?"

"You call me 'Fat Leon.'"

"Everyone calls you that."

"Do I look fat to you?"

"No, but..."

"There's a phrase, from the French: '*fait accompli*.' It means 'done deal.' They don't call me 'Fat,' they call me '*Fait*,' which can also mean 'fact.' And when you say '*Leon*,' you don't realize you're mispronouncing the French word for 'lion.'"

"So your nickname means what? Done Deal Lion?" Cedric made a face. "That don't make no sense."

"That doesn't make any sense, you mean, but you're wrong. In fact, it does make sense. My business associates know I always get the job done and I'm no coward."

"*Fait Leon*." Cedric mulled it over. "So are you French Cajun?"

"No."

"Creole?"

Leon shook his head.

"Where you from, then?"

"I'm a Brew City transplant."

"Huh?"

"I'm from Milwaukee."

"Where's that?"

"Wisconsin."

Cedric scowled. "It sounds like you're making crap up just to mess with me."

The rumble of a diesel engine interrupted further discussion. The pair climbed the stairs to see who'd pulled into Leon's driveway.

***

"We got an item needing discrete, permanent disposal. You the right guy to talk to?"

Ernesto and two others Cedric didn't recognize stood at the mouth of Leon's driveway. Ernesto did the talking. A pear-shaped man in needle-sharp black shoes and a porkpie hat stood beside him. He fixed his gaze on Leon and didn't blink. Cedric's twin—if Cedric stood half a foot taller and weighed about eighty more pounds—stood near a shiny red pickup truck. They exchanged guarded glances.

Leon approached the nearer pair. "Will the cargo pose a health hazard to me or my associate?" His *associate*? Cedric felt a flush of pride.

Ernesto shook his head.

"How heavy is the cargo?"

"Let's say at least two-sixty."

Leon nodded, as if crunching numbers in his head.

"You want it buried in the ground or should we dump it in the swamp?"

"Sink it in the swamp," Ernesto said. "The deeper the better." He reached into his pocket and withdrew a tightly wound roll of green bills. "And forget where you sink it."

"Do I need to worry about cops or the government showing up and snooping around?"

The fat man reached out the touched Ernesto's sleeve with a stubby thumb and forefinger.

"No more questions," Ernesto said. He peeled three bills from the roll and handed them to Leon. Then he addressed the hulking man nearer the truck. "Wilf, unload it."

***

Leon piloted his airboat in a circuitous route deep into the swamp. From time to time, he consulted the map he'd folded up earlier inside his cabin.

A heavy oil drum sat on the airboat's deck. Cedric slouched on the passenger seat between the drum and the driver seat. He massaged his forearm. He thought he might have pulled a muscle during the loading process. The damned thing felt full of bowling balls. He felt thankful Leon had a moving dolly or he didn't know how they'd have gotten the drum down to the dock and onto the airboat.

Cedric let his eyes travel over the drum. He wondered how much Ernesto had paid Leon, but didn't ask. He shivered from the cool air hitting his sweat-soaked skin.

At last, Leon eased off the control lever. The propellers slowed and stopped. The airboat rocked in the murky black water as the pair moved toward their cargo.

"This spot should be deep enough," Leon said. "We'll tip it on its side and roll it."

They worked together, Cedric pushing and Leon pulling. When the drum tilted, several objects shifted within and rang against the steel wall. Leon gritted his teeth. His biceps bulged, and the veins above his wrists stood out as he eased the drum to the deck. He nodded at Cedric.

"Roll it off the port side, into the water."

Cedric hesitated. When he leaned against the drum, Leon stopped him. "Switch sides. Port side is to the left." Cedric switched sides and tried to roll the drum. Leon had to help. With each revolution, the center of gravity changed, and the pair had to exert themselves to keep up the forward momentum.

"Sounds like a handful of rocks in a clothes dryer." Cedric joked. Leon grunted with effort and gave the steel drum a final shove. It hit the water's surface and sent a wet spray into the air. Cedric watched as it sank into the murk. It left no trace.

***

They stood in front of Leon's cabin. The sun neared the western horizon. Leon offered Cedric a lukewarm Coke from a cooler half-filled with water. Cedric cracked the can open. The sweet fizz that filled his mouth tasted terrific. He noticed Leon staring down at his battered work boots and realized the older man had something on his mind.

"Some things I do aren't always strictly legal." Leon lifted his sweat-stained trucker cap and scratched his scalp.

"That ain't exactly news," Cedric said. "I know how to keep my mouth shut. You know that."

"That's not what I'm getting at. Those guys we just did a job for, they're bad news."

Leon peered at him. Cedric said nothing. He didn't intend to admit he knew Ernesto.

"I've seen the talkative one around, but the others are new. The fat guy in the hat gave me bad vibes."

"Yeah." Cedric didn't know what else to say. In truth, he felt much the same. He hoped neither of the others would be around when he sought out Ernesto for a fix.

"Your life has potential, you realize that?" Leon caught his eye before continuing. "Don't get involved with people like them. They're poison."

"Okay, but—"

"You're wondering why I took their dirty money. Well, times are tight and sometimes a man has to do things he doesn't want to do just to survive."

Leon's sunburned face now looked pale. "You still got a chance. Keep your nose clean."

He stood and walked over to where Cedric sat. He handed him a damp one-hundred-dollar bill and gave his shoulder an awkward squeeze. He went into his cabin, closing the door behind him.

***

Cedric shuffled up the sidewalk toward home.

He'd stopped at a 7-Eleven to buy a box of coconut patties and a Yoo-hoo to wash them down. He'd divided the resulting broken bills between his pockets. Sixty bucks plus change waited in his right pocket to give to Gran, because it was the *right* thing to do. Thirty bucks sat in his left pocket because that was what he had *left*. With that thirty, he'd get a quarter of crystal from Ernesto. With *that* in his system, he'd be ready to work like a pack mule tomorrow. More work, more money, more crystal; it made for a good cycle. Cedric felt contented with his plan.

Cedric reached his grandmother's house at dusk. The house stood dark, and Cedric frowned. He pushed open the front door. "Gran?"

No answer came. Cedric stopped in the kitchen. The breakfast dishes sat piled in the sink, untouched. He spun on his heel and checked the living room. Gran's purse sat on the coffee table, undisturbed.

Cedric's heart started racing. It felt like being on crystal, but with fear simmering in his brain. "Gran!" he called again, louder this time. If she was napping and he disturbed her, so what? Let her be mad. At least then, he'd be able to relax.

He found her bedroom and the bathroom empty. Cedric even checked his room, just in case. Maybe she'd found the magazines he had stashed under the mattress. Or she'd found his old glass pipe. Something like that might give her a heart attack.

Cedric stopped short. *A heart attack.*

Gran said she wanted to put in a brick pathway in the back yard. She'd asked for his help and he'd told her to wait...

Cedric raced down the hall, through the kitchen, and out the side door. He sprinted into the tiny back yard, scanning the ground for what he dreaded finding. His eyes adjusted to the gloom. He saw no sign of his grandmother.

The boy scanned the narrow yard again. Wooden fence; bird feeder; bed of yellow flowers; wheelbarrow; bed of blue flowers; bird bath; the other fence. *No Gran.*

Cedric looked again at the wheelbarrow. It sat empty. Missing were the bricks intended for a decorative path between Gran's flowerbeds.

Enough bricks, he realized, to ensure a busybody snitch sank to the bottom of the swamp.

THE MONSTER'S LEATHER APRON

The moment Edward completed work on his fifth artistic endeavor, he sensed the wheels of fate beginning to turn. Ginger, she had called herself, though he doubted that had been her real name. What a filthy, ignorant wretch she'd been at the start. Like the others, she'd been an unwieldy hunk of sculptor's clay, rough and unfinished. He had carved with his blades until he found her true essence. No masterpiece, he had to admit, but a vast improvement and a strong artistic effort given the resources available at his disposal.

And yet, a mounting sense of dread compelled him to flee Whitechapel in the black of night, while her blood still soaked into the straw mattress where she lay. He'd stowed away in the back of a peddler's creaking wagon. He couldn't afford to be seen. Not that he feared recognition; published eyewitness accounts varied. He'd wanted to escape notice because he'd kept his leather apron and knives with him when he'd fled. He could not bear to leave them behind.

Edward smiled in the darkness. Scotland Yard, and the insufferable Abberline, had attempted to place him under surveillance. Though his name had not yet made the papers or the latest edition of *Puck*, Edward felt the noose closing around him. Abberline, Moore, and the others would doubtless be enraged to find that their quarry had escaped. How far would their pursuit extend? When, Edward wondered, could he stop running? A nagging, yet comforting idea came to him. *Perhaps others will take up my work.* Edward contemplated this as the wagon he rode in reached the outskirts of London with the first gray light of dawn.

The fugitive fought the needling panic that came with the approaching sun. He scanned the empty streets, unfamiliar with this borough's layout. Edward spotted a small shed and leapt from the still-moving wagon. His boots scraped the cobblestone, but he kept his feet beneath him and ran. The unwitting peddler never looked back. Edward could see a frumpy woman inside her shop. The enticing aromas of meat pies and fresh bread invaded his flaring nostrils as he ran. Edward glanced around then stole into the dank confines of the shed. He crouched behind a stack of crates, sending a trio of rats scurrying for the corners.

Ensconced in darkness, Edward tucked his knees under his chin and contemplated his situation as morning broke. Despite the cramped quarters and preternatural knowledge that he'd be discovered soon if he didn't leave London, he managed to doze. He'd rested for an hour before he received unwanted attention.

"What are you doing in there? And who the devil are you?"

Edward sat up, his mouth parched, pupils contracting from the invading light. The sunshine turned the figure into a black silhouette blocking his only means of escape.

"Why are you in my shed?" The figure's strong Cockney accent was shrill, grating.

"A trio of unsavory characters beat me and robbed me on Wapping High Street. I remember one of them had a cudgel." The lie came easy. Edward pressed a hand to his temple and shaded his eyes as if in pain. In truth, he covertly examined his inquisitor, who seemed to be alone.

The woman—whom Edward was certain he'd seen in the bakery window—seemed nonplussed. "Wapping High Street, you say? Then why did they dump you here?"

"I don't know, mum. I don't even know where I am."

"Blackwall. Near the docks." The wood creaked beneath the woman's shifting feet. "You can't stay here."

Edward nodded, winced, and said, "I think my kneecap's dislocated. Will you help me stand?"

The woman sighed but moved toward him, skirts rustling

against crates. She bent and held out an arm.

Edward took it, twisted it, and drove the woman face-first into the shed's wall. He maneuvered behind her and snapped the woman's neck. He staggered to the door and pulled it nearly closed, allowing only the thinnest line of sunshine to reach the interior. Edward crawled back to the woman and withdrew a blade from his leather apron. It felt comforting to touch. So would the woman's inner workings—once he had arranged them just so.

He paused, reflecting. This would not do. He could not leave a trail. Lips pressed together in a tight line, Edward fought against, and resisted the nearly unbearable compulsion to use the woman as his canvas of flesh. Sighing, he put his knife away.

Edward stood and eased up to the crack in the door. He closed one eye and surveyed the street. Horse-drawn wagons passed in either direction; nearly all were filled with goods. Here and there, a carriage held occupants, but most of the traffic here seemed to be commerce-related. Edward thought of the docks, now within walking distance. Did he have enough money for passage across the ocean? He believed so. Perhaps he could pick up work along the way. Edward slipped from the shed and strolled with his hands in his pockets, his treasured knives rolled up in his leather apron, tucked in the crook of one arm. He decided upon a destination as he walked to the docks.

***

Ten years later and half a world away, Edward still fled fears of detection and incarceration. He also fled his own reckless urges. Edward had traveled in a restless zigzag across America in a fruitless attempt at leaving suspicion of his previous crimes—and tempting, new flesh canvases for his blades—behind him. He sought only solitude.

Edward had taken notice of the newspaper reports detailing the discovery of gold in the Klondike region of the Yukon. This region appealed to him. There, he thought, he could avoid the slatternly women who too often caused him unbearable temptation. With no small amount of luck and a great deal of hard work, Edward might return reinvented, a wealthy man.

This morning, however, Edward lay silent, listening to the sounds of betrayal.

"Hurry up and get the other dogs harnessed. The more ground between him and us when he wakes the better."

"It doesn't bother you to leave him?"

"Edward's a monster. I won't be the one to stop him, but I won't be around when they hang him, either. They might want to string us up just because we're with him." The man grunted with exertion as he hefted something onto one of the sleds. "Besides, once we're home, won't half of the gold spend a lot nicer than a third?"

Though the other man did not respond, Edward knew his Klondike prospecting partners meant to abandon him, to leave him starving, feverish, and alone against the elements.

He lay in his tent, wakened by their stealthy movements as they broke camp. His partners, Sheldon Winslow and Morgan Lynch, expected him to die—and soon. Edward meant to prove them wrong.

He'd paired up with Sheldon in Portland at the start of the trek north. They'd met Morgan in the Alaskan port city of Skagway. The trio formed an alliance marrying their fortunes, literal and figurative. The prospecting and survival supplies, the food and rations, the cold weather clothing, the purchase of good sled dogs, and a hundred other expenses they hadn't counted on had depleted their existing funds. Yet they'd been lucky. Edward and his partners had been among the first to stake a claim on the newly christened Eldorado Creek, and had mined more gold than those earlier arrivals who worked claims on the famous Bonanza Creek. Most of the other fortune seekers found nothing at all, save for frostbite on the Yukon Trail and syphilis in Dawson City's brothels.

Because of the brothels, Edward came face to face with what he loved, and loathed, most. He should have known. Wherever men and money were found, there too would flocks of soiled doves congregate, feeding off the men like parasites. Poisoning the men with disease and insanity. These women needed reshaping. Edward knew he was the perfect man for the work. No one else had his experience, his pedigree.

He'd removed his leather apron from where he had kept it hidden deep in his pack. The blades sang to him as he picked each one up in turn, examining them for sharpness. One artistic endeavor led to another, and soon he had equaled his Whitechapel output.

Recently, Edward had been battling a fever. Now his prospecting partners meant to take advantage of his situation, meant to leave him behind.

The pounding headaches, the burning throat, and the muscle stiffness he could bear, and had. Fever dreams plagued him at night, but he'd felt sure recovery was imminent. It had now become obvious that his partners disagreed.

Edward regretted last night's outburst. They'd just crossed the Yukon River. Fort Yukon lay behind them. Dawson City lay ahead. The trip south across the river had seemed endless—to Edward. His illness, apart from taking a toll on his body, had begun to take a toll on his mind. Every few minutes, he felt convinced that he could hear the river's ice cracking beneath their feet. He fought the waves of panic, letting the dogs find their way. At last, they set up camp on the other side, nestled amongst the spruce timberland. Sheldon and Morgan had wanted to go on, but Edward insisted on stopping. Once the tents were pitched, he had crawled inside his, legs dragging, body shaking with exhaustion.

When Sheldon brought in strips of bacon on a tin plate for him some time later, Edward mistook the food for strips of human skin. "You're supposed to leave those whores to *me*!" he shouted. "It's my blades that cleanse, not yours!"

Sheldon had withdrawn from Edward's tent, thin-lipped and glowering.

Fever dreams and jumbled recollections plagued his sleep. He had started awake, only to find he'd left one nightmare to enter another. The sounds of their furtive movements drifted into his dark tent. He lay there hearing so much, but seeing so little.

Now, driven by equal parts fear and fury, Edward finally threw off the clinging blankets and crawled toward the tent opening. He tried to shout through the walls of his tent. But his throat only made a dry clicking. One of the dogs whined. One of the men grunted as he lifted something heavy. The sounds all had a muffled quality, as if already fading from memory. He tried to call out, but all that escaped his mouth was a cracked whisper. He fumbled in the darkness for the opening of the tent.

"Mush!" Morgan's voice commanded. The sound of one of the sleds began to diminish as it moved away from camp and found the trail. Edward heard more whining. He wondered if it came from Iluq. The squat, gray malamute with the missing tail had always preferred him to the other men. Perhaps Iluq would be his ally now, refusing to budge until Edward had joined them. He felt a flicker of hope.

A whip-crack pierced the air, extinguishing Edward's short-lived optimism. The jingling of leather traces was enough to convince him that the second sled had joined the first in their exodus of betrayal. He still had his knives, always kept them nearby in their leather apron. If they came back now, Edward vowed to slice them both open out of spite. Take a blade across their throats and another across their bellies. Let their steaming entrails flash-freeze in the sub-zero conditions. *And all that gold!* That, too, provided Edward with incentive to survive.

He fumbled with the tent flap and winced at the burst of frigid wind that slapped his face when he pushed it through the opening. The air felt so cold it burned. He hadn't appreciated the comparative warmth of the interior of his tent until now.

No clouds floated in the Arctic sky, yet no sun shone either. Except for the spruce trees, the world seemed to exist in shades of gray. Steeling himself against the cold, Edward crawled on his elbows the rest of the way through the tent opening.

"Morgan! Sheldon!" This time he had mustered a feeble cry, but nothing close to an actual shout. He spat in disgust and his saliva cracked before it hit the snow. He realized that meant it was colder than fifty degrees below zero.

The sled tracks led down a deep ravine. Terror at the prospect of spending his final minutes helpless gripped him. He cursed his former partners. They'd left him. He still had his blades, but what good could they do him now? He had no means of escape. How long could he survive in fifty-degree-below-zero conditions without food or supplies? Edward let the thought go. He squinted across the ravine and saw no dogs or men, only a serene landscape of spruce trees and snow. He crawled into his tent, deciding it would be his sanctuary until death came.

"Our father in heaven, hollow is thy name," he croaked aloud. "Now I lay me down to sleep in a frozen tomb, dark and deep." He closed his eyes. Strange how cozy his hiding spot now felt. After all he had witnessed, he decided death itself wouldn't be so bad as long as he met it on his own terms. Edward considered stripping naked and laying outside on the snow but couldn't summon the strength he needed to execute his plan.

He concentrated on the drifting sensation that now buoyed him, curled in his murky womb. *A womb or a tomb?* Perhaps they were the same.

He drew his knees up to his chest. He felt safe. *White surrounds me, yet I see only darkness.* Edward smiled at the gentle incongruity.

Time passed. Edward slept but did not die.

"You, in the tent. Are you awake?"

Edward struggled into a sitting position, his mouth parched and his pupils contracting from the invading light. Someone held the tent flap open. The sunshine turned the figure standing before him into a black silhouette. A sickening sense of déjà vu swept over him. For one moment, Edward thought himself back in the shed beside the bakery in Blackwall—the past ten years a dream. Then he realized the truth. A wiry, dark-skinned man crouched, looking into the tent.

No sound of breaking branches or inhuman roars came to his ears.

He glanced back at the newcomer—an Inuit. He seemed to be melting, his substance fluid. Edward's mouth went dry. He shook his head, as if willing his mind into coherent thought.

"Sick. Fever," he rasped. "Need help." He collapsed again and allowed darkness to cradle him.

***

His companion seemed to fade in and out of sight as he told the tale of a vicious and violent demon named Kigatilik. When the apparent shaman referenced The Claw People, his gnarled hands twisted into hideous pincers. He said he had once encountered a pair of prospectors lying naked in the snow, entwined in each other's arms, and frozen stiff. These stories and more replayed themselves with feverish repetition on a stage in Edward's mind. He tried to tell the strange man to stop but couldn't find the words. The faces and forms of his victims interspersed themselves in the scenes of mythological depravity and carnage. Blood-soaked figures contrasted with endless white mountains in Edward's nightmares. Had the demon, Kigatilik, wreaked this havoc?

"No, Edward," said a pulpy red maw that once anchored a face. "Not Kigatilik, but *you*."

Edward awoke from this most recent dream with a start. It had felt more like a visitation. Like the long-ago Sunday school story of Paul on the road to Damascus, the scales had fallen from his eyes. He'd been going about it all wrong. Nevertheless, the great god Kigatilik had come to him, had demonstrated for him.

"My god has taught me how to prey," Edward marveled.

"You're awake. Good."

Edward recognized the speaker but tensed when he realized he didn't know where his leather apron and knives were. Without them, he felt naked, exposed.

"Who are you?" Edward asked the stranger.

The old man sat down across from him. Between them a campfire blazed. "I am Sawaya, a Yupik shaman."

"What do you want?" Edward's eyes darted around, taking in his surroundings. He'd been moved, he saw. His location had changed, and the absence of his knives troubled him.

"Have no fear," the older man said. "If I wanted to kill you, I would have already done so, using a ceremonial ivory-bladed knife given to me by Tagish, one of the tribe's hunters, in exchange for healing his sick child."

"Or you could have bored me to death with another story like that one."

The shaman leveled his gaze on Edward. "I have kept you warm and safe as you thrashed and sweated. The stars have appeared and danced their dance in the sky five times, and I have watched over you. The caribou hide blanket you have curled under I have brought for you. I hunted to keep you fed, not a simple task since you scared away most of the wildlife with your ravings."

Sawaya rose and approached him. The old man fingered his carved-stone orca amulet with one hand and withdrew the ivory blade with the other. He crouched beside Edward, brandishing the weapon.

"Better put that thing away," Edward said. "Or I'll take it—and the entire arm holding it—as a souvenir."

The Yupik paused, considering. Then he sheathed the weapon. "You do not understand. I act as a go-between, serving my people, the Yupik, and the spirits of the sea animals."

"What do you want me for, a ritual sacrifice?" Edward felt his lips pulling into a humorless smirk. "I'll never let it happen. I've walked away from much worse."

"No. I dragged you away from worse. That is the truth. I mean you no harm. That also is the truth."

"How is it that you speak English?"

"I interact with those in the white people's village."

"Dawson City?" the words were out of his mouth before he could stop them. Edward winced; he didn't know if his description had made the rounds.

"Yes. The place you have fled."

An icicle of fear slid down Edward's spine. "How do you know that?"

"I've been watching you since you arrived. The first time you arrived," the old man said pointedly. "I witnessed your violent actions toward the woman on that first night and toward the others on nights that followed. I hope my silence, despite my knowledge, has helped build the level of trust between us."

"You saw the things I did. And yet you sought me out. You said you wanted to test me. Why?"

"I consult dreams. I listen to the spirits. I often know more about people than they themselves know."

"If you're trying to get me to pay you for your silence, your minutes are numbered, old man."

"You radiate a power unlike anything I have experienced. The only word I can use to describe it is *otherness*. You wish to feed your dark instincts."

"I fought against them," Edward admitted. "But then..."

"You had a vision," Sawaya finished.

Edward nodded.

"You saw Kigatilik."

Edward remained silent.

"Few see him. Fewer still see him and live. This is why I believe you can help me." Sawaya knelt and stirred the campfire with a stick. "There's someone else nearby who would interest you."

The shaman had piqued his interest. "Tell me."

"He is powerful, like you," the shaman said. "Mumetaq is the largest and strongest of our tribe. He towers over all others by two heads. But he attacks his own people. He was once a man, now he is a monster."

Edward felt his nostrils flare, his eyes narrow. He couldn't tell if he felt insulted or intrigued. A mix of both, perhaps. "Why is he like me?"

The shaman flushed. "Alike, yet different."

"Where?"

"He wanders, but can often be found near the seal camps. It's where he preys; where he eats."

"He kills seals? That is of no concern to me. You've wasted enough of my time." Edward cast the caribou pelt aside and stood.

The Yupik raised both hands in a warding gesture. "Mumetaq kills members of his own tribe. He eats them. He eats *us*." Sawaya grimaced. "He went hunting but returned possessed by the demon spirit we call the Wendigo. The transformation was instant, his hunger relentless. I tried everything I could to heal him. Nothing worked."

"And this Mumetaq, he still terrorizes your tribe?"

"Yes. He is a monster, with the strength of a polar bear. He does not protect us, does not honor our ways. Only a monster attacks, kills, and eats his people."

"Why tell me?"

"You can save our dwindling tribe." The Yupik clutched his orca amulet. "You alone have the expertise needed to do the job. I'm asking you to spare me and kill him instead. Consider it a challenge."

Edward grinned. "First, you will return to me my leather apron and knives. Next, you will lead me to your cannibal giant, old man. And then you will leave us alone."

***

Coming to him for help would prove to be the worst mistake the Yupik shaman had ever made. Of this, Edward felt sure. He sneered at the old fool's sincerity as he tracked his quarry. He had to give the old man credit, however, for the herb-infused stew he'd prepared for him. Edward had wolfed it down and his fever had broken. He felt like a new man as he took a deliberate step into Mumetaq's field of vision.

The giant lunged and swiped at him with polar bear-like ferocity. Edward dove into the sparse scrub cover provided by the tundra. His attacker lumbered toward him, but Edward darted out of harm's way.

Edward studied the other man's enraged visage. Bulbous tumors pushed out from his head in every direction. This was certainly the murderous outcast, Mumetaq. The shaman had described him well. His arms were enormous, his fists like limestone blocks. His sinewy legs looked like they could carry him a hundred miles before tiring.

The giant focused on Edward, bellowed, and charged.

Knowing he faced imminent danger, Edward reached into his leather apron and withdrew six blades, three wedged between the fingers of each hand.

Mumetaq's brutish eyes widened. The big man slowed, stopped, and then drew back, not out of fear but apparent reverence. Edward gave his first convert a beatific smile. He flicked the blades, quick and effortless, and saw how the mad cannibal admired how they reflected the starlight.

Edward had decided to serve his own purposes by not complying with the shaman's instructions. He offered Mumetaq his largest knife. The other man received it and an immediate change came over him. The perpetual look of rage drained from the big man's face. A look of malicious glee replaced it. The Yupik outcast sat down and looked at Edward, eyes agleam.

Edward flicked his wrist. He mimed approaching someone and slitting their throat, their chest. He showed the giant cannibal how to carve a body, and the important role the blades played. Edward pointed at himself. Then he pointed at Mumetaq, who now trembled with excitement. Edward pointed in the direction of the mining camp.

The giant grinned. A slaver of drool from his mouth caught the starlight. Edward realized the cannibal was literally hungry for action. *Come to think of it,* Edward thought, *I could go for a bite, myself. A special variation of steak tartare perhaps. Or fresh tongue. Why be afraid to try new things?* He turned and began walking across the tundra back toward Dawson City. Mumetaq rose to his feet and followed.

***

Gladys Beasely bundled against the night's bitter chill, marched along the all but deserted road on the edge of Dawson City. She'd been out late, speaking with other like-minded citizens about cleaning up the town's vices: the gambling, the dance hall girls, the drinking. Someone had inferred that some of the dance hall girls did more for the miners than just dance. For Gladys, that had been the last straw. She meant to confront these women of ill repute immediately, and either drive them from town or compel them to kneel and pray for forgiveness. She'd learned of the location of one of the largest brothels from a red-faced man, who had quickly clarified that he'd overheard some other men talking about it but had never visited the location himself.

Gladys knocked on the door of the establishment, but no one answered. She vowed not to give up. She hammered on the door. Still no one came. "I know you're in there!" she called. Her skin prickled with anger. When they opened the door, she'd be ready with Word and the wrath of God. She gazed at the door. Nothing happened.

Then she heard approaching footsteps. They rounded the corner of the building. Gladys flushed and turned to face the street, ready to explain. Two men, obscured by the night, approached. One towered over the other. Something hovering near the smaller man's midsection glinted in the starlight.

"On your way out, mum? I know this place," the shorter man said, "and I must say it is an affront to your better nature which, I've no doubt, lies hidden deeply within. Fortuitously, I am just the man to help you find it."

Gladys's knees threatened to buckle. She found herself unable to speak, unable to breathe. The giant savage intimidated, yes, but the shorter man with the English accent infused her with deep, penetrating dread. His eyes glittered maniacal, monstrous. He wore, she saw, a leather apron. In each hand, he held two menacing blades. He twirled the knives with ease and tossed them each aloft in turn, like a juggler at a carnival. It was quite a feat. One, she realized belatedly, that she'd never have the chance to see again.

Gladys fell to her knees on the frigid, muddy ground. Movement had become impossible. She gazed straight ahead as they approached, until all she saw was the monster's leather apron.

BLIND FAITH

The day Juleen Hardgrove's life changed, the midday sun cast its heat with palpable force. Juleen paused midway between the farmhouse and the well and let the empty water pail hang limp in her hand. She gazed at the Ridgeback Mountains jutting out of the earth on the far side of the valley. The scene never failed to inspire her. Someday, she'd cross those mountains. Someday, she'd build her own life.

The Hardgroves kept to themselves. Pa tended to the crops he coaxed from the fields. He worked dusk to dawn, as the unpredictable Montana weather allowed. Juleen didn't find that unusual. She had no knowledge of how farming was done elsewhere, and never questioned her father's nocturnal habits. He slept days. When his family had bathed and turned in, he rose and went out to work the fields.

Ma was a silent woman, taciturn, but loving toward her children. Juleen had never heard her mother speak. Each day she cooked, cleaned, tended the garden, and tackled a dozen other duties and chores. She and Juleen had worked out a series of hand gestures for when she wanted or needed help.

Elsabeth, Juleen's older sister, sat in her corner and sewed. The girl looked like a beautiful store-bought doll. Her sister had creamy, perfect skin, full lips the color of red ribbon, and bouncing sweet corn-yellow curls. Elsabeth sewed clothing for the entire family. She created fluffy quilts that staved off the bitter winter cold. She knitted with incredible speed and created breathtaking embroidered scenes. She did it all by touch. Elsabeth could not see. Juleen's sister wasn't just blind, Elsabeth lacked eyes. Sometimes Juleen cast surreptitious glances at her sister's face. The disconcerting pockets of darkness lurking behind her half-closed eyelids marred her otherwise remarkable beauty.

Juleen—boyish and stocky—often thought of herself as apart from the others. Every day and night, she struggled with a restless feeling. She wanted to travel the wagon-rutted trails that narrowed out of existence in the direction the sun rose, and in the direction the sun set. Juleen wanted to see more of the world.

Twice a year, on the vernal and autumnal equinoxes, Pa hitched their mule to the wagon and Ma made the journey to the nearest town. She'd leave at sunup and return at sundown. Pa never went, owing to his preference for the night, but he always labored over a handwritten list of supplies to be purchased. Juleen had a dozen questions. Did her mother speak in town? Did she simply show the shopkeepers the list? How did stores work? Did her family have money Juleen didn't know about? Did her mother trade for goods? The wagon always left empty and returned piled with supplies. Though Juleen begged each time to accompany her mother, her parents had never let her leave their homestead.

Juleen sighed, tore her longing gaze away from the sawtooth majesty of the Ridgebacks, and resumed her journey to the well.

Juleen turned the crank to lift the heavy wooden bucket from the aquifer deep in the ground. Motion on the horizon caught her attention. A colorful wagon came into view, an iridescent beetle trundling along the trail. Juleen kept her eyes on the slow-moving object as the bucket rose. She dumped the water from the well bucket into her own pail. Then she secured the rope and peered again at the approaching wagon. It rolled along, still miles away. Juleen carried the pail of water back to the farmhouse.

Excited to be the bearer of news, Juleen pushed open the door. "Ma, there's a—" she broke off when she saw her mother standing at the far window, watching the wagon's approach.

Juleen put the pail on the table and joined her mother. Ma put a finger to her lips and cast a meaningful glance at the room where her husband slept.

"Who is it?" Juleen whispered. "Can you tell?"

Ma's lips pressed into a thin line. She made a brisk motion with one hand. *Salesman.*

***

As the wagon neared, Ma and Juleen busied themselves preparing for a guest, or possibly, guests. In her corner, Elsabeth sewed in placid silence. Ma swept the floor while coffee brewed. Juleen couldn't stop herself from looking out the window to mark the wagon's progress.

At last, Ma signaled Juleen to go outside; it fell to her to greet their guests.

Shivering with anticipatory delight at the break in monotony, Juleen paced in the dooryard's dusty heat. She kept glancing at the wagon on the trail, the same way her tongue strayed to the empty socket whenever she lost a baby tooth.

As the wagon neared, she picked out more details. The wagon itself was black, but garish and colorful lettering decorated the side that she could see. Four horses—three black, one a dark brown—pulled the wagon. The man at the reins wore all black, with an old-fashioned stovepipe hat pulled down to his ears. The wagon slowed and the horses turned toward the farmhouse. The driver must have noticed Juleen standing in the dooryard watching, because he twitched the reins and the horses began to prance.

She studied the driver's face as he approached. He had smooth, sun-darkened skin. His dark eyes, shaded by his hat brim, conveyed both warmth and danger. His high-bridged nose sat atop a dark brown mustache that spread over soft lips like sleek bat wings.

Juleen's insides felt tingly. Her heart raced. The stranger pulled at the reins and the horses came to a standstill. The man doffed his hat and made a deep bow. He grinned.

"Hello, darlin'. Is your father here?"

"Pa's sleeping like always, but Ma has coffee ready for you."

Juleen said. Caught up in the wonder of the moment, she added: "I'd like to see what you got inside your wagon!"

One side of the stranger's mouth lifted in a half-smile.

Juleen felt her face flush with embarrassment. "Beg your pardon. We don't get many guests." Not knowing what else to do, she kicked at some pebbles and waited for the visitor to speak.

"Well, now," the man atop the wagon said. "I'm always glad for such an enthusiastic greeting. Why don't you introduce me to your mother and we'll see about satisfying your curiosity later."

Juleen nodded. The man placed his stovepipe hat on the seat beside him and climbed down from the wagon. Juleen led the way into the house. Her mother rose from her seat at the kitchen table as they entered.

"Allow me to introduce myself. I am Doctor Alfred Moyle, madam." The stranger gave her a deep bow. "I am so pleased to make your acquaintance."

Ma acknowledged his bow and motioned for him to sit. Then she signaled to Juleen to speak on her behalf.

"Ma doesn't talk. She..." Juleen realized she couldn't explain something she didn't understand. "My mother's name is Judith Hardgrove."

Her mother smiled at their guest and poured him a mug of fresh-brewed coffee, which he accepted.

"Thank you, madam. And what is your name, young miss?" he asked.

"Juleen."

"And your father?"

"Sleeping, like I told you."

Moyle laughed. Juleen glanced at her mother, who gave her a reassuring smile.

"Yes, of course, but what is his name?" Moyle pressed.

Juleen's cheeks burned for the second time in as many minutes. "Pa's first name is Aleister."

Moyle sipped his coffee and then asked, "Is he ill? Perhaps I can be of service. I have with me a wide variety of miraculous cures gathered from the ends of the earth."

Juleen shook her head. "He isn't sick. He just sleeps during the day."

Moyle peered first at Juleen and then at her mother. "I see." He said at last, though Juleen realized Moyle found her father's habit unusual.

"Well, I don't," Elsabeth exclaimed, "because I can't!" She laughed at her own joke.

Moyle started in surprise. Juleen felt sure he'd have spilled his coffee if he hadn't set it aside. He stood up fast enough to send his chair skittering backward.

"I beg your pardon," he said, looking at Ma. "I didn't realize someone else was present." Moyle walked over to Elsabeth's corner.

"My! Aren't you the picture of beauty?" He bent and kissed her small white hand. "On my honor, you are as lovely as a porcelain doll." He took her other hand and kissed that as well. Elsabeth giggled and Juleen felt a prickle of envy.

"She's eleven," Juleen blurted. "And I'm nine." Moyle straightened. Ma sat rigid, watching Moyle. Juleen sensed something had gone wrong. Was it her fault? "My sister and I have the same birth month. Isn't that interesting, Mr. Moyle?" She knew she was babbling but didn't know how else to smooth things over; the mood of the room had changed.

Their guest strode back to the table and reclaimed his seat. "It's *Doctor* Moyle." He pinned her to her chair with a withering look. "I hope I won't have to remind you again."

"I'm sorry... Dr. Moyle." Juleen felt shocked and close to tears.

Ma made a pair of quick hand gestures and Juleen slid from her chair and left the table. A weight lifted from her spirit and buoyed her steps. Ma had told her to wake her father. Pa would set things right.

She tapped on his door. When he didn't respond, she knocked. "Come," he said, his voice groggy from sleep. Juleen entered her father's dark, windowless room. She closed the door behind her. *This is all Elsabeth ever sees,* Juleen thought. "Pa?"

"Yes, lamb?" her father still sounded drowsy.

"There's a man here," Juleen whispered. "He rode up in a funny looking wagon."

"I need my rest." She heard her pa yawn. "Are you sure you can't handle him yourself?"

"He's actin' fresh." Juleen danced from one foot to the other, anxious to have the stranger gone.

"With your ma?"

"With Elsabeth."

Her father made an inarticulate sound as he considered her words. She heard the whisper of his blanket and he drew it aside to climb out of the bed. "I'll get dressed."

Juleen left the blinding darkness of her father's room for the silent oppression of the kitchen. On her way, she passed her sister. Elsabeth stitched the hem of a gingham dress and kept silent.

Juleen gazed at her mother as she reseated herself at the table. She didn't look at Dr. Moyle. Awkward silence reigned.

At last, Juleen heard her father's approach. Moyle turned his head and broke into an impolite smirk he didn't try to disguise. "I see now who the living doll takes after!" he said, and followed his remark with a guffaw.

Unused to the light, Pa blinked like a mole as he surveyed the room. He reached Ma's chair and stood on tiptoe to kiss her cheek.

Then he made his way around the table with cordial solemnity and extended his hand to shake with Moyle. "I am Aleister Hardgrove. How do you do, sir?"

The doctor rose from his chair, towering over Juleen's father by more than two feet. Moyle went through his introductory speech again.

"Don't think we need any of what you have for sale, sir," Pa said, his tone mild but unapologetic. "We make do for ourselves. My wife, bless her heart, makes the most of the local herbs."

"Haven't met anyone yet who didn't end up buying *something* from my traveling medicine show." Moyle scowled down at Pa. The big man seemed to be taking mental inventory of his wares: "Pills, tonics, elixirs, remedies, cures, pamphlets, novelties, and entertainment."

Ma gestured and Pa spoke in reply. "That is a splendid idea, my dear." To Moyle he said, "Won't you stay for dinner?"

Moyle gave everyone in the room an oily smile. "Don't mind if I do. I take my steak rare, madam."

"There will be only stew, I'm afraid," Pa said. "But we'll have something made in no time, won't we?"

Ma nodded her assent, rose, and busied herself about the kitchen.

"Juleen, would you see to Dr. Moyle's horses?" her father said. "I'm sure they'd appreciate some fresh water."

Juleen rose and walked to the door. To her dismay, Moyle followed her.

"It's too late to move on tonight," he announced. "I'll just bed my horses down in your stable and be on my way in the morning."

Without waiting for a reply, the big man caught up with Juleen in three long strides. He grabbed her shoulder and spun her around to face him. Moyle bent and spoke into her ear. "Whatever you think about me, put it out of your head. I'll have what I want soon enough and then I'll be on my way."

***

"We're simple folks, Dr. Moyle," Aleister Hardgrove said. "Keep to ourselves most of the time, unless a neighbor needs help with a barn raising or Judith takes Elsabeth to a quilting bee."

Moyle studied Elsabeth for longer than Juleen thought gentlemanly. "That's why you know nothing about life," he said. "Out there is a world you cannot imagine." Moyle pointed expansively with his fork, a piece of potato still stuck in the tines. "I've been across this land and have learned a great deal." He shoved the bite of potato into his mouth and helped himself to the last of the stew. "Take those hills, for instance." Moyle indicated the general direction of the Ridgeback Mountains with his chin. "I bet you think they're something special. They're not." He slurped water and belched. "You ought to see the Rockies. Now those are *real* mountains."

Juleen noticed her pa hide a smile behind his hand and

wondered what he found amusing.

"No one knows as much about medicine as me," Moyle announced. "Not bragging, just stating a fact. The list of folks whose lives I've saved with my expansive knowledge and expertise would fill your living room walls."

Juleen refused to swallow this obvious lie. "I don't believe you."

Moyle's face paled. Ma set down her coffee. Even Elsabeth recognized the insult and stopped eating, her head cocked.

"Now, Juleen," Pa said. "Don't disrespect our guest."

Moyle drew himself up in his chair and locked eyes with Juleen from across the table. "Explain your insolence," the doctor said coldly.

Juleen hadn't heard the word before but guessed its meaning.

"You talk real big, but I think you're a liar. If your medicine really worked, people would come to *you*. But you keep moving from place to place, and that proves you're nothing but a cheat."

The words Moyle said next dripped venom. "You are a loud-mouthed, rude, and stupid little girl, in need of a thrashing."

"She'll get one," Pa said. Juleen wilted. She could stand up to Moyle, but her father siding with the stranger stung.

Her mother tried to console her with covert hand signals but Juleen stared at her plate, her eyes swimming with tears. She refused to be consoled.

"An unfortunate way to end the evening," Moyle said. "But I suppose acknowledgement of one's betters is too much to ask of back-country yokels." He pushed back his chair and stood. "I'll be gone by morning's light."

As Moyle strode to the door, Pa spoke. "Juleen, help your mother wash the dishes. Then change clothes and meet me at the woodshed." His features looked solemn, even grim. "After twenty lashes from my belt, you'll be helping me in the fields tonight."

***

It took Juleen a moment to realize her father had trudged past the woodshed without stopping. Had he forgotten the whipping he'd promised?

The moon glowed overhead. The stars winked and sparkled in the heavens as father and daughter made their way through the wheat field. The crop's leaves brushed their legs, and the heads, heavy with kernels, bowed as if in deference as they passed.

Pa entered a small clearing and paused. Juleen reached his side and gasped.

An oblong stone of the darkest black lay at the center of the clearing. Juleen's immediate emotion was one of amazement. Then she realized this was where her father would beat her, and her muscles tensed.

Standing shoulder to shoulder, her father met her gaze. As if reading her mind, he said, "I have no intention of thrashing you, despite that traveling charlatan's outrage. In truth, I am glad you stood up to him. He's an empty-headed braggart."

Juleen felt weak with relief. "But why did you take his side at supper?"

"I needed an excuse to have you join me here—at the Sacred Shrine," her father said. "Time is short. We must offer a sacrifice tonight."

Juleen's fear returned—and multiplied.

"Steady, my daughter," her father said. "Surely you noticed your mother does not speak. She sacrificed her tongue. Last year, Elsabeth sacrificed her sight by giving up her eyes."

Aleister reached into his satchel and retrieved a jar containing an herbal mixture of his wife's creation. He removed the lid, dipped his fingers into the sticky paste, and smeared sigils onto the surface of the shrine.

"Our rites are based upon an ancient Eastern maxim about seeing, speaking, and hearing no evil. We sacrifice a sense in order to gain insight into—and power over—evil."

Juleen remained silent and wide-eyed. She'd never seen this side of her father.

"Are we bad people, Pa?"

"Not at all, lamb!" he laughed. He finished his ministrations and closed the jar. "We are warriors, in opposition to evil. But I made a mistake; I delayed the completion of the rite, and now I fear we could pay a terrible price."

"Because of Moyle?"

"Yes, but if not him, there would have been another. It's my fault for letting you keep your hearing as long as I did. I will rectify that tonight. Once I have completed the rite, we will have one family member who is adept at each skill, and our power to stifle evil will triple."

Juleen opened her mouth to respond when an orange glow on the skyline over her father's shoulder arrested her attention.

Pa turned to look. Ma, her dressing gown billowing behind her in the night air, dashed toward them. She kept making a series of gestures with her hands.

"He's set the house ablaze," Pa translated. His lips pressed into a tight white line and his features darkened in anger. "And he's taken your sister—by force."

Juleen felt sick.

Ma arrived, gasping for breath, and fell to her knees, into Pa's arms. He held her until she broke their embrace.

"We cannot wait a moment longer," Pa said. He dug in his satchel again and withdrew a long-barreled revolver. Juleen felt her skin grow cold.

"Daughter," her father's words were gentle, "are you willing to make this sacrifice?"

***

Juleen stretched across the surface of the Sacred Shrine. The stone had soaked up the sunshine all day long and radiated heat beneath her, chasing away the chill she had felt.

What if Pa is crazy and all his talk is claptrap? Would Ma still allow him to do this? We need to save Elsabeth, not do this! And our home is burning to the ground!

Juleen gazed into the endless night sky and fought to silence her thoughts. The image of Elsabeth, held captive in Moyle's departing wagon, stuck in her mind like a cocklebur.

Ma spoke to her father through a series of gestures.

"No, she's *not* out of reach," Pa said. He peered into the darkness. "Moyle has his horses at a full gallop, but he's still well within striking distance."

Juleen had no cause to doubt her father; his night vision was much keener than theirs.

He dug once more in his satchel and withdrew something Juleen couldn't identify. He held his hand out to Ma. "Judith, take some beeswax to protect your ears during the ritual."

Juleen's eyes shifted between her parents as they pressed the beeswax into their ears. Her heart raced. *Please let the waiting be the worst part of this*, she prayed, although Juleen did not know who she expected to acknowledge her.

Ma took her hand. Juleen, despite her mounting trepidation, felt comforted.

Pa used his thumb to cock the hammer of the revolver. He placed the gun uncomfortably close to her ear and pointed the barrel away from her, into the wheat. He uttered a strange series of words Juleen couldn't understand.

He pulled the trigger while still speaking. Juleen's entire body jerked in shock. Her eyes watered—or perhaps she wept. Both seemed plausible. Her father had placed his free hand between the weapon and her face to protect her from the worst of the recoil. Juleen trembled. Her ears rang. *Just one*, Juleen realized. *The ear on Ma's side still works.*

The moment she realized this, her parents switched places. Ma took her hand again. Pa leaned down and spoke into her ringing ear. "Thank you for your noble sacrifice, my daughter. I love you."

He straightened, repeated the incantation, and pulled the trigger.

Utter silence fell.

No echo, no ringing, no humming. Juleen heard nothing to indicate even the absence of sound. She had entered the domain of ineffable silence.

Her parents helped her into a sitting position. Ma pulled a kerchief from the pocket of her dressing gown. She wiped away wetness from Juleen's ears and cheeks.

Juleen stole a glance at the kerchief and her stomach gave an unhappy lurch when she recognized her blood. She'd hurt herself before, was no stranger to blood, of course. This blood, however—trickling from deep inside her skull—seemed more intimate, more precious, somehow.

Pa knelt at the head of the altar. Ma took the space to his right. He motioned for Juleen to kneel at his left.

Take your father's hand and close your eyes, Ma signaled. When Juleen reached across for her mother's hand, Ma shook her head. She pressed her free hand against the black stone surface. Juleen did the same and closed her eyes.

Seconds later, she felt a dizzying sense of motion. She panicked and opened her eyes. Her father squeezed her hand in a gesture of reassurance. Both Ma and Pa kept their eyes closed. Their features seemed serene.

Juleen closed her eyes and the sickening motion returned. It lasted only a few moments before a shape swam into focus. *It's a glass jar,* Juleen realized. It held dried seedpods. The view changed, and Juleen was ready for the motion this time. It took getting used to, but she no longer felt quite as sick. More jars and bottles nestled against each other in carpetbags and crates. Juleen saw Elsabeth's delicate hands lashed together with strips of rawhide. Juleen leaned her forehead against the stone altar, stunned. She understood she was seeing what her sister would have seen—if she still had eyes.

That's part of the sacred magic, a woman's voice said. *Now that we are connected, we all see what she can't; we all hear what you can't; and I can speak here, but only because you are all with me.*

Though she had no memory of ever hearing it, Juleen knew this was her mother's voice. Girlish excitement intermingled with sorrow over their situation and threatened to overwhelm her. It was too much to take in; she couldn't—

"Juleen, look at all this neat stuff!" Elsabeth thought. "Thanks to you, I can see it!" She scanned the interior of the medicine show wagon, revealing animal pelts, antlers, exotic fruits and vegetables that neither of the girls recognized, and more. A pair of marionette puppets danced frenetic jigs as the wagon jounced over the trail. Juleen laughed, despite herself. In the semidarkness, they identified a deck of playing cards, a white banjo, a dark shotgun, and an assortment of other fascinating objects.

Then Ma's voice came again. *All right, girls. You've had a gander at Moyle's treasures. It's time we put an end to this.*

"Will you come rescue me, now?" Elsabeth asked.

We're sending help, Ma said. *Everyone be silent, but stay connected. Your father and I must converse with Awaxaawé and plead our case.*

***

Juleen never forgot what happened that night, nor did she ever fully understand it. Her perceptions of the events were like individual puzzle pieces but try as she might, she never assembled the puzzle into a coherent picture.

The name her mother had used was, "A-wa-ha-wa," but more nuanced and guttural in her pronunciation.

Juleen kept her eyes closed, kept holding her father's hand. She braced herself against the stone altar.

Pa seemed to be speaking to Ma in the real world, and Ma, in turn, communicated with their mysterious benefactor on the family's behalf. Awaxaawé's responses made Juleen feel as if an angry porcupine kept bristling inside her skull. She tried to understand its language but comprehended nothing.

Then, for a single prolonged moment, everything lapsed into darkness and silence.

The world beneath her quaked and shook without warning. The ground fell away, then rose and struck her. Juleen hurtled through the air, flailing her arms and kicking her legs. She tumbled and rolled through the wheat field like a dirt clod in a dust storm.

She lost sight of her parents and the black stone altar. Her skin stung from various scratches and scrapes. The nausea bothered her the most. Her mind's eye, like a looking glass, duplicated her physical state, and Juleen tumbled through endless inner space.

Her instinct toward self-preservation forced her eyes open. If she could get her bearings, she reasoned, maybe the dizziness would subside.

The earth's violent tremors continued, as if following a pattern. The ground heaved like storm-tossed waters. She tried to tuck into a ball to protect her head and limbs each time she fell.

Then Juleen misjudged her position and hit the dirt hard enough to drive the air from her lungs. She lay on her back, fighting for breath. Juleen sought the moon for comfort—but could not find it. Even the twinkling stars had disappeared. Then the moon emerged from behind a towering cloudbank and glowed high in the sky. Some of the stars reappeared as well, while others disappeared. The ground shook, and Juleen bounced and rolled. Now, however, she kept returning her gaze to the night sky. Something out there was moving: something colossal. *It blotted out the moon just now*, she realized.

A fresh shockwave sent Juleen airborne. When she landed, her head struck a solid, smooth surface. She fell unconscious before her brain realized she'd returned to the Sacred Shrine.

***

Juleen awoke to the touch of her mother's hand on her cheek. Her eyes fluttered open. Ma's face was smeared with dried blood and her hair was tousled and mottled with wheat kernels. Pa stood nearby, squinting at the sun's brilliance. He smiled at Juleen then turned his attention back toward the horizon.

Her mother stroked her face and helped her sit. Juleen saw Elsabeth riding toward them, astride the brown horse, and clutching its mane. The trio of black horses followed. Juleen remembered Moyle and chewed on her lip, contemplating his fate.

Elsabeth leaped from her perch and Pa hugged her tight.

The family faced each other. Pa said something and Elsabeth smiled. Ma gestured an approximation of his words for Juleen's benefit—something about riding the tail of a comet. To her right, a wispy column of smoke rose and smudged the sky. Their home,

Juleen knew, lay in smoldering ruins.

The brown horse had wandered in close to the group and nuzzled Elsabeth.

Ma's hands flew, and Juleen tried her best to decipher her communication. *We'll ride the horses to the next homestead and seek help there. Moyle is dead. Elsabeth is safe. We, the Hardgroves, have won.*

Juleen didn't feel like they had won. She felt dazed, battered, and exhausted. She gazed across the valley at the Ridgeback Mountain range and frowned. Her perception of the world around her had altered, though she could not articulate how.

***

Fifteen year later, Juleen woke to the motion of her husband lunging from their bed. She sat up and watched Jeff pull on a pair of trousers. He grabbed his shotgun from above the door and hurried out into the night.

Juleen sat awake, waiting until he returned.

A fox outside the chicken coop, Jeff signed when he reentered the house. *I shot it.*

Juleen pondered the hens. Jeff had heard them, but she could not. Suppose they had not had the ability to communicate their terror in a way Jeff understood? How much damage could the fox have done, if left unimpeded?

Jeff returned to the bed they shared. He gave her a quick but loving kiss on the cheek and settled in beneath the blanket.

Juleen observed her husband as he curled back into the same position in which he'd lain before waking. Even though she had witnessed it, she perceived no discernable evidence that he'd roused, risen, dealt with the disruption, and returned to his slumber.

Suddenly, Juleen found it hard to breathe. Her pulse raced. In her mind, she returned to the night when the earth had rumbled and shook. She remembered the man who had destroyed their home and had tried to steal her sister. He had disappeared from the face of the earth. Juleen considered the moon and stars, blotted out for a moment, and then reappearing. She thought about the sawtooth peaks of the Ridgeback Mountains, mere miles from her childhood home. Nothing had looked, or felt, quite the same to her after the earth-shaking events of that night.

Sunrise found Juleen still awake, pondering the night she learned faith could move mountains.

WENDIGO, GOING, GONE

"**M**r. Ziebart, I'm Jacqueline Swift. Feel free to call me Lin. I'm one of the resident directors here at Great Lakes Funeral and Cremation Services."

She shook hands with her final client of the afternoon.

"One of my assistants, Josephine Fiddler, is attending to other business. Other than Josie, we have the place to ourselves. You are my last appointment of the day, but don't feel like we are in a hurry. I am happy to provide as much information as possible regarding our services and can answer any questions you might have. Please have a seat."

She indicated the chair opposite her. The man, Bob Ziebart, seated himself. He had purple crescents under his eyes and a disheveled head of brown hair. His off-the-rack suit was rumpled. Ziebart glanced at the arrangement room's ceiling, the understated artwork that hung on the walls, the vases of fragrant flowers, and finally, the floor. He looked everywhere except at the woman who would help prepare his deceased wife's funereal arrangements.

Lin had grown used to it. Many clients, men especially, expected to meet with a man. One dressed in a tasteful dark suit, hair silvering at the temples, perhaps the third generation of a family-run business. Lin knew about family traditions; hers went back more generations than she could count.

"Just to share a little about my background," Lin said. "I've been in the business since I turned twenty-two. I started at a crematory. Before long, I realized I wanted to do more to help the families and to help the decedents." She paused, gauging the man's reaction. His eyes darted, caught hers for an instant, and then he returned his gaze to the floor. She continued. "We strive to give the person what they wanted in death, even if it was never possible for them to get everything they wanted in life."

"That's a beautiful sentiment," Ziebart murmured. "But she hated the idea of being buried in a casket, lavish or otherwise."

"We pride ourselves in offering more contemporary options, and a healthier grieving experience. Death is natural and shouldn't have such a stigma—"

A muffled crash—the sound of a cadaver gurney tipping over—came from the next room and Lin paused. For the first time, her client was looking at her and holding her gaze. "What was that?" he asked.

That, Lin thought, *sounds like my reckless assistant letting her hunger get the best of her.* Aloud, she said, "It was probably a gurney bumping against the wall. Nothing to worry about."

Lin gave the man her most reassuring smile and continued with the topic at hand. "While we do offer traditional embalming and funerals, green funerals are rapidly gaining in popularity. They're aimed at making burials low-impact on the environment, and you can be assured your loved one will return to the earth naturally without any embalming chemicals or invasive procedures."

The man began to turn his head but caught himself and looked down into his lap. Lin understood; he was about to defer to his wife, ask her what she preferred—and then he'd remembered.

"If your wife enjoyed the outdoors and loved nature, she might appreciate that option. We offer decomposable wicker caskets and biodegradable shrouds."

Ziebart seemed distracted. He hunched his shoulders and crossed his arms. "Is it cold in here? I feel a sudden chill."

Lin allowed herself an inward sigh. Unlike the antlers or hairy bodies, this was an aspect of the folklore that held a basis of fact. A sudden, unseasonable chill signaled the presence of those like her, especially when feeding. *To say nothing of the foul stench*, Lin mentally added. It was why her kind had begun infiltrating the business of death; it was the perfect place to hide in plain sight. She had clouded her client's mind, but her assistant wasn't shielding herself at all. *Reckless.*

"We're adjacent to a refrigerated area. If Josie is working in there and inadvertently left the door open, it can create quite a draft." Lin forced a smile. "We can relocate if you like?" She lifted the final word to reframe her offer as a question, but the man shook his head.

"No, no. I'm fine." He took a deep breath. "I think I'm just beating around the bush. This isn't the type of conversation one enjoys having."

"I understand completely," Lin said. "Are you leaning more toward a green burial, then?"

"My wife didn't know that was an option." Ziebart paused, seeming to contemplate. "She always like the quote about 'ashes to ashes, dust to dust.'"

"Cremation," Lin said. "Certainly. We offer those services as well. We have a cremulator on the premises. Another opportunity for the families to be more involved—if they want to be involved, of course. Everyone's comfort level is different, but I believe it helps the grieving process. You, and your wife's friends and relatives, may choose to decorate her cremation container. If you have children or grandchildren, they can draw pictures, for instance. You can put flowers on top or tape notes to the side. Loved ones can write farewell messages on it... you get the idea."

The man nodded. Another blow against the other side of the wall caused Lin to make a quick decision.

"I've given you a lot to think about," she said, rising from her chair. "Here are brochures explaining each of the options we offer. I'll give you a few minutes to think it over, and then I'll be back to answer any questions you might have. Please excuse me for one moment."

Lin exited the room and pulled the door closed behind her. She hurried a few paces down the hall and pushed open the door to the preparation room. What she saw appalled but did not surprise her.

Her assistant knelt on the floor, crouching over a cadaver. Josie felt her presence and looked up, her face and hair clotted with gore. She tried to appear apologetic, but Lin wasn't buying it.

"Have you lost your mind?" Lin hissed. She clenched her hands into fists. "I have a client in the next room! We wait until nightfall to feast. This has always been the rule!"

"I'm sorry! I had a lapse in judgement," Josie's shoulders sagged. "I got back from a pickup at Regional Hospital, and they had seven new cadavers for us to take. I lost control. I'll stop."

"Damn right you will. Get that one on a drawer in the cold chamber," she nodded in the direction of one of the large morgue refrigerators. "And wash your face; you look beastly."

She left the room and hurried back to her waiting client. *Seven decedents in one trip? That's got to be a record.* She only had a moment to puzzle over this before turning the knob and reentering the arrangement room.

"I'm so sorry for the delay," Lin gave the man a comforting pat on his shoulder and resumed her seat beside him. "Do you have any questions I can answer for you?"

"Well..." Tinges of pink brightened the man's pale cheeks. "I'm thinking she'd like a green funeral, with a wicker casket, maybe. But how much is that going to cost?"

"In general, a traditional embalming and casket funeral will be the most expensive. Cremation will be the least expensive, with a cost differential of about a thousand dollars. Green burials end up somewhere in between. I'm happy to get you a specific cost breakdown that you can take home and examine. Then, when you've decided, we can meet again to discuss—"

A moan of anguish so loud it sounded like the roar of a wild animal drowned out her words. All color drained from Ziebart's face. "I... I'd better go, uh, p-perhaps I've come at a b-bad time." He finally managed.

Lin couldn't blame him. An unpleasant chill emanated from the shared wall. The room reeked. Josie had obviously failed to keep her promise.

Lin set her jaw and rushed to the preparation room. If the man left while she was gone, so much the better. She threw open the door. "Josephine! I warned you—" The words died on her lips.

Bitter cold filled the room. Their exhalations crystallized in the air. Blood, scattered bones, and ragged lengths of hair covered the floor. Two gurneys had tipped on their sides. Even the walls were spattered with gore. Doors to multiple cold chamber slabs hung open like the mouths of shocked passersby. At the center of it all, gnawing on stringy remnants of meat from someone's hipbone, sat Josie. Her assistant had completely given in to the Change.

Josie's altered frame was gaunt to the point of emaciation. Ash gray skin pulled itself tightly over her bones. Josie's eyes had receded deep in their sockets, where they glittered from within the shadowy darkness. Her sore-covered flesh gave off an odor of decay. Her bloody lips pulled back from her gore-clotted teeth in a threatening, possessive snarl.

Lin fought to maintain her composure, but her entire body trembled. With each cadaver Josie had devoured, her hunger had grown. That was their curse: to grow in proportion to their last meal so that one could never be full, never be satisfied. Gluttony was punished with starvation.

"Damn your greed, damn your lack of self-control," Lin shouted. "And damn *you!*"

Josie responded by lifting the bone to her bloody maw and scraping off another bit of meat with her teeth.

"Wendigo psychosis! My god! I always thought it was either just a metaphor or a convenient excuse for someone who'd gone mad with starvation."

Appalled, Lin turned to look at the speaker. She hadn't heard the grieving man's approach. He looked past her, and surveyed the room, wide-eyed.

"Native American folklore has always fascinated me," Ziebart said. Despite the carnage, his voice was calm. "I've studied it extensively, in fact. The police won't understand. I should stay until they arrive. I can help explain. She shouldn't have to face the death penalty if she genuinely believes she's a Wendigo."

"Windigoag." Lin said.

"No," the man said. "I've studied the etymology of the various words from the different tribes. They all mean the same thing, but the word you just used is actually the pluralized form."

"I know that." Lin felt as if she wanted to tip her head back and unleash her sorrow and frustration in the form of a scream.

"But that would mean—" Ziebart looked stricken. He took a fearful step backward.

"That's right," Lin said.

She lunged.

***

Lin sat alone in the office where the only illumination came from the city lights shining in through the window. She pondered the events that had transpired.

Seven new bodies. At once. Josie had looked at the sudden influx and seen a feast. She hadn't been able to resist. Lin, who had learned how better to control her appetite, had brought down her lone victim with more regret than hunger.

The telephone on the desk rang, startling her from her reverie. She let the machine take the call. "This is Summerside Retirement Facility calling. We need to schedule a pickup at your earliest possible convenience..."

Lin rested her forehead on her fingertips and massaged her temples with her thumbs as the voice provided the particulars. Lin realized she'd have to call someone in; she didn't trust Josie to make another run. The caller hung up. The phone immediately rang again.

"This is Regional Hospital. We have nine more deceased needing immediate retrieval..."

What the hell is going on out there? Lin frowned and gazed out the window, as if the night skyline would somehow provide the answers she sought.

Lin heard Josie moaning from down the hall. Her victims numbered seven; thus, her suffering was sevenfold. Josie deserved it for showing such a horrendous lack of restraint. She'd made a series of poor decisions today. *Let her think on her misdeeds.*

The telephone rang again. "Uh, hi, this is Good Shepherd Nursing Home. We have half a dozen deceased that we'd like you to pick up. Tonight, if possible. If you wait until morning, there will likely be several more. You have our address on file."

Lin lurched from her seat. She left the office, sped past the arrangement room, and reached the preparation room, where she'd left Josie with strict instructions to clean every inch of the floor and walls. "This room better be spotless, because every drop of blood is evidence," she had said. Lin had then taken several boxes filled with remains to the cremulator. The machine had been working on reducing bone, hair, and tissue to ashes ever since.

Now, in the doorway, Lin stopped short. Josie had done next to nothing. Instead, she sat on the floor, slumped against a wall. She turned her ghastly, emaciated face toward Lin and coughed. "I'm sick," she said, in a timid, helpless voice.

"You ate too much," Lin replied. "You know how the hunger grows."

Josie shook her head and then coughed again. She wiped the back of her hand across her mouth. "This is different. I'm *sick.*"

Lin felt her blood run cold—or colder than normal. "Josie, what did the paperwork say?"

Josie gave her a blank look. "I didn't check."

"You didn't—" Lin's rage boiled. "Seven new cadavers in one trip, and it didn't occur to you to look to find out what had killed them?"

Her assistant made no reply, only stared down at her blood-sticky hands. She coughed again.

From the office came the shrill ringing of the telephone.

Lin considered. Something truly terrible was happening across the city. People were dying in alarming numbers. And instead of benefitting from this catastrophe, Lin and Josie were only going to suffer. They were responsible for eight missing persons. Tomorrow, the building would likely be teeming with law enforcement. *We've finally found a way to survive, maybe even thrive, and now it's all going to hell.*

Lin's frustration gave way to horror as the death rattle of Josie's final breath broke the silence. Lin touched the door jamb, irresolute.

Wide-ranging emotions quarreled for supremacy within her. Lin mourned her Wendigo sister, but for a moment, she hated her too. That hatred quickly found a new focus. *Humans,* Lin seethed. *Humans are the real problem, the real threat. They've unleased some new plague.* Had she already contracted it? She shivered.

Lin felt weak. Her breaths came in gasps. She sank to the floor, put her face in her hands, and wept.

Down the hall, the phone began to ring.

ANIMATE OBJECTS

"Everybody in here avoids you." The pale woman leaned in close, filling Debra's field of vision. Her breath soured the air. "I want you to tell me why."

Debra Montez, known to the screws as inmate 37829, looked up at the blond woman who had approached her in the concrete confines, charitably referred to as "the yard." Debra appreciated the sixty minutes of fresh air and sunshine afforded to her and the other inmates of B Wing each morning after breakfast. She didn't appreciate the skinny woman's intrusion. The newcomer had the hungry, darting eyes of someone looking to make a name for herself. *A freshie,* Debra thought. *And scared.*

Silver Mountain Women's Correctional was fraught with interpersonal politics. Debra had learned from hard experience that whenever she found herself surrounded by others, trouble often followed. She met the newcomer's gaze. "I avoid people, and people avoid me. That's just the way it is. It's for the best."

"Yeah, but I wanna know *why.*" Blondie took a step closer. Her pale skin set her apart from most of the inmates at Silver Mountain. Debra wondered what crime the woman had committed. She looked too healthy to be a meth head. The woman kept clenching her right hand, curling her wrist toward her hip. *She's hiding something in her sleeve,* Debra thought. *A shiv?*

Blondie sat down cross-legged across from her. "So, what's the story? With you, I mean."

Debra shook her head. "It doesn't matter. We're here to do our time. If you're looking for protection, I'm sure you—"

The other woman interrupted. "I'm not trying to be your *friend*. I just wanna know what you did to wind up in here."

"I did nothing."

Blondie snorted. "That's what we all say, right?" She glanced around, as if gauging the yard. Different groups congregated in different areas. Plenty of eyes lingered on the two of them. Debra understood. This one hadn't found a group to accept and protect her. So she had targeted Debra, another loner.

"You're one of the few who has a cell all to yourself." Blondie pressed. "Why?"

Debra did not intend to reveal her past. The prison psychologist, Hoglan, had told her many of the inmates had a history of mental issues. He'd included her with that group, thanks to details revealed at her trial. Debra herself wasn't convinced.

"If I had a cellmate, they might not always be safe."

"So you're the baddest bitch on the block, huh?" Blondie's lips twisted into a sneer. Debra tensed, ready to react if the other woman tried to attack.

"I don't want to explain. You wouldn't believe me anyway." Debra tried to stand, but Blondie leaned in fast, close enough to touch.

"Damn it! I asked what makes you special." Her voice cracked, betraying her rising anger. "Last chance to talk before I lose my shit."

Debra pictured what the woman might have hidden up her sleeve. She eased herself back. She didn't fear the woman; freshies like her were easy to read. Debra hoped if she humored her and told her story, Blondie might write her off as cracked and decide not to make an enemy of her.

"I'm here because I was late for work one too many times," Debra said. "I thought my boss had it out for me, but I was wrong." She sighed and stared at the ground, thinking. "Maybe it'd make more sense if I told you about my home life first."

***

The alarm clock slumbered, shirking its duty. Debra knew she had set it, but the damned thing hadn't rung. She'd overslept for the second time in a week. Debra sat bolt upright with an oath. The bedding twisted around her legs, tried to pull her back into bed. She disentangled herself and slid into her waiting slacks. She glanced at the clock. At least it kept accurate time. If she hurried, she'd only be about ten minutes late—as long as she didn't miss the bus.

Her job at the call center wasn't demanding and she had no major complaints, except that Lang, the floor supervisor, seemed to have a problem with her. As a rule, she made few mistakes and gave him little reason to reprimand her, but lately she found arriving at work on time difficult. Debra appreciated her cozy apartment. She felt fortunate to have a full-time job that paid her bills, but sometimes wondered if, deep down, she dreaded going to work more than she dreaded losing her job.

Debra found her loafers halfway across the floor and stepped into them. She hurried from her bedroom, through the living room, and into the open kitchenette. She drew a glass of water straight from the tap and gulped it. Debra shrugged into her jacket. She reached into the pockets for her apartment keys. Her heart sank. The keys were not where she had left them. Debra's shoulders slumped. She had even triple-checked before bed.

"Not again," she murmured. "*Not again.*"

***

The optimism of arriving at work ten minutes late had deflated like last week's birthday balloons by the time she discovered her key ring underneath her bed.

She bolted from her apartment and, in her hurry, made another catastrophic error. She took the elevator. This elevator gave her fits. It often ran slow, or stopped between floors for no apparent reason. As if on cue, the cube lurched to a stop between the fourth and third floors. Debra's unease at running late only increased her feeling of helpless claustrophobia. She pressed her sweating forehead against the cool metal of the elevator door and forced herself to relax. She didn't carry a cell phone and couldn't call ahead. Instead, she had to content herself with mentally rehearsing the conversation she would have with Mr. Lang when she finally arrived. The elevator, as if sensing her predicament, restarted its descent.

Debra's journey became a mirror image of itself.

Elevator. Sidewalk. Bus aisle.

Seat.

Bus aisle. Sidewalk. Elevator.

Lang.

Her supervisor stood waiting at her cubicle when Debra scuttled into the call center. She felt her stomach drop. "I'm so sorry, Mr. Lang, I had some trouble—" Debra stopped when Lang raised his hand.

"The first time you came in late, I let it slide. The second time, I had to give you a verbal warning." He brandished a sheet of paper. "This written warning is a Plan for Improvement." He handed Debra the page. She glanced at it and looked again at Lang, who had kept talking. "If you arrive more than five minutes late any time in the next thirty business days, we will take further action up to, and including, termination of employment."

A verbatim quote from the employee handbook, just for me. Oh, joy! Aloud, Debra said, "I understand, Mr. Lang. It won't happen again." She scribbled her signature on the sheet. "My alarm didn't sound this morning and then I couldn't find my keys. Some mornings, it seems like everything conspires against me."

"I don't need to hear excuses. I need productivity." Lang glanced around and lowered his voice. "You answer to me, but I answer to *him.*"

Debra followed her supervisor's glance down the hall to the executive suite where the corporate president lounged like a malevolent ruler behind perpetually closed doors. She'd never met the man face to face but had caught glimpses—and had heard stories. "He's not big on diversity," Lang murmured. "He's on my case all the time to facilitate turnover among certain...

demographics."

Debra felt her cheeks growing hot. The inside of her mouth dried. "That's discrimination. He can't fire people without cause."

"Exactly." Lang nodded as if the conversation had concluded. "So make every effort to be at work on time. And no more flimsy excuses."

He strode away and Debra sat down at her desk. She focused on controlling her breathing. Debra glanced around her cubicle, barren save for a laptop, phone, and headset. She appreciated the risk Lang had taken by revealing the ugly truth of the matter. She craned her neck and made a mental inventory of the men and women who'd populated the workstations around hers when she first started working there. Blond and bubbly Sue still occupied the cubicle to her left. Paul, who spoke with a charming Aussie accent, answered calls from the cubicle across from her. Scanning other cubicles, however, Debra realized several other faces were absent. *So it's true.* She pressed her lips together in a thin line and booted up her computer.

She took calls for the rest of the morning, most from customers who needed help troubleshooting issues with their appliances or had questions about warranty coverage. She fielded a smattering of unavoidable complaints, and one woman grumbled about her accent, but Debra kept her cool, followed her scripts, and made it to lunch.

She took off her headset and looked up to see another cubicle neighbor, Muhim, waiting. "You want a coffee or a tea?" Muhim asked. "Come on, I will walk with you."

Debra rose. "Coffee sounds great." They walked side by side to the staff break room.

"I noticed you were late again," Muhim said. Her Somali accent ran her words together in a way that Debra secretly found charming.

"Yeah, Lang noticed too." Debra said drily. "He wrote me up."

"What if he fires you? What will you do then?" Her colleague's eyes betrayed a sense of vicarious excitement. Debra knew Muhim lived with several extended family members in an apartment on the lower South side, just as her companion knew Debra lived alone. Muhim had inferred, correctly, that Lang firing her would be catastrophic.

"He just doesn't understand the things that happen to me." Debra hugged herself and frowned.

"Like what?" Muhim tucked a stray lock of hair back under her shash and reached for the coffee pot. She poured two cups as Debra struggled to explain.

"I know it sounds crazy, but it's like, if I set my keys down after work, they won't be in the same spot when I wake up in the morning. Or my shoes will be missing. Things like that."

"But no one is there to move your belongings, Debra." Muhim gazed at her over her steaming coffee cup, her dark eyes dancing with excitement. "Unless you think someone is breaking into your apartment. Do you think your building super might be using a master key to sneak in and watch you sleep?" She shivered in exaggerated revulsion.

Debra stifled a giggle. She shook her head. "No one's doing it. It's just... happening." She sipped the steaming brew. As the pair strolled back to their cubicles, an idea came to her. "Hey, will you do me a favor?"

"You want me to hide in your closet and watch to see who is moving your belongings?"

This time Debra did laugh. "If I give you my phone number, will you call me in the morning? I don't trust my alarm clock to wake me."

***

As Debra approached her apartment building that evening, an elderly man limped toward her from the opposite direction. White tufts of hair bristled from beneath a tweed ivy cap. Laugh lines surrounded his twinkling eyes. A brown paper bag of groceries filled each arm. He looked familiar, but Debra had no name for the face. He looked, to Debra, like the stand-in for Santa Claus in a Norman Rockwell painting.

"Let me get the door for you." She smiled at him and hurried ahead to unlock the street-level entrance. She stood back, holding the door open. The white-haired man glanced at her, gave a curt nod and a grunt, and sidled inside the vestibule. He panted as he approached the elevator door.

"Would you like some help with your groceries?" she asked.

He glanced up at her face. "No, thank you." Still holding the bags, he pressed the call button with his elbow and turned his back on her.

"I don't mind." She moved toward him. "I'm Debra Montez. I live on five." The elevator doors opened, and the man stepped into the car.

"You look like a nice enough girl." The old man stood near the doors. His wide-legged stance and the grocery bags prevented Debra from entering. "But one never knows." Before she could reply, the elevator doors closed on the old man's unsmiling face.

***

The rebuff of her friendly gesture, coupled with the fear of arriving late again and thus losing her job, kept Debra from falling asleep for hours. She tossed and turned long into the night, kicking at the covers, adjusting her pillow. She couldn't get comfortable, and her mind wouldn't let itself rest. At last, she dropped off into a fitful doze.

Debra woke to the somber grey light of dawn and to the grating jangle of her clock's alarm. She felt surprised it had done its job. Debra blinked several times, trying to lubricate her eyes. She sat up and stretched.

The telephone gave a shrill cry and leapt from its place on her nightstand. The phone landed on the floor.

"Come here, you stupid thing." Debra said. She reached for the receiver, but the phone rang again and it skittered across the bedroom floor, as if startled anew by its own ringing.

Debra scrambled on her hands and knees toward the phone. "Why are you doing this?" she cried. Exasperation lifted her voice up two octaves. "Just because that might be Lang calling doesn't mean—" *No, not Lang,* she realized. She'd asked Muhim to call.

She dived with arms outstretched, and caught the phone on its third ring, skinning her knee on the floor in the process. Wincing, she lifted the receiver. "Hello?"

"Hello, Debra?"

"Hey, Muhim," Debra rose to her feet with a huff of exertion. "Thanks for calling."

"You sound out of breath. Everything okay?"

"Yeah, just chasing my stupid phone."

After a long pause, Muhim responded with a laugh that sounded uncertain. "Well, you said to give you a call, so... See you at work?"

"Sure. Thanks again."

Debra made it to work on time, and Lang, seeing her at her desk, nodded and returned to his office. Debra booted up her computer and adjusted her headset. "I appreciate your service and your professionalism," she murmured, nodding at each apparatus in turn.

The workday progressed without incident.

***

As soon as Debra unlocked her apartment door, her key ring leapt from her hand and skittered across the floor. Debra sighed. "You want to travel? Fine with me. But you better be where I need you to be when I wake up in the morning."

She closed the blinds, but they refused to rest and opened themselves again. Debra flopped onto the couch and kicked off her loafers. The microwave oven beeped, inviting her to heat up some food.

"I grabbed something from a taco truck after I got off the bus," Debra announced. The microwave beeped again and fell silent. Debra knew if she wanted food later, the microwave would refuse to work.

The television, as always, seemed eager to please. It was an outdated model with a fuzzy picture by today's high def standards, yet Debra had put off discarding it. She turned on the television and settled onto the couch. The book on her coffee table riffled its pages. Debra had to turn up the television's volume with the remote.

"I swear, some of you make me crazy," she muttered. She thought of Mr. Lang's Plan for Improvement and addressed the room. "If I'm late for work again, I'll lose my job. Then I'll have to move somewhere else, somewhere smaller. Most of you will have to be sold, or taken to the dump."

The riffling book fell silent. The blinds closed. She watched her keys slink across the floor toward the front door. Satisfied, Debra squinted at the television's faded picture until her eyelids felt heavy. She closed her eyes and let herself drift.

Just after midnight, her alarm clock's battery died, and it stopped ticking.

***

"Debra, I need to see you in my office." Mr. Lang's expression told her everything she needed to know. *He means to fire me.*

She looked around at her colleagues in their cubicles. Never before had she observed them so studiously focused on their duties. *I guess I face this alone.*

She hurried into his office and closed the door. "Mr. Lang, I am *so* sorry."

He pressed his lips in a tight white line. He slid a sheet of even whiter paper across his desk toward her. Debra ignored it and kept speaking.

"I talked to them last night. I told them they needed to behave, and to stop working against me. I explained what was at stake." Debra knew she was babbling, but she couldn't stop. "I got through to them, I'm sure of it. They mean no harm. But it died overnight. No one could foresee that."

Lang's eyebrows knit together in apparent consternation. "What died?"

"My alarm clock. The other times, it was just being lazy. That was its personality. And my keys—they love to travel. That's why they're never where I leave them. But I talked to them all last night, and I *told* them—"

Lang shook his head. "I don't have time for this." He withdrew an expensive-looking fountain pen from his desk drawer. "Sign your termination at the bottom of the page."

Debra felt her heart pounding in her chest, a panicked bird in a cage. "Mr. Lang, *please*, you don't understand. Objects, when they're around me, reveal their inner personalities. Some of them have minor faults, just as everyone does. Some are disorganized, others are weak, and a few shirk their duties."

Lang's cheeks had reddened. "Just sign the paperwork, Ms. Montez. I don't want to hear another word!"

***

"So what the hell happened?"

Debra considered before replying. Reliving the past had left her drained and she felt a headache coming, thunderclouds on the horizon.

"He didn't hear another word," she finally said.

"Why not?" Blondie prodded.

"His fancy ink pen revealed its personality. It was..." Debra found herself reliving the humiliation of the prosecution's mocking cross-examination during the trial. "It was violent. And evil."

A wide grin transformed Blondie's face. "Holy shit. You stabbed him with it."

"No!" Debra grimaced. "I didn't do anything. The pen—"

"Did you go through his eye into his brain and kill him instantly, or did you stick it in his throat and watch him bleed out?"

Debra wished the other woman would shut up and leave her alone. She longed to be back in her barren cell. She closed her eyes, blocking out her surroundings. *Bunk, toilet, basin, bench,* she thought. *Nothing there can get me in trouble.*

"You murdered your boss just so you could get three hots and a cot!"

"No..." Debra mumbled, shaking her head. Danvers in her memory again, wide-eyed, and spouting his psychobabble nonsense about "malicious psychokinesis." She squeezed her lids tighter. "No, not me."

"I'm kinda pissed you tried to sell me your crazy 'the pen did it' bullshit, though." Blondie said. Debra registered the threatening undertone creeping into the other woman's voice. "You and I need to come to an understanding. From now on, I—"

Debra heard the other woman yelp. She opened her eyes.

Blondie was staring down at the makeshift weapon buried deep in her belly. Blood soaked the fabric of her jumpsuit in a widening oval. As Debra watched, the liquid seeped into the small white bristles. Blondie whimpered. Red droplets began to drip from the bristles, the protrusion jutting from her belly now mimicking a leaky faucet.

"Hey!" a voice shouted. One of the screws had finally noticed. "Break it up, goddammit!" He came at them in a full run. "*You* again!" he exclaimed when he recognized Debra. A second guard arrived and pinned her to the ground. Debra did not resist. She'd get time in solitary, but she didn't mind. She kept her gaze fixed on the shiv. Debra reflected upon the incongruity between its sunny yellow hue and the deep scarlet seeping from the woman's ugly wound.

A thought came to her, and she clung to it with desperation.

I didn't do anything. It's the toothbrush that's bad, not me.

BEHIND HIS SMILE

There are only three of us staying in this dilapidated little roadside motel. It's a sad indicator of the shortened attention spans of people today. There was a time when—thanks to the Mothman legend—this motel would be flashing their NO VACANCY sign for most of the year.

The man in number twelve interests me a great deal. Twice now, we've passed each other, crunching across the motel's dusty parking lot. He glanced down at me and offered a tentative smile as we passed and I nodded cordially in return, but that was all. His overall appearance was rather off-putting, but I've decided I would like to visit with the fellow. His presence in this lackluster place interests me. The only other guest is an elderly woman, who is staying in room six. With me staying in room two, it makes me wonder if the clerk made a conscious decision to keep us as far apart as possible. Could the walls be that thin?

Perhaps they are; I've made frequent trips to the soda machine that bakes in the sun on the far side of the motel, and every time I've passed the closed door of number twelve, I can hear the tall man speaking. He says things that I can't quite grasp; poses questions I have no answers for. It's like trying to follow a conversation with an astrophysicist who barely has a handle on the English language. I wonder if he's crazy.

But what if the man in twelve is here for the same reason I am? He might also be marking the anniversary of the first sighting of the Mothman. Plenty of people have heard about the mysterious creature, but precious few seem to be interested this year.

I mentioned the man's incessant muttered questions, but I suppose his eccentric appearance is what most people would remember. He's deeply tanned and quite tall: my opposite in these respects. His long dark hair is combed back, and he wears a glittering green full-length coat that looks to me like what they call a duster. I've never seen him without it. He wears a wide black belt that matches his deep-set eyes. Now that I think about it, when he smiled at me that first time, I thought he rather looked like an aging shock rocker. The man's clothing and demeanor are terrifying and ridiculous in equal parts.

The motel is a throwback to the heyday of Route 66 when men still wore hats. The rooms form an L shape. The office squats apart, close to the curb. My room is shabby and exudes a musty odor that I imagine spans back decades. It's the type of place one imagines has seen better days, but even those days weren't much to celebrate. The prices are quite reasonable however, and the sweaty, morbidly obese man who tends the motel office was quick to volunteer directions to the nearest "gentlemen's club," which I understood was meant as a friendly gesture. I asked the clerk, who introduced himself as Dewey, about the Mothman, but he only shrugged the rolling hills that were his shoulders.

"Just moved here about a month ago. Never heard of no 'Moss Man.'"

He seemed sincere, so I didn't bother to correct him.

A vacant strip mall molders next to the motel on one side, and a decrepit warehouse leans in from the other. Drive a few miles north of here on Route 62 and you'll encounter the abandoned remnants of the West Virginia Ordnance Works. Travel a mite farther and lose yourself in the McClintic Wildlife Area. I suppose it's not a typical tourist destination. But I'm not a typical tourist. Nor, I would wager, is the man in twelve.

Perhaps we are kindred spirits, pilgrims still searching for the truth about the Mothman. If I could devise a way to "accidentally" encounter the grinning man, perhaps I could engage him in conversation. If I turned the topic of conversation to the Mothman, we might share our experiences and anecdotes with each other.

***

I've been here over a week and still haven't met a friendly or talkative person besides the corpulent motel clerk. The servers and store clerks pretend not to hear my questions concerning the Mothman. I find their collective silence rather perplexing. Much to my surprise, the statue depicting a rather sensationalized artist's rendition of the Mothman has been removed, perhaps even demolished. Gone are all the souvenirs. The fact is I can find no trace of the legend, though I know it exists. I wonder at this sudden change.

I drive my car around town and the surrounding area, wandering and exploring each day until late into the evenings. The cherished notion that I might miraculously encounter the Mothman is never far from my mind.

In fact, as I turned into the motel parking lot after another disappointing and uneventful day, a strange figure froze in the glare of my headlights. My heart leapt into my throat. *There it was!*

My eyes had deceived me. I hit the brakes and stopped only inches short of the tall man from room twelve. Despite the close call, he grinned when he recognized me. His green duster sparkled in the illumination and billowed behind him in the breeze like wings. No wonder I'd been fooled. The dark man nodded at me and, still grinning, strode across the lot. My radio erupted with crackling bursts of feedback from several stations, all talk radio programs by the sounds of it. I fumbled with the volume knob, but the sounds seemed to diminish of their own accord. I glanced up in time to see the tall man push open the door to room ten and disappear inside the rectangle of darkness. Surprised at his apparent room change, I drove the last few yards in uneasy silence.

***

I wonder if the man in the green duster is here without

transportation. I have yet to run into him at any of the diners or convenience stores around town. I've described him to people. I assumed a fellow that eccentric looking was bound to get local tongues wagging, but all I got were blank stares in return.

He must not have been satisfied with room ten either. I could hear him running through the litany of his incessant questions as I passed room eight this afternoon on my way to the soda machine. I felt half-tempted to simply knock on his door and use his room hopping as an excuse to start a conversation, but I chickened out again and kept moving. Headaches arise with each trip to the vending machines, but I can't decide if it's more or less caffeine my body craves.

***

This is strange; the man with the perpetual grin now occupies room six.

An ambulance arrived early this morning and a pair of sleepy attendants wheeled the old woman out on a collapsible gurney and hoisted her body into the back of the vehicle. I say "body," because if she were alive they certainly wouldn't have zipped her into that telltale black bag for the trip.

The motel clerk didn't know the cause of her passing, even after I had offered him a ten-dollar bill for his trouble, so I again took him at his word.

As I climbed into my car the next morning, I sensed someone watching me and looked up. The new occupant of room six stood in the window, parting the curtains and grinning at me. He acted as if he and I shared some ghoulish secret and I felt my heart start to race. I backed out and sped away down Route 62.

***

Today while hiking in the McClintic Wildlife Area, I had a chance encounter with a park ranger. The fresh air cleared my head and I felt great, as I often did during my time away from the motel. I'd been wandering along a nature trail, and the ranger marched in my direction from deeper in the brush. We exchanged greetings and mild pleasantries. His name, he said, was Simon. He explained that part of his job included ensuring the deer hunters followed the appropriate laws.

"Need a special permit to hunt out here," Simon said. "Only bucks with an antler span of fourteen inches or greater can be kilt."

How he pronounced "killed" somehow put me at ease. Whatever coldness had infected most of the town hadn't affected the park ranger, at least as far as I could tell. I broached the subject of the Mothman.

"Wasn't a moth, wasn't a man," Simon announced. He hitched up his belt in a way that reminded me of Barney Fife. "It was a bird."

"I'll be darned," I commented, lapsing into a folksy delivery that matched his. "Must've been awful big." I still had my own ideas about the creature.

"Oh, it was," Simon agreed. He leaned in and lowered his voice though we were alone. "My daddy was a park ranger here in the sixties and seventies. He passed on in '82, but he told me the truth about the Mothman a few days before he died." I held his gaze and waited for the second-generation park ranger to continue.

"The Mothman was just a mutated bird. Looked like a giant Sandhill crane. The damned thing had two necks and two heads! My daddy swore to the fact on his deathbed. Said the thing had a wingspan of thirteen feet. He thinks the red foreheads accounted for the red glowing eyes folks claim they saw."

"How'd a giant two-headed crane disappear like it did?" I had started to think there might be something to Simon's story.

"Just a few days after some folks saw it roosting on the Silver Bridge, it flew into a power line. Blew out the 'lectricity in Point Pleasant and burnt itself into a crispy critter. Animal control called in the Park Service to have a look-see. What was left of the bird stunk to high heaven and was barely recognizable. The feathers had melted together like wax. My father said they'd kept the bird spread out on the concrete floor of one of the old ordnance buildings at the TNT factory for just a day before it decomposed into ash." He shook his head as if to clear it. "Happened so fast that no one ever got a picture of it, but it was a bird. I'd swear on my daddy's grave."

"I'm sure that won't be necessary," I said. "Nice chatting with you." We shook hands and parted.

**

I arrived back at the motel to discover the grinning mystery man had turned the corner and now occupied room four.

Not that this should have surprised me. I would have been more astonished had he *not* moved. I've given up on understanding his eccentric actions. Now I simply accept them. Given the grand scheme of things, switching rooms at a seedy motel isn't unheard of. Maybe he's just bored. Or he could be trying to find a cleaner room. I haven't seen a maid or housekeeper since I checked in.

Still, his manner is decidedly strange. Take his odd clothing for instance, or the unceasing stream of questions I hear every time I pass his room. What would a face-to-face conversation with the grinning man entail?

**

I feel hung over, though I didn't do any drinking last night. This morning I awoke face down on the worn and musty fibers that pass as carpet here and staggered to the bathroom sink to splash my face. I had tossed and turned all night. The noise from room four had me gritting my teeth and wrapping the lumpy pillow around my ears. When I did manage to drift away my sleep was plagued with nightmares.

"*Drovizel! Where is you?*" The voice had sounded like it belonged to a chain-smoking caveman filtered through an old drive-in movie speaker. The sound had scrambled my brain like a relentless fever dream. "*They bolted. I lost them. Drovizel, where is you?*" If the sound had gotten any louder, I thought the grimy mirror in the bathroom would shatter. That, or my eardrums would burst. The motel room door had burst open, and a sparkling green figure towered in the doorway.

The mysterious man's dark eyes dragged around the room. Never in my life have I seen such a haunted, ghastly face. "*Drovizel! Is you here?*" he cried out as he raked his long fingers through inky black hair.

I realized two things in quick succession: first, that the man's lips did not move as he spoke.

Then I realized I wasn't asleep.

***

I've stayed in bed all day today. I'm not by nature a hypochondriac, but right now, I believe something must be wrong with me. Perhaps lack of sleep makes me paranoid. Dewey somehow squeezed through his office door and waddled across the parking lot to check on me. Sweat droplets jettisoned off my shaking body and pattered onto the carpet as I stood leaning against the doorframe, listening to what he had to say. He wanted me to seek medical attention. I told him that I simply had a bug and would be right again in no time. I felt guilty for lying. He probably feared having a second guest die at his motel in less than a week. I, meanwhile, feared leaving before I could unravel the mystery of the motels' only other occupant.

***

The rest of the morning, the grinning man in the sparkling green duster subjected me to a barrage of questions that my mind could not grasp. My nose bleeds intermittently, and my head hurts so badly a migraine would be an improvement. The man has introduced himself to me several hundred times over. His name is Indrid Cold.

Around noon, I gave up trying to rest and summoned all my strength. I hoisted myself out of bed. Indrid Cold's voice reverberated in my head as I staggered across the gravel to the motel office. Dewey looked up in surprise and reached for his old wall-mounted phone. I held up a hand.

"You can call an ambulance after you answer a couple questions for me." I paused to catch my breath. Indrid wasn't as audible here. The motel clerk nodded.

"You hear that television blasting all the time?"

"Nossir."

"Hear anyone yelling or talking?"

The clerk shook his head.

"Dewey, did you ever serve in the military? Were you ever injured in combat?"

The obese man just looked at me as if I were crazy.

"I'm wondering if you happen to have a metal plate in your head."

Dewey's eyes popped open in a mix of delight and dismay, like I'd just offered him a box of chocolate-covered cockroaches. "I was in a bad car wreck two years ago," he said. Dewey rapped his knuckles on the back of his skull and produced a flat yet metallic tone.

I nodded. "Second question. What do you know about the man in room four?"

The clerk stared at me blankly. "Four is vacant."

I shook my head. "Mr. Cold is in there now. He occupied room twelve when I first checked in, but he's been making his way—"

Dewey furrowed his brows. "You're the motel's only guest."

"I've seen him on several occasions! I hear him rambling on like a lunatic every day!" I leaned against the counter. "He's been changing rooms and getting closer to mine!"

The clerk threw up his chubby hands. "You're crazy, man! You prob'ly got hallucinations from your fever or something."

I spun around and tottered out of the office. My walk back to my room felt like climbing a mountain in the face of a storm, but I pushed on despite the pain. I needed closure.

I know Indrid Cold does not intend harm. I feel his sorrow and his confusion. I believe he may have gone mad. Cold is a stranger in this world. I believe he lost something of great sentimental value a long time ago. I visualize a beloved and cherished pet scampering away from a station wagon during a family vacation in a remote wilderness. I believe something similar happened here all those years ago.

The mood of the townies makes more sense to me now. As Indrid Cold rambles about, he inundates minds with endless headache-inducing questions. The locals—some consciously, others perhaps unconsciously—have developed a Pavlovian response to him. By denying the Mothman's existence and shutting it out of their thoughts, I bet that Cold tends to leave them alone. Yet I think about the Mothman often. It's possible the old woman in six died of a brain hemorrhage when Cold got too close for too long. I blame myself. My interest in the Mothman somehow drew Cold to me, and she paid the ultimate price as a result.

Why he chose to approach me room by room down the length of this dilapidated motel I cannot explain. Moreover, does he realize the damage he is capable of when he tries to communicate? If Cold sees me as a kindred spirit and has the urge to confide in me, I will not deny him. A frown of anguish hides behind his perpetual smile, and I believe I understand why. I try to remember the details Simon, the park ranger, shared with me. Indrid Cold will want to know them. Perhaps he'll finally find some measure of peace.

I stand at the door of room two. *My room.* My brain feels like it wants to boil out of every orifice in my head. During the brief time that I was gone, Indrid Cold has moved in. I am his ultimate goal. I steel myself and turn the knob. When the door swings open, I hope I will be able summon enough strength to return his trademark grin.

A FROZEN MOMENT

Brandon Bouchard stood facing his adversary. Two thousand restless, shouting Kazakhstani waited in anticipation. The opponents did not look at each other. Instead, they stared down at their blades hovering inches apart. Brandon tensed and tightened his grip.

The linesman dropped the hockey puck and Brandon reacted a fraction of a second quicker than his opponent. He drew the puck toward him with the blade of his stick. He passed it to one of his teammates, Zach Cullen, a winger from Minnesota. The kid skated well and had what Brandon's teammates back home in Toronto called "soft hands." Cullen outmaneuvered his defender and turned up the ice.

Brandon spun, intending to follow, but a scowling player from the opposing team caught him under the chin with an elbow. Brandon's head rocked back, and his knees grew watery. He sprawled face-first onto the sheet of ice. Dazed, he wiped ice shavings from his helmet visor in time to see that Cullen had passed the puck to Viktor Antropov, the other forward on their line. The pair had just crossed the blue line into the attacking zone. Brandon leaped back up and skated as hard as he could to rejoin the play.

***

Brandon liked to think of the ice rinks as battlefields: each game was a battle to win, each season of hockey, a war. Two evenly matched sides fought to achieve victory. The coaches were the generals. They drew up the battle plans and shouted commands. Each goal scored signified a step toward conquest. Each army went through boot camp, training exercises, drills, and gathered intel about their adversaries. Instead of local recruits, the teams were mostly comprised of mercenary soldiers. The players who skated out with fresh legs during a line change entered the fray like reinforcements. Brandon dreaded suffering an injury; no soldier wants to get wounded. Most of the players played through pain and did everything they could to stay in the game. To Brandon, the worst feeling *wasn't* the pain that usually came with an injury, but the frustration in having to sit and watch from the stands.

Brandon, playing nearly 9000 kilometers from his Ontario home, saw himself as the ultimate soldier of fortune. He didn't speak the local language, but understood the universal language of hockey, and they paid him to play it.

Brandon had just celebrated his twenty-forth birthday; he wasn't a kid anymore. This might be a make-or-break season. He always hoped to turn heads, get an offer to play for more money in a better league. And Brandon still had his looks. At least, based on the attention he received from young—and sometimes not so young—female fans, he assumed he did. He still had a straight nose, never broken; he was a sniper, not an enforcer. He'd never dropped the gloves for a tilt. He only had a single scar along his left jaw line from when a stick blade caught him up high his first semi-pro season. He considered himself lucky. Brandon sometimes wondered how much longer his luck would continue.

***

Cullen and Antropov cycled the puck around the net with Daniel Jarvis, one of their defensemen. Brandon stayed back at the blue line until he and Jarvis could switch places. Then he saw an open spot and drifted toward it. For the moment, the opposing team had lost track of him.

Across the ice, Cullen raised his stick blade to the rafters, as if readying for a thunderous one-timer shot. Brandon broke toward the net, his eye on Antropov. His teammate sensed his presence and found him with a perfect saucer pass. Brandon settled the puck, noted the goalie out of position thanks to Cullen's distraction, and fired a slap shot. The goalie adjusted too late to make the save and Brandon watched the puck hit the back of the net. He always carried with him a frisson of unease until he or someone on his team scored a goal. Then the uneasiness lifted, replaced by a feeling of relief—until the next face-off.

Brandon passed the net, but before he could raise his arms in celebration, someone drove a crushing blow into his lower back. He hurtled toward the ice rink boards that surrounded the playing surface. For one frozen moment, Brandon mentally celebrated his goal. Then he struck the boards headfirst.

The soldier hears the crack of cannon fire and realizes he's been hit. His rifle falls from his senseless hands. He topples to the battlefield, rolls, and lies still. Staring up, he sees the artillery explosions lighting up the sky overhead. He wants to close his eyes, but there's something up there... something falling out of the sky. He can't move out of its way. It's his helmet, knocked from his head by the initial impact. It blots out the sky and then lands on his face, turning everything to darkness.

***

Brandon couldn't remember a damned thing. He didn't *need* to remember to know he'd suffered a horrific injury. The wheelchair he sat in confirmed that for him. Brandon couldn't feel anything from his waist down. He felt hopeless and alone. He was overseas on a temporary visa. He'd have to get in touch with his agent, or his parents, and alert them to his situation. He couldn't stay; he needed better medical care than they could provide here. Brandon willed away the tears of self-pity that threatened to spill down his cheeks. He looked around him, craning his neck in hopes of sighting a familiar landmark.

The scene was so bright and clear he had to squint. Sounds seemed more like noises. Smells hit him with near-physical impact. Everything he experienced felt bolder and sharper, as if his brain compensated for its loss of mobility by sharpening the focus of his senses. His brain had dialed everything up to an eleven.

Brandon raised his voice. "Does anyone speak English? I need help."

Passersby hurried past him. None of them looked him in the face or acknowledged his presence. They simply streamed around him. Brandon wheeled the chair toward a street corner and peered in each direction. Nothing looked familiar. Crippled, ignored, and now lost. He bowed his head and seethed. No one in Ontario would ever act this discourteously.

After a few minutes, Brandon straightened. His resolve had returned. He needed to find a location he recognized. The arena, the players' living quarters, even a familiar grocery store would help him get his bearings.

Swarthy-faced men, women, and children surged past him, traveling in both directions. Brandon rolled forward at a deliberate pace, afraid of running over someone's foot. As he crossed an empty street, an automobile sped straight toward him, and he pushed the chair's hand rims in a frantic, adrenaline-fueled attempt at reaching safety. The car's side mirror clipped one of the push handles on the back of the chair and spun him around, hard and fast. For one frozen moment, Brandon felt sure he'd tip and topple into the street. It didn't happen.

He shouted an incoherent string of curses at the receding vehicle. He looked around for a sympathetic face but found none. Everyone ignored him as if afraid his paralyzed condition might be contagious.

***

Hours later, soaked in sweat, his arms trembling with exhaustion, Brandon caught sight of the ice arena. He summoned his last remaining vestiges of energy and wheeled toward the welcoming sight. He knew his teammates weren't on the ice practicing this late in the afternoon, but he hoped he'd find Coach

Popov in his office. Maybe Kenes, the team trainer, would still be around the locker rooms. One of them could help him.

Brandon reached the entrance and fumbled with the arena doors. With no one in the vicinity, he had to maneuver his way through by himself. At last, he got through the door and wheeled down the concourse toward the locker rooms and hockey operations offices. Brandon reached a black vinyl curtain and paused to collect himself. He pulled the curtain aside and rolled through, only to face another set of doors. Again, he fought the door until he had made his way through and rolled down the hallway toward Coach Pop's office.

He reached his coach's—*former* coach's, he mentally amended— door and saw a thin line of light beneath it. Brandon rapped on the wood but received no response. He knocked again, harder this time. Pop didn't respond. He rattled the knob but found it locked. "Coach! Come on, open the door!" The door remained closed to him. Puzzled, he slumped against the chair's backrest.

Brandon admitted defeat and rolled out of the arena as quickly as he could.

***

At least he'd regained his bearings. He'd roll to the apartments and find Cullen, or one of the others who spoke English. He knew they wouldn't be as cold as Pop had been. By now, the sun had dipped close to the horizon and a chill had infused the air. His sweat stains chilled his skin. Brandon ignored his discomfort and rolled onward with dogged determination. Even stuck in this chair, unable to walk, he was still a hockey player, and hockey players had more grit than anyone on the planet. This he believed. *One of the boys will help me out,* he told himself. *I'll call my folks tonight and be on a plane home tomorrow.*

His hopes were dashed yet again. Brandon found the entrance locked. He shouldn't have been surprised. This was a standard precaution in a neighborhood with a less than ideal reputation. Brandon sat, considering. Some of the guys had likely turned in for the night, while those who had opted to go to a club wouldn't return for hours. He was stuck.

A minor glimmer of hope came. He recalled a corner store a few blocks from the apartments. Outside that store sat a phone booth with a working payphone. Back home, such a relic would be a rarity, but here in Kazakhstan, many still lingered. He ignored the dull ache in his arms and rolled toward the store.

***

Brandon wanted to scream. Part of him also felt like weeping. He did neither.

Instead, he stared dully at the payphone. Someone had ripped off the receiver. The cord hung like the drooping tail of a chastised dog. *It doesn't matter anyway*, Brandon thought. He realized he didn't have money or a calling card to place an international call. In the end, he didn't shout or sob—he laughed. His chest shook with rueful guffaws that bordered on hysteria. How could his current predicament get any worse?

As he pondered this, his gaze landed on a group of approaching men. His laughter ceased. Brandon could tell just by how they carried themselves—the drunken swagger, the boorish bravado—that they hunted trouble. At a club, surrounded by his teammates, he would have felt no fear. Here, at night, alone and crippled, he wanted to disappear. Not knowing what else to do, he rolled his chair backward into a recessed doorway.

There were five of them. Brandon's eyes jumped from face to face. Wiry black hair, beetle brows, narrowed eyes, sneering lips. One guy chewed on a wooden toothpick. Another slammed his elbow into the side of the phone booth, cracking the glass. Four of them wore motorcycle boots. Brandon doubted they rode. Instead, they probably favored the boots as a fashion choice and because the heavy soles could inflict tremendous damage to a ribcage, for instance, or to a face.

The group reached his doorway. Two of the men turned their heads to look in his direction but looked away after only a passing glance. He realized he was quaking.

The men passed him. Brandon waited, barely daring to breathe. He expected them to turn on him at any moment. Instead, the sounds of their empty boasting faded, and the group disappeared into the night. They'd shown him mercy.

***

Brandon wandered. He rolled through neighborhoods he'd never seen, never knew existed. When the sidewalk disappeared, he adjusted his trajectory and rolled his chair down the side of the street. He rolled well out of the way whenever a vehicle approached from either direction. But it was late, and traffic was light.

Brandon paused and gazed at the moon. It was nearly full and lent a ghostly iridescence to the tableau before him. He marveled at the idea that his family could look upon the same moon from their part of the world. There was a ten-hour difference between here and home, but Brandon could never quite reconcile in his mind which country was ahead of the other. He estimated it was close to midnight here. That meant, for his parents back home, it was closing in on 2:00 p.m. The facts surrounding the moon's orbit remained elusive to him. Would his family see the moon as he saw it later that night? Or had they already seen it during what, to them, was *last* night?

Brandon tried to feel closer to his family, but the attempt backfired. Now, he felt the distance between them even more keenly. Tears trickled down his cheeks and he wiped them away. For the first time, he realized he couldn't remember the last time he'd eaten. Nor could he remember the last time he'd used a bathroom. An appalling scenario came to him: if he couldn't feel his legs, then maybe he couldn't tell when his bladder was full. And if that was the case—

Brandon felt his crotch and found it dry. This should have comforted him, but it did not.

A terrifying idea presented itself, but Brandon rejected it hard and fast, like hip-checking an opponent into the boards. He grabbed the hand rims and pushed his chair down the road. He kept on at this pace until his arms felt weak and rubbery. He rolled to a stop to let his aching muscles rest.

The lit end of a cigarette glowed in the darkness. After a few moments, a querulous voice called out to him. Brandon felt so relieved at the acknowledgement of his presence that he didn't hesitate. He rolled toward the voice.

An elderly woman hunched on a dirty wooden stoop. She wore a shawl over her bony shoulders. The elapsed decades had whitened her hair. Her face was a wrinkled roadmap of her life. She squinted at him and exhaled a cloud of tobacco smoke. Then she mashed the cigarette out and beckoned him to come closer.

Brandon wheeled so near their knees might have touched. "Do you have a phone?" he asked.

The old woman held up a gnarled hand in a gesture demanding silence. She examined his face, like a painter trying to determine if he was fit to serve as the subject of her next portrait. Then she took one of his hands. After only a moment, she let him go, broke their contact.

"*Sen öldiñ*," she announced.

"Sorry, I can't understand you." Brandon's frustrations reared up again. He hadn't realized before today how much he'd relied on translations from his teammates.

The old woman rooted around in her wrappings until she withdrew a small pouch from some hidden pocket. The pouch was tied with a length of what looked to Brandon like leather, or rawhide. "*Sen öldiñ*," she said again. This time, the words seemed to carry with them sympathy, even a degree of warmth. Yellowed fingernails loosened the strings. She reached into the pouch, and withdrew something that might have been dust, or ashes. The old woman repeated her words a third and final time and threw the powder into Brandon's face.

His eyes burned, and he squeezed them shut. He heard her words again, but this time understood their meaning. "*Sen öldiñ*— you are dead."

A blinding white light blazed behind his eyelids. Then all became darkness.

***

Brandon's body reposed in the peace imparted by death, his neck broken. The empty vessel lay surrounded by teammates and opponents alike, their heads bowed, kneeling in respectful silence on the ice. The murmuring fans fell silent when the paramedics moved his inert form onto a spine board. One opponent sat weeping, apart from the others. Brandon knew, even without recognizing him, this player had dealt the deathblow.

Brandon Bouchard's spiritual essence considered the scene for one frozen moment. He drifted toward the rafters of Kazakhstan's Owl Creek Arena.

N.O.A.H.'S VOYAGE
(A FUTURE FABLE)

The derelict docked at sundown, though no one knew at first that the enormous hovercraft was empty. Everyone assembled on the dock assumed N.O.A.H. had brought another group of passengers safely across the boiling lava seas. The Nautical Overland Airborne Hovercraft's automated process of docking took less than three minutes. Porters stood waiting at the end of the gangplank, ready to carry any luggage the immigrants aboard might want help with. Drivers waited in their transports, ready to take the newcomers to houses, motels, or even a consulate building.

Minutes passed. No one disembarked. The usual cluster of porters—mostly rhinos and hippos—waited expectantly. A rhino porter coughed to show his impatience. The drivers, mostly springboks and impala, began to take notice, alerted by the inactivity of the porters. Two passing dockworkers, a jackal and a hyena, exchanged knowing glances, though in truth neither knew what to make of the situation. Along the dock, necks craned, and eyes rotated in sockets.

A passing giraffe made the most of her advantageous view and told anyone who would listen that the hovercraft's deck was "most certainly empty."

Someone must have contacted the shipping company because a chimp and a lioness arrived after ten minutes and took charge of the situation. They enlisted the help of a few volunteers—the jackal and hyena who'd exchanged glances among them—and seven inquisitive creatures marched up the gangplank to look for signs of life.

*****

Githa, a porcupine, trundled up the gangplank behind a family of antelope. She held her boarding pass up to be scanned, and then stretched out her neck to receive the electronic collar. According to the information packet she'd received, the collars were some sort of safety device. Githa suspected they also tracked their movements while aboard N.O.A.H. This vessel, she knew, was part of an entire fleet of automated transports, programmed to move Earth's surviving animals to areas of safety.

Some of the animals preferred to go below deck where they felt more comfortable while others stayed on the spacious deck of the hovercraft. Githa scanned the motley gathering of refugees, all hoping for a better life far away from the place mankind had called the North American continent. The eruption of the super-volcano beneath Yellowstone had rendered a large portion of it unlivable.

Lumbering bison, barking prairie dogs, sly coyotes, regal elk, and dozens of other animals both familiar and unfamiliar shared the deck. Squirrels scampered and scolded. Agitated rattlesnakes coiled and rattled a warning to careless passersby. A lone wolf skulked away looking for solitude. Githa found a corner and settled in for the journey.

The vessel launched without fanfare. A fawn, gamboling about the deck, lost its footing when the ship surged forward, and slipped between the deck and guard rail. It fell toward the molten lava, but only for a moment. Saved by its magnetic safety collar, it landed back on the deck, where it stood on trembling legs until its mother stepped forward and guided it to an area farther from the railing. Githa observed the entire scene unfold and felt thankful they'd averted disaster.

The continent receded behind the vessel and soon, Githa could make out nothing but the boiling morass of lava stretching to the horizon on all sides. According to N.O.A.H.'s information packet, the journey would only take a matter of hours. During this time of relocation, all truces and treaties were to be observed by all aboard. Food was supplied, including meat for the carnivores, and no hunting was allowed.

The animals milled around the deck and time passed.

***

A cursory examination of the vessel found nothing amiss. Food and water were present in plentiful supply. Luggage was still present and undisturbed. No damage to the vessel seemed apparent.

The chimp used his tablet to interface with the hovercraft's systems. First, he examined the ship's passenger list. "Two-hundred fifty souls aboard," he said.

"Full capacity," the lioness noted.

"Indeed," the chimp said. "So where did they all go?"

"Perhaps the vessel departed by accident before the boarding process began," the jackal said, trying to be helpful.

The lioness glowered at him. "Impossible."

The jackal noticed the hyena take a slinking step away from him and frowned. The two were drinking buddies and this betrayal stung. He stiffened his neck and focused on the chimp examining the data on his tablet.

"No problems reported upon launch," he said. "Wait a second..."

"What is it?" the lioness asked.

"According to the log, a fawn fell overboard upon launch."

One among the group, a hippo, opened his jaws wide for a sympathetic wheeze.

"But," the chimp added quickly, "it happened so soon after departure that most of the passengers were still on deck. N.O.A.H.'s magnetic safety system kicked in and the fawn was pulled back to safety well before it touched the molten lava."

The volunteers assembled murmured their relief. The lioness remained silent.

The chimp kept scanning the automated logbooks from the vessel's voyage. He seemed about to set his tablet aside when something arrested his attention. He frowned and squinted at the screen. As he kept reading, the chimp's eyes widened in apparent horror. At last, he let his long arms drop. The tablet struck the hovercraft's deck with a sharp clack. The chimp looked up at his colleague, his face stricken.

"They're all gone." His words were quiet, heartbroken.

"Gone where?" the lioness asked.

The chimp waved toward the expanse of molten, bubbling lava. It was a helpless gesture. "Under. They're dead. All of them."

***

Githa had been dozing, so she didn't see how the trouble started. She awoke to bleats of sorrow, and angry shouts and growls.

"Someone killed a fellow passenger!" one voice shrilled.

"Who broke the truce?" another voice demanded.

Githa trundled toward the voices, confident she could defend herself if necessary. A large grouping of animals stood in a semicircle near the stern. On the deck lay the bloody remains of a mule deer. Githa slipped between the massive hooves of a moose to get a closer look. She realized a large contingent of hoofed animals—deer, elk, moose, antelope, and bison—had surrounded a pack of coyotes, and a trio of wolves. The canines snarled. Their hackles were raised.

"Murderers!" someone bellowed.

"Not I," countered a wolf.

"Nor I," said a coyote. Others echoed similar declarations.

"Silence!" a buck elk with a magnificent rack of antlers shouted. "One of your kind has murdered one of our kind. We must have vengeance!" Many of the gathered animals joined their voices together in agreement.

Githa waited for the sound to diminish. Then she asked, "Who is the guilty party? Surely we can find the culprit."

A mountain lion leapt from the bridge and sauntered forward. In a silky voice, she said, "We know their type. They're all dirty and lazy. They're not like the rest of us. They connive and take advantage of the system. They shouldn't even be allowed on this vessel."

"Lies!" The wolves howled in disgust. The pack of coyotes yipped and bared their teeth. "We did nothing wrong!"

But the hoofed animals were focusing their attention on the mountain lion.

"We let them mingle with us, we trusted them. And look what happened. One of them took a life. They all should share the blame. And you know it won't be long before another one of them attacks one of us."

"Throw them overboard," said the deep, rumbling voice of the moose standing above Githa. She glanced around and noticed more feline carnivores—bobcats, lynx, and additional mountain lions—had insinuated themselves into the group surrounding the canines. Something didn't feel right. Her mind raced.

The elk who had called for silence earlier surged toward the pack, his head down. The coyotes tried to leap out of harm's way, but the circle of animals kept them penned in. The elk scooped up one of the coyotes with its antlers and flipped it over the rail.

The angry mob acted as one, surging forward, forcing coyotes and wolves over the vessel's railing in rapid succession. The first couple thrown overboard came back, apparently saved by their collars, only to be thrown over again. The feline predators and even some of the smaller animals joined with the hoofed creatures to create insurmountable odds for the canines. In a matter of seconds, the coyotes and wolves were dispatched into the sea of lava below the vessel.

Then something strange happened. Githa observed the large elk flip over the rail. Then a pair of deer and a moose plunged into the molten liquid. Animals scrambled away from the rail, but it was too late. Anarchy and chaos ruled.

More creatures went overboard as if dragged by an invisible force. *It's as if we're all tied together*, Githa the porcupine thought.

Then she realized the truth.

A moment later, she felt an unseen force grab the collar around her neck. She went airborne, hurled toward the molten lava. The agony seemed to last forever. At last, mercifully, her brain boiled itself to liquid, and her awareness ceased.

***

"They *all* went overboard?" The hyena's voice caught in his throat. This revelation was shocking, even for the likes of him.

"I'm afraid so," the chimp said. "The magnetic safety system is designed to save one or two animals at a time, not a large group."

The lioness growled her frustration. "The fools doomed themselves by turning on each other."

"And they went to their deaths in rapid succession," the chimp said. "Even those below decks could not fight the magnetic collars' pull once the majority had gone overboard."

"Dragged like links of a chain," one of the rhinos said.

"Indeed."

For a time, quiet reigned. Each animal ruminated in silence.

"I suppose there's nothing we can do about it now," the chimp said at length.

"This vessel is meant to save lives," the lioness said. "Back out it must go."

"I'll plot new coordinates," the chimp said.

"Send it to the continent mankind called Europe this time," the lioness instructed. "And let us hope the animals there who wish to make the journey can behave in a more civilized fashion."

TRY TO REMEMBER

"There's no use calling. Your wife isn't coming home. Not tonight and not ever." The snarling voice in the receiver's earpiece rose, sounding gleeful yet cruel. "Do you want to know why?"

George perched on the seat of his recliner, stunned into silence. He forced a single word, which fluttered from his mouth like a dazed moth. "I..."

"Your wife is dead, defiled, and buried in a shallow grave in the woods behind my house. I murdered her!" The speaker lowered his voice to a sandpaper whisper. "Every day, before I leave for work, I stop and urinate on the spot where I buried her."

George heard a click and a moment of silence, followed by the insistent drone of the dial tone. Scalding tears welled and rolled down his wrinkled cheeks like blood beads gliding from a deep scratch. With shaking hands, he fumbled the receiver back into the cradle and sank back.

Dead! Dear God in Heaven. He ran trembling hands through his lank white hair. *What can I do?*

George gazed around the dimly lit study. The clock on the mantle indicated the time: ten o'clock, on the dot. His stomach gurgled. Was his hunger to blame for his sense of unease? No, now the unwelcome emotion was fading. George frowned. *Had* something gone wrong? He no longer felt sure. The feeling slipped away like a dream forgotten upon waking.

From somewhere distant, the muffled notes of a melody came. Distant, George decided, because the notes came from another room in the rambling manor, and distant also because he couldn't place the once-familiar song. George closed his eyes and focused on the tune. He'd try to remember.

The song, George decided at last, came from one of Tchaikovsky's ballets. But wasn't he alone in the house?

George shuffled to his study door and turned the knob. To his astonishment, he found it locked. He jiggled it again, harder this time, but the knob refused to turn. In his consternation, he lost track of the distant strains of music. His gaze roved around the dim room.

Night had fallen like a blacksmith's anvil, heavy and black. No stars or moon lit the sky outside the solitary window, and the bulb of the reading lamp next to his chair did little to chase away the encroaching shadows. A serving tray stood near him, beside the closed door. A covered platter sat atop the tray. He lifted the silver cloche to find a light meal of chicken-fried steak, green beans, and mashed potatoes with gravy on a plate. He shoved a fingertip into the mashed potatoes and found them still warm. George frowned and licked his fingertip.

He did not recall preparing any supper or bringing the tray into the study. Who, then? He reached out and twisted the door's brass knob once more. It didn't budge. He tapped on the door, feeling foolish. How had he managed to lock himself in his own study?

He could pound on the door and shout until Laurel heard his cries. But what would she say? Would she accuse him of going senile? Would Laurel even hear him? She'd been deaf in one ear for decades, ever since the day he'd—

George pushed the memory away. Across the room, he noticed a notepad on the end table beneath the lamp. Seized by sudden curiosity, he left the tray and returned to his chair.

George lifted the notepad and stopped short. Someone had tucked a note between the pages. The note was addressed to him.

A hand-written message seized his attention. He read:

LAUREL IS DEAD AND GONE. YOU DID THE DEED YOURSELF. DO NOT PANIC. YOU MUST CALL 911 AT TEN O'CLOCK EVERY NIGHT. BE PROMPT. THEY KNOW ABOUT

YOUR CONDITION. CALLING EACH NIGHT TO INQUIRE ABOUT HER IS OF UTMOST IMPORTANCE IN MAINTAINING THE ILLUSION OF YOUR INNOCENCE.

George's hand rose to his mouth, as if to stifle a cry. None came. He sank onto the recliner and reread the message. He felt shocked, frail, and befuddled. *Laurel, dead?* It was dreadful. But if he'd killed her, accidentally or otherwise, they couldn't expect him to live out his days in prison.

Had he called the authorities already? He hadn't eaten. Perhaps he'd called while his food cooled. What "condition" had he referenced in the note? The old man furrowed his brow, deep in thought.

His wife was dead, and he had killed her. *But when? And how?* The question of why didn't bother him as much. He'd always had a vicious temper; shame on her for not remembering to tread lightly.

His dinner forgotten, George sat holding the notepad, rereading the words. He glanced at the clock on the mantle. Ten o'clock, right on the dot. He lifted the receiver and began to dial.

"Smithville Police," said the voice on the line. "Please state the nature of your emergency."

"This is George Price. I'm calling about my wife."

"What about the old broad?"

George took umbrage to the dispatch operator's snide remark but let it pass. His mind raced. He'd seen the time and panicked. Should he feign complete ignorance? How much did the authorities know?

"She's not here," George said. "I had hoped you could send an officer to my—to *our*—home to investigate."

"What'd I tell you last time?"

"Last time? I don't—"

"I told you she's in love with me now and she doesn't want to hear from you anymore. Why can't you let her go? Leave her to her happiness."

While the male voice was speaking, George heard a feminine voice in the background, voicing something in good-natured protest. *Laurel?*

"Is my wife there with you?" George's hands shook, not in sorrow over his wife's betrayal, but with rage. *How dare she?* "Put her on the phone. I demand I speak with her."

"Sorry, wrong number!" George heard the other man break the connection. The drone of dial tone mocked his anger and confusion.

That ungrateful witch. George seethed. *After all I did for her.* He slammed the receiver back onto the cradle and massaged his temples. George sank back in his recliner. He needed time to think. Something seemed wrong. His thoughts were a darting school of minnows. But one among them was a decoy. If he could reach into the water and pluck it out...

George took a deep breath and opened his eyes. He felt disoriented for a moment, but then the details of the room resolved into clarity. He was in his study. A serving tray stood across, beside the closed door. A covered platter sat atop the tray.

He had dozed, and Laurel had brought him his supper.

***

"You're a total ass, you know that?"

"Yeah, I know it," Mike replied, glancing at his girlfriend as she reentered the dispatcher's area. "Because you always remind me."

Shirley twisted the cap off the diet soda she'd just bought from the vending machine in the hallway. The release of carbonation hissed like an irate tomcat. She flopped into a rolling chair at another station and swiveled toward Mike.

"Why do you torture that poor old guy like that?" She scrunched her nose and frowned in disapproval. Her expression only turned him on.

"*He's* torturing *me!*" Mike pantomimed shooting himself in the temple with one hand. "You know that crazy old shit calls here at least dozen times every goddamned night."

Shirley took a long pull on her soda, swishing the liquid around in her mouth before finally swallowing. This too, aroused Mike.

"You're lucky the 911 calls aren't recorded. Most places they are, you know."

"I guess living in a podunk town has *some* advantages." He attempted to sneer, but in his current state, it manifested as a leer.

"I still feel bad for the guy."

"He can't remember what happened two minutes ago." Mike said. "I bet he already forgot he called me. He doesn't remember calling last night, or any other night. And I guarantee he'll be calling again tomorrow night with the same sob story. Sheriff Ramsey says to just humor him, but not to send units out there anymore."

"But why is he calling over and over?"

"I don't know. That's a new twist. Once a night is bad enough."

"You better promise me you'll be nicer to him when he calls again." Shirley gestured with the plastic bottle, nearly splashing the fizzy green liquid onto her yoga pants.

Mike rolled his eyes. "I'll try to remember."

***

Three months prior, George called 911 for the first time.

The dispatcher notified Sheriff Vince Ramsey, who drove to George and Laurel Hostetler's residence himself. It was the only time he made the journey with lights flashing and siren wailing.

Laurel met him at the door, eyes wide. "Why, Sheriff Ramsey, what's wrong?"

Vince frowned. "George called," he said. "He told my dispatcher that you had... met an untimely end."

If the old woman was shocked or startled, she didn't show it. Instead, her shoulders sagged, as if bearing a heavy burden. "Perhaps you'd better come inside, Sheriff."

Vince removed his hat and stepped into the Hostetler home. Laurel beckoned him to follow as she climbed the stairs to the second floor. He trudged up the steps, gazing around as he did so. To his eye, nothing seemed amiss.

Laurel reached George's study and knocked on the closed door.

"Enter," said the gravelly, masculine voice within the room.

The old woman turned the knob and opened the door. "George, Sheriff Ramsey is here." She stepped aside so Vince could enter.

George's white hair stood in wild, greasy tufts. He wore a silk smoking jacket that might have been fashionable forty years ago. *He looks unkempt,* Vince thought. George's face betrayed his obvious surprise, but only for a moment. Then the successful businessman and civic leader reappeared.

"Good evening, Sheriff." The old man extended his hand and the two shook. "What can I do for you?"

Vince let his hand drop. "Just following up on a call we received." He glanced around the room. Other than several sheets of paper strewn across a large mahogany desk, the room was immaculate in appearance. And yet, something nagged at him.

"A call?" George gave him a blank look.

"Someone called 911 this evening," Vince explained. "They claimed there'd been foul play. Here."

Vince caught George's irritated, questioning glance directed at his wife. Then he returned his attention to the sheriff. "Someone playing a prank, obviously," George said.

Vince considered this. His new dispatcher, Mike, had told him the caller had been a distraught-sounding old man who had identified himself as 'George Hostetler.' Vince considered revealing this but held his tongue. "I suppose you're right. It's obvious you are both safe. Sorry to have bothered you."

The two men shook hands again and Laurel led him out into the hall. He followed her wiry, stooped frame down the stairs. "I have a tea kettle on the stove," Laurel said. "Won't you join me for a cup?"

"Oh, thank you, but no," Vince said. "I better get back to the station."

Laurel turned to face him. The pain in her expression caught him off guard.

"Five minutes, Sheriff. Will you give me that?"

Not able to find a way to politely extricate himself, Vince nodded.

Laurel made her way to the kitchen and removed two fragile-looking teacups from the dish rack. She served him tepid, tasteless tea and a plate of sugar cookies that were, to his relief, delicious.

Thinking she had something on her mind, Vince tried to engage her in conversation without success. Laurel responded to his questions and comments with brief, distracted replies. Why had the old woman insisted he stay, only to spurn his banter? Laurel glanced at a clock hanging above the stove and rose. Relieved, Vince swigged the last of his tea and stood as well.

"Thank you for your hospitality," Vince said as he followed her through the living room. "I'm sorry to have bothered you."

Instead of seeing him to the door, Laurel moved to the stairwell. At the banister, she turned to face him. "Would you like to say goodnight to George?"

Something in her tone gave him pause. "Yes, of course." For the second time in ten minutes Vince found himself following Laurel up the stairs to the second floor.

She reached George's study and knocked on the closed door.

"Enter," said the voice within.

The old woman turned the knob and opened the door. "George, Sheriff Ramsey is here." She stepped aside so Vince could reenter.

George's face betrayed his obvious surprise, but only for a moment. "Good evening, Sheriff. What can I do for you?"

And finally, Vince understood.

***

George Hostetler suffered severe short-term memory loss. Laurel explained their plight to Vince in hushed tones as they stood together at the foot of the stairs.

"He remembers a business rival who slighted him thirty years ago but can't remember what I made him for breakfast ten minutes after he's finished eating."

"But why would he call us thinking you were dead?" Vince asked.

Laurel shrugged. "I have no idea. Something misfired in his

brain. Hopefully, it doesn't happen again."

But it did happen again. On his next visit—the next evening, as it turned out—Vince didn't bother with the lights or siren. By the end of the week, he didn't bother responding at all. He briefed his deputies and dispatchers about the old man's mental state and instructed them to log the calls but not to send a unit for a false alarm.

After a couple weeks, the old man settled into a routine of calling every night at ten o'clock.

***

George lifted the silver cloche from the covered platter to find a light meal of chicken-fried steak, green beans, and mashed potatoes with gravy on a plate. He frowned and looked closer. Laurel had marred the potatoes by sticking a finger in them. Her careless, unhygienic conduct was unacceptable. He'd make sure she understood.

George grabbed the doorknob and scowled when it refused to open. His irritation grew. He rattled the knob and then pounded on the door. "Laurel!" he bellowed. "This goddamned door is stuck!"

He scanned the room for something he could use to spring the lock. His eyes fell upon a handwritten note beside his recliner. Curious, he picked up the page. As he read the lines, he sank into his chair. He felt shock, sorrow, defiance, and fear in quick succession as his mind processed this new information. Cold sweat droplets formed on his forehead. His hands shook, his breaths came in gasps. He looked at the clock and gasped. *Ten o'clock, on the dot.* Time to place his call. Heart aching, thoughts whirling, he reached for the phone.

George called the police and reported his wife missing. According to his note, the authorities already knew Laurel was dead. George suspected he might be suffering from minor memory lapses, hence the repeated phone calls asking for help. Calling was supposed to help reinforce their belief in his innocence. But something had gone wrong.

"You're a dirty liar, George. We know you murdered your wife." George recognized the anger in the dispatcher's voice. "We have several units on route, in full riot gear. Sheriff Ramsey told everyone to shoot to kill."

George couldn't speak. His tongue seemed to thicken. His throat closed. How could he begin to explain what he hardly understood himself?

Now he understood the locked door: he'd barricaded himself in.

The dispatcher had broken the connection. George replaced the phone's receiver with shaking hands. His chest ached. He covered his wrinkled face with his hands, letting fear and self-pity sweep away his self-control. Sobs wracked his bony frame.

***

Laurel pressed her good ear to the door and held her breath. Inside the den, her husband sobbed and muttered. Laurel waited. She'd become adept at waiting. At last, her ear attuned itself to the snores coming from within the room. She turned the key and eased the door open.

George slumped in his recliner, moaning in his sleep. His wrinkled cheeks shone with fresh tears. The lone lamp shone like a prison spotlight on the notepad still lying on his thigh. A dull pang of guilt jangled her heartstrings, but only for a moment. Laurel, not conscious she did so, touched a hand to the ear that no longer worked; the ear her husband had struck with an open palm the night she'd burned his pork chops. Thirty-two years ago, that had been, but she remembered it like it had happened yesterday.

Laurel closed and locked the door behind her. She carried the serving tray back to the kitchen, reflecting. He'd cut her with words, had bruised her with fists. In some ways, the words had been worse. She wondered if he ever felt remorse or regret when he read the words she'd inscribed on the notepad. She hoped so. They saw each other—every day, in fact. She still cooked for him, though her arthritis flared like lit matches in her fingers these days. She cleaned, kept him entertained, and kept him safe. Not that he showed any appreciation. Still, she carried out what she saw as her wifely and household duties.

Evenings and nights, however, belonged entirely to her. She prepared him his supper and locked him away in the den. Then she tried to forget about him. He certainly forgot about her.

Laurel listened to classical, jazz, or standards depending on her mood. She read the special large print books she checked out from the library. She'd drink her tea out on the patio or watch a musical on television. She *lived*. Laurel cherished the time she allotted herself.

Sometimes she let George out, guiding him to the guest bedroom to sleep. Most nights, however, she left him locked away, trapped within the room—and within his bewildered, fearful mental loop.

Laurel preferred this arrangement. She breathed easier, even found she could smile and enjoy life. *Better in my twilight years than never at all*, she reflected.

She scraped George's untouched food into the garbage and rinsed the dishes. She found herself thinking about the den where the beast she had married spent so much of his time. The furniture there needed dusting and the rug needed vacuuming. She'd been meaning to change the burned-out light bulbs as well. She'd noticed that only the lamp remained lit.

The clock on the mantle had stopped at ten o'clock. Laurel flushed when she pictured it. In truth, she had moved the hands of the clock to their present position to match the time designated in the counterfeit note. Perhaps that had been a tad too cruel. Nothing she could do about it now. The clock needed fresh batteries, and she had none in the house. She'd add them to the grocery list tomorrow unless it slipped her mind.

She told herself she'd *try* to remember.

PEST CONTROL FOR DUMMIES

Matthew Bachman's skin tingled from the tension of the approaching storm. He peered at the looming thunderclouds and increased his pace behind his new push mower. He wanted to finish the backyard before the storm broke.

Matt paused, stooped, and picked up a branch the last storm had stripped from an oak that loomed in the center of the yard. A distant rumble rolled across the sky. He glanced around for Darren but did not see his young son. Matt released the blade stop to kill the motor and shouted his son's name.

The boy came around the corner of the flat-roofed garden shed. Darren held a fist-sized neon orange bouncy ball in one hand, an overpriced souvenir from the last time the family had gone out for pizza.

"You need to stay where I can see you," Matt scolded.

He pulled the starter cord and the mower roared to life. From the corner of his eye, he saw Darren scurry down the hillside toward the towering oak, where he had not yet mowed.

"Hey!" His son turned. "Not down there, you dummy! Up there!" Matt stabbed his finger at the area he'd just completed.

Five more minutes—if he hurried—and he'd beat the storm. If Nick hadn't decided to go grocery shopping right after work, Darren would be inside with him, occupied with a cartoon or a coloring book.

Matt cut a strip of grass then turned for another pass. It amazed him how smooth this new mower handled. His old self-propelled model seemed to drive like a tank in comparison.

Thunder rolled, closer this time. Matt wondered what Nick had in mind for dinner. A rain droplet hit the lens of his glasses and clung there. He felt the mower's front wheels lift as he stooped to snatch up another downed branch at his side.

The mower handle jerked in his grasp and Matt guessed the blade had chopped a panicked garter snake. A large one, Matt guessed, based on the meaty *thwack* that came from the mower's undercarriage. Matt straightened and saw Darren crouched beside the roaring machine. Had he been chasing the snake?

Wasn't a snake, he realized. Darren had stayed on the freshly mowed portion of the incline, but when the bouncy ball rolled away, he forgot his father's instructions.

Matt's numbed hands finally released the mower's blade stop and momentary silence fell.

Darren looked as if he wanted to cry but was too shocked to do so. The boy sagged until his backside sank into the grass.

The mower blade had made a clean diagonal cut, leaving his thumb and the fleshy part above his wrist, but Darren's fingers were gone. All four fingers, Matt realized, and the knuckles and joints that connected them to the rest of his hand. Bloody rivulets weaved and intertwined down his son's upraised forearm.

At that moment, the storm clouds opened. An icy spray drenched them. Matt stood motionless and indecisive. His chest felt tight, his mind had gone blank.

Matt knelt and lifted his son. The boy had wet his pants and his face was chalk dust white. His entire body trembled. *Shock*, Matt realized. He placed his thumb and fingers in a tight grip around Darren's wrist. Not a perfect tourniquet, but it would have to serve.

Matt knew he had to call 911. He tried to remember where he had left his phone. He found himself cursing Nick for taking the car. He wondered how long it would take for an ambulance to arrive. Matt's eyes fell on his new mower. He never wanted to touch it again. The dripping rain spatters on his glasses marred his vision. He swept them off with his free hand and gazed down at his son. Darren's wan features swam back into focus. The rest of the world receded.

Guilt filled him. As a younger man, he hadn't wanted children. He sought to avoid the responsibility of parenting. Then he had met and fallen in love with Nick. Soon after, thanks to repeated discussions, Matt had softened his stance. Nick's presence put him at ease somehow, gave him a sense of peace, optimism, and well-being.

It took four long years of paperwork, expenses, and patience. At last, they adopted a boy from within the state's foster system. Darren, their son, was now five. Nick took to parenting naturally while Matt had remained more aloof.

He squeezed his hand tighter around the boy's wrist. His life wasn't over, it *couldn't* be. Nick would never forgive him for his negligence.

He had to get their son to the hospital.

Driven by a newfound clarity of purpose, Matt straightened. With Darren lolling in his arms, he took a step. Something clacked on the shed roof. Matt heard two more sharp cracks, followed by rolling clatter. Nestled in the grass near his feet lay what looked like a misshapen golf ball.

"Daddy?" Darren roused but did not open his eyes.

"S'okay, buddy. I'm gonna get you to the doctor."

The clamor increased. A shower of mutant golf and ping-pong balls tumbled across the lawn. *Hailstones,* Matt realized. *Biggest I've ever seen.* He shielded his son as best he could and hurried toward the house's back door. Matt knew hail this size could break a window or crack a windshield. He couldn't bear the thought of one of these frozen projectiles hitting and further injuring his son.

He reached the door and twisted the knob with his free hand only to find it locked. Matt cursed. He huddled so the screen door acted as a makeshift barrier between Darren and the onslaught of hail and rain.

They would have to go around so he could try the front door. Matt hoped he'd left it unlocked. He readjusted Darren, tucked the boy's head protectively under his chin, and dashed around the corner of the house. Matt's breathing came in gasps by the time he reached the corner of the house that would take them to the front yard.

A burst of wind and rain buffeted them when they turned the corner. The sight of the wind-driven hail made Matt feel like a space pilot navigating an asteroid belt. He kept his head up, ready to dodge, and rushed across the lawn.

The ball of his left foot came down on a fallen hailstone and the entire world slanted at an odd angle. Father and son skidded across the rain-soaked grass and Darren's injured hand squirted from his grasp.

On his hands and knees, Matt scrambled toward his son. Just as he reached him, a hurtling hailstone the size and shape of a peach pit struck him square on his right eye. A moment later, an invisible nail gun shot a projectile of pain deep into his skull. The blow brought with it an unpleasant memory of violence endured as a teen. For a moment, Matt's vision grayed, and he feared he'd faint. Perhaps he did; when he looked around, he was surprised to find his thumb and fingers clasped once more around Darren's wrist to stanch the flow of blood.

"Mister!"

It took a moment for Matt to register the shout amid the clamor of hail slamming on the rooftops and sidewalks. The shout came again, and Matt looked toward the street. A rusty pickup truck sat idling at the curb. A hard squint gave Matt the impression of a brawny man behind the wheel. A black and acrid cloud of exhaust plumed from the tailpipe.

"Do you need help?"

"Yes!" Matt called. He collected Darren's drooping limbs and drew him into his arms. Another oversized hailstone thwacked him in the small of his back. Matt gritted his teeth and pressed on until he sidled up to the waiting truck.

His smarting eye had already begun to swell shut and without his glasses, he struggled to make out the driver's features. "My son needs a doctor. Could you drive us to the hospital?"

"I believe we could." Something about the man's features struck Matt as strange. It seemed as if someone else in the vehicle had spoken. He stepped closer and squinted to bring the driver better into focus. He wore oil-stained navy blue coveralls. The man stared straight ahead. Matt peered into the truck, and what he glimpsed perched in the big man's lap made him gasp.

A grinning cherub's face met his gaze. Large round eyes, painted a watery blue, shifted in a sidelong glance at his bulky handler. The eyes returned to Matt. "You will have to excuse him; he does not say much." Maraschino cherry lips opened and closed with staccato rapidity. "Hurry up and get in!"

Darren roused in his father's arms. "Daddy, it hurts real bad."

Matt set aside his feelings of misgiving and hurried around the front of the truck. He cast another questioning look at the driver, but the man didn't move or react.

Matt threw the passenger door open and clambered into the cab. He adjusted Darren in his arms, tightened his grip around the boy's wrist, and turned to the man behind the wheel. "Thanks for stopping." He pulled the door closed and raised his voice against the din of the hail. The man had shifted his arm, so the ventriloquist dummy faced them again.

"We've had a terrible accident," Matt said. "We gotta get to the hospital."

"I can see that." The dummy said. The man steered the truck back onto the empty residential street and they accelerated away from the house. At the next corner, the man took a right.

Matt stiffened. "Hey, the hospital is the other direction," he told the driver.

"Listen, *friend*," the dummy's inflection betrayed his apparent irritation. His tiny arm stretched out, revealing a rigid hand with four fingerlike extensions fused into one. Involuntarily, Matt glanced again at his son's maimed hand. Burgundy fluid still seeped from the open wound. The blood would not clot; the injury the boy had suffered was too severe.

"From now on," the dummy said. "You talk to me, not him. Show me respect and I will respond in kind."

The driver made another hard right. The sudden motion pressed Matt and Darren against the dummy. Matt cringed. *This guy's reckless* and *crazy*, he thought.

"There is much more to me than you perceive." The dummy pantomimed smoothing his tuxedo sleeves and adjusting his red bow tie as he spoke. Matt wondered how the driver managed simultaneous control over the mouth and arms. Another block passed in a blur. "I am no dummy."

Matt felt a pang of guilt and gazed at the doll-like face. Its eyes seemed to hold a knowing gleam. *Just a fluke*, Matt thought. *He doesn't know what I thought.*

"The man behind the wheel is *never* kind to strangers," the dummy said. "I sensed your distress and made him stop. In fact, I am keeping you safe. My exertions are stopping him from hurting you."

Matt's gaze traveled up to the driver's face. The big man stared straight ahead, his features impassive. The honking horn of an angry motorist blared; the pickup truck's driver had ignored a red light and sped through the intersection. Matt glanced at the steering wheel and noticed the man's free hand. It gripped the wheel with white-knuckled intensity.

The truck traveled another block farther away from the hospital. Matt's injured eye ached. Darren hung limp in his arms, pale and shivering, his lips now tinged with blue. The hail had abated but rain still fell, and thunder boomed.

"I have a plan that can save your son," the owner of the clattering red mouth announced. "Do you trust me?"

This is crazy, Matt thought.

"I do not think your son will last much longer without medical attention," the dummy said. "You must decide."

Matt swallowed and his throat made a dry click. He had to humor the man, pretend to believe his insanity, in order to get help. Matt looked not at the driver, but at the wide-eyed doll seated between them. "Yes, I trust you. What's the plan?"

"There is no room for error, and we must act fast."

Houses and trees grew and receded in a dizzying procession. Matt squinted at the speedometer but couldn't bring its digits into focus. In his mind's eye, Matt watched the hospital dwindle to a pinpoint of white.

The dummy blinked and the white light disappeared. Matt came back to himself.

"He is rebelling," the diminutive figure said. "He drives while he can. Now, listen."

Darren shivered in Matt's arms. He stroked his son's forehead and cheeks with his free hand and waited for the dummy to continue.

"First, I will reassert control over him. I will force him to turn us around. As we draw near the hospital, I will exert all my influence. He will stop the vehicle, but he will fight my control. This is the crucial moment when you must act."

Matt felt his heart racing, as if they planned to rob a bank, only the prize to be won or lost was not money but his son's life. "What do I need to do?"

"When we stop, you must grab me. Put your hands around my middle and pull quick and firm. Do not let go, no matter what you think you feel. This one will react with anger and violence." At this, the dummy glanced up at the driver again. "Move fast, all in one motion. Lift me and place your son's injured hand within me. The access point is through my lower back. And you would do well to remember what I told you; there is more to me than what you can see."

Matt's swollen eye ached, but he vowed to power through the pain for Darren's sake.

"Do you agree?" the dummy asked.

"Yes." Matt drew Darren up against his chest. His son's closed eyes hid in pools of shadow. He prayed he'd see them open again. Matt had kept his hand clamped around his son's wrist for so long, he wondered if his fingers would respond to his brain's command when the moment arrived.

"I must go back inside," the dummy murmured. "I will make him take us to the hospital." The gleam in his animated blue eyes faded and the lids drifted shut.

A moment passed.

The truck began to slow.

***

A steel-gray work van with the words Gio's Pest Control stenciled on the side slowed and pulled to the curb in front of Matt's hail-strewn front lawn. Gio himself, wearing a yellow rain slicker and brown dungarees, emerged from behind the wheel. He paused to sniff the air and then walked to the back of the van.

"Our quarry was here, and recently, judging by the odor lingering in the air." The white-haired man paused, as if waiting for a response from within the cargo area. Then he said, "Patience, my friends, patience."

The rain slackened, and then abated. The thunderclouds scudded away across the sky. Tendrils of mist floated in the air.

Gio paced around the lawn. On occasion, he stooped to examine markings in the grass. He found traces of blood among the hailstones and followed a series of depressions around the corner of the house.

In the back yard, he zeroed in on the lawn mower and walked over to it. The rain has washed most of the blood spatter away, but Gio saw enough to piece events together in his mind. He knelt in the wet grass beside the mower and tipped it backward to examine the undercarriage. He removed the clippings bag and opened it. Gio rolled up his sleeve and sent his gently questing fingers through the piles of damp grass. He found what he sought near the bottom of the bag. He removed the object and slid it into the slicker's pocket.

Gio returned to the front yard. A dark-haired man stood on the sidewalk between a newly arrived but otherwise unremarkable car and his pest control van. He held plastic bags of groceries in each hand.

"Can I help you?" the young man asked.

"No, but I believe I can help *you.*"

"Who are you? What do you want?"

"I am Gio." He gestured toward his name emblazoned on the van and bowed. "And I am at your service."

The dark-haired man shifted the grocery bags and frowned.

"You re-shingle roofs after hailstorms or something?"

"Forgive my directness, but do you know where the rest of your family is?"

"Inside the house, I suppose. Look, I'm sorry but we aren't interested in buying anything—"

"A terrible accident happened in your back yard." Gio paused to make sure his words had impact. "It involved a lawn mower."

Nick paled. Gio could see his mind working, envisioning any number of gruesome scenarios. One of them, Gio knew, was likely the truth.

"This might be hard to believe," he said, "but the danger relating to the mowing accident is secondary to a greater threat."

He watched incredulity slacken the young man's features. "I don't understand."

"I believe your child suffered a grievous injury." Gio wrung his hands in a gesture meant to convey his sympathy. "I found evidence of an accident in the back yard. I also found a pair of eyeglasses?" He raised the last syllable so that the statement became a quest for information.

"My... husband wears glasses," the young man said.

"I believe your husband accepted a ride from someone he shouldn't have."

Nick dropped the grocery bags and dug in his pants pocket. "I should call the police..."

"That won't help," Gio said. "But don't despair; I know where they are headed."

"Where?"

"The hospital. That's where I'm going now. Would you like to ride along with me?"

Nick wasted no time in deciding. "Make a U-turn and head north at the intersection," he said. "The hospital's less than a mile from here." He left the groceries on the sidewalk and rushed to the passenger side.

Gio slid behind the wheel and keyed the ignition. "Hang on tight!" he shouted.

"Don't worry," Nick said as he fastened his seat belt. "I can take care of myself."

Gio repressed a smile. "I wasn't talking to you."

***

Matt recognized their street as they passed it. *We're finally back where we started*, he thought. He gritted his teeth and prayed they wouldn't be too late. The pickup's tires chewed up another block and the driver sped through a yellow light.

Matt's mind drifted back to the house. Nick would have arrived home by now, he realized. Matt wondered what he would think when he found the house empty.

Another block passed. Then Matt noticed an old man in a van keeping pace beside them. Nick—*his Nick*—sat in the passenger seat. Nick turned his head and his eyes widened when he saw Matt. Matt saw his partner's lips move, but he had no idea what he might be saying. The van slowed, fell back.

Then he heard metal strike metal. The pickup careened and the silent driver fought for control. The truck bed spun in an arc until the pickup jumped the curb at an angle and smashed into a light pole. Matt's head cracked against the side window.

Darren's injured hand slithered loose from his grip. Matt thought he heard the tinkling of broken glass, but when the sound continued, he realized his ears were ringing. Matt closed his eye. They'd had an accident; all he had to do now was wait for an ambulance.

"Make the switch now!"

Matt roused and opened his uninjured eye. The ventriloquist dummy came into focus. It stood on the seat, shouting, its features splattered with blood—Darren's blood. *Gotta stop that bleeding*, Matt thought.

The dummy kept shouting. Matt reached for the dummy, paused, then changed his mind and reached for Darren's bleeding hand instead.

"No, you idiot! Grab *me*!" The dummy screeched. The driver's head rested on the steering wheel, not moving. The dummy's eyes made panicked back-and-forth motions. Its tiny hands reached for Matt, as if imploring him to act. *My God, this thing is actually alive!*

"Your son needs me!"

Matt, believing for the first time, reached out with both hands and tightened his grip around the dummy's middle. He felt an unusual vibration, like a nest of angry hornets, and the dummy's earlier admonition sprang to mind. *No matter what you think you feel...*

He looked again at his son's wan features, the purple half-moons under his eyes the only aspect hinting at any color. Blood dribbled and pooled on the floor mat. If his son's breathing became any shallower, he wouldn't be breathing at all.

Though it felt endless, Matt's indecision lasted only a moment. He plucked the dummy away from the unconscious driver. Its head rolled; its limbs flopped. Matt felt surprised at its weight and warmth—warmer, in fact, than his son. He lifted Darren's injured hand and guided it into the narrow orifice in the dummy's back.

Nothing happened.

Matt's good eye darted back and forth between Darren and the dummy.

Nick arrived at the pickup's passenger door and threw it open. "What happened to Darren?" Panic raised his voice several octaves. "Let me hold him."

Nick lifted their son from Matt's lap. He knelt with him on the cracked sidewalk and started crooning to the boy. The dummy still hung from the boy's arm like a lifeless doll. For a horrible moment, Darren looked just as lifeless. Matt wondered again if he'd imagined his interactions with the dummy after all.

The old man who'd forced the crash arrived, panting. He gazed down at Nick, Darren, and the dummy. His lips tightened in a straight white line. "I wish you hadn't done that, mister. You made things a whole lot worse."

"I didn't have a choice," Matt said. He felt defensive. "Thanks to you, we crashed four blocks from the hospital. The dummy—or whatever it is—offered to stop the bleeding."

"That thing's dangerous. It's a parasite." The old man muttered.

"Though it doesn't realize the harm it causes."

"But he already looks better," Nick said. He'd been staring intently at Darren's face. His words carried with them an undercurrent of cautious hope. Matt looked down and he too noticed a change in their son's appearance. Darren's cheeks had regained some color. His breathing had steadied.

As they watched, the dummy opened his eyes. His grin now looked malicious.

Nick reached out a hand to push the dummy aside, but it lashed out at him, knocking his hand away with shocking ease. Matt searched for the white-haired man who had stood behind Nick, hoping the guy would step in and help.

But the old man had disappeared.

Matt stared in horrified fascination as the doll shivered with apparent delight. He tried to lift Darren away, but the doll swatted his hand. *It feels like my skin is burning*, Matt thought.

"Daddy, my shoe's untied." Except for the wriggling doll attached to his arm, Darren looked normal, in the peak of health.

"We'll deal with that later, buddy."

"He's right," Nick said. "We need to get you away from this... whatever the hell this is, first."

"But my shoe!" Darren seemed agitated now. "It's *untied*, Daddy!" A jolt of realization made Matt lunge for his son's sneaker. He pulled it off his foot and frantically started yanking at the laces.

***

"Get ready to grab your son and don't let go!"

Matt glanced over his shoulder. The old man had returned to his van. He reached the rear doors and threw them open. Dark brown objects tumbled from the van's cargo area. Matt thought they looked like deflated footballs until they started skittering across the asphalt toward them. He marked four oblong bodies, each trundling on stubby tan legs, antennae extended straight ahead, their black eyes gleaming.

Matt noticed Nick hadn't seen them coming. Before he could

warn his partner, one of the creatures clambered over Nick's legs, and he let out a shrill scream.

***

"Grab him now!" Gio shouted.

The dark-haired young man recovered from his initial shock and reached for his son. Gio noted the shoelace dangling from the other man's hand and nodded his approval. "As soon as you have him, use the shoelace to make a tourniquet."

The termighties, as he called his hybrid creations, fell upon his failed experiment. Each attached its black, pincer-like jaws to a thrashing limb. He'd bred his newest creations to eliminate their target with speed and efficiency. He hoped the lives of the boy and the original victim, the pickup truck driver, could be saved. Gio felt a twinge of sorrow and remorse; for a short time, the struggling, shrieking parasite had been like a son to him.

***

Nick pulled Darren's legs, fighting to regain possession of their son. Giant bugs pulled the dummy in different directions as they gnawed at his arms and legs. The bugs were low to the ground, thick-built. The dummy raged and squealed. The motion of its eyes and mouth became so swift that its features blurred.

Matt leaned forward and joined Nick. They'd decided to adopt and raise a son *together*. They would save his life the same way. He put his hands around Darren's waist and pulled. As he strained, and the weird bugs savaged the dummy, Matt thought he heard the wail of approaching sirens. By now, even Darren had joined in the fight. He'd wrapped his free hand around the dummy's neck, as if trying to choke it. The dummy moaned and seemed to weaken.

Matt's good eye swept over his partner, their son, the dummy, and the giant bugs. The violence struck him as both shocking and surreal.

We're playing tug of war for our son's life, Matt thought. *Dear God, I hope we win.*

***

"They amputated his entire arm from the shoulder down." The policeman wrinkled his nose. "Gangrene."

Matt shuddered.

"Will he survive?" Nick asked. He held a cold compress to Matt's puffy eye.

"He's malnourished, but they said he should pull through."

"Did anyone find out his name?" At Nick's question, Matt squinted to read the cop's nameplate.

"Barney Severson, a diesel mechanic from Denver." Jones, the policeman, said. "Wife reported him missing last week."

"Will he be charged?" Matt asked.

Jones nodded. "A number of traffic citations for sure. We have a lot of questions. I hope Mr. Severson has adequate answers."

Matt shifted and winced. Now that his adrenaline had subsided, his entire body seemed to throb with aches and pains. "I'm willing to speak on his behalf despite the fact he kidnapped us. I think he was just confused, and still under the influence of... some outside force."

"So you say."

An awkward silence spun out between them.

A surgeon approached. "Misters Bachman? Your son is awake, if you would like to visit him."

Nick helped Matt stand and the trio left Officer Jones in the lobby.

As Matt made his way into the recovery room, he felt shocked at how small the figure lying beneath the starched white hospital sheet looked. His eyes traveled upward and froze when they reached the red bow tie.

"Dad-eeee!" The eager cry filled the room. Matt saw a grinning mouth and a pair of blue eyes that danced with merriment. His knees buckled and Nick grabbed him. "Whoa! You okay?" His partner's face conveyed only concern and sympathy. Had he not seen?

"Maybe you ought to sit down." As Nick dragged over a chair for him to sit on, Matt looked again at the figure on the bed. It was Darren, of course. *But for a second there*—Matt supposed frayed nerves were to be expected after an ordeal like this.

"Do you like my boytie?" Darren asked, fingering the red bowtie with his free hand. "I took it from that mean guy when we were wrestling." His face glowed with pride.

Matt felt like he had a mouthful of sand, but Nick stepped in. "It looks cool, kiddo! And we sure taught that bully a lesson, didn't we?"

"Mm-hmm," Darren's eyelids drifted half-shut.

The doctor addressed the pair. "We should let him rest. He came through surgery like a champ." He lowered his voice and continued. "We provided your son with a transfusion to alleviate his blood loss. Due to the severity of the wound, and the lack of any fingers to reattach, I shortened the bones in his hand. Then I performed what is called a reconstructive flap surgery. Given the extent of his injury, your son's recovery thus far is remarkable."

"Daddy?" Darren had roused himself. All heads turned toward the boy.

"Yeah, buddy?" Nick asked, but Darren was looking at Matt.

The boy's eyelids drifted closed again. He opened them with obvious effort. "I don't like it when you call me a dummy."

Matt's cheeks burned with shame. "I promise I'll never do that again."

The surgeon ushered them from the room. Nick asked a lot of questions, but Matt lagged, thinking. What had happened between the dummy and his son during those few minutes they had merged? He made a mental vow to keep a close eye on Darren. *Just to make sure.*

***

Gio accelerated his pest control van—which wasn't a pest control van any more than Gio was a man—merged with the

Interstate traffic and headed west toward the Rockies. His termighties had performed their duties admirably. They slumbered in the van's cargo area. Gio allowed himself a few minutes to bask in the sense of accomplishment the termighties' success gave him. Then he turned his thoughts toward the one he had lost and allowed himself time to grieve.

Wood had not worked. Something had corrupted the process.

Next time would be different. Gio kept one hand on the wheel and slipped the other into the pocket of his rain slicker.

When his gently questing fingers touched the small fingers concealed within, his features relaxed, and he smiled.

THE MASKS YOU WEAR

That's you behind the obstetrician's mask, helping deliver yourself. You hope witnessing how you emerge from your mother's birth canal will help you understand why you cannot fall asleep on your back. Then perhaps you can avoid the marital complications your insomnia will cause.

Here is another. You don't recognize yourself behind this mask, either, but you should. You've replicated the wicked features of that movie villain who gave you nightmares as a child. You lurk, meaning to frighten yourself away from the junk-filled vacant lot six blocks from your childhood home. If you stay in your own backyard, maybe you'll never meet the curly-haired kid who lived alongside the lot in the enormous white ice block of house. All the drama and heartache that followed that summer can be avoided, erased.

That's you behind the sneering, pimpled face, and greasy hair, bullying yourself in the middle school cafeteria. You hope the harassment will lead to an aversion to eating. Then maybe you can spare yourself the constant cycle of comfort eating and yo-yo dieting.

That's you, behind the wheel of the excrement-brown Mustang with the bad shocks and four bald tires, chasing yourself home from high school. Don't just throw a fearful glance, gaze back at the driver. The edge of the mask has curled away from your chin. Even if you don't recognize yourself, pause to appreciate the irony of the glowering features of the mask *revealing* your cruel intentions instead of hiding them.

You cannot change the biological factors that shape who you are, so you interfere with and manipulate situational factors at every opportunity.

That's you behind the false smile, gaslighting yourself, treating yourself like a gullible fool. It's a preemptive strike to prepare you for when it happens again, when it's *not* you behind the mask.

Every day, on your way to work, you cut yourself off in traffic. You have your reasons.

Sitting in a confessional's semidarkness, you've listened to your own sordid secrets.

When each lifetime ends in failure, you are reborn. All the preexisting versions of you adjust their masks in preparation for the hapless new arrival.

That's you behind the postal carrier's blank stare, delivering the letter you wrote warning yourself not to move out of state. That's also you, skulking up the walk five minutes later wearing the disguise of a package thief to make sure you never get that letter.

That's you wearing the mask with the disapproving frown, the mask of derisive laughter, the mask with the pitying stare, the mask of angry challenge.

You, behind these various facades, are by turns intelligent, insightful, intrusive, and insane.

Behind so many masks, that's you, psychologically abusing yourself with false flags and deliberate misinformation, all in the vain hope you'll somehow see the truth.

Sometimes, you help yourself make the right decision. You vandalize your own car, smashing the windows of your red compact two-door, to warn yourself away from someone who wants you to have an affair.

Who fires you from the occupation you think you'll love, but will end up hating? Twitch aside their mask and see.

You'd like to give yourself sage advice more often, but another incarnation of you has other ideas. You are the helpful stranger, and the backstabbing friend. You strive to be the ghost in your own machine, but never succeed.

You shamble through life, chained to archaic, toxic baggage.

You don't even know who you are anymore, nor do you remember if you ever knew at all. You are a pinball, bounced and battered through an existence that offers endless free plays, but never a prize. You've achieved an immortality you never sought.

Try as all of you might, you can't get it right. Your life repeats on a Mobius strip. You didn't understand the blessing, and now it has transformed into a curse.

Skulking behind your assorted masks, you seek to put right the wrongs in your life, to redress your grievances. Each time you fail, your life begins again. Each failure becomes an emblem, a mask you wear. They keep stacking up, like empty egg cartons, rising into the sky.

You don't understand the rules. You don't even comprehend the object of the game. You are fixated on your own persecution and perspective. You attempt to toughen yourself against others hurting or wronging you. Instead, you should make amends to those *you* have wronged. This is the secret to a life well lived.

You intend to tell yourself all of this; to break the cycle of futility with wisdom shared from behind a mask of pure empathy. However, another you, hiding behind a stubborn and prideful mask, shoots yourself to prevent the transfer of secrets. You are forever at odds with yourself, destined—and perhaps *predestined*— to disagree.

That's you guiding, leading, chasing.

That's you scheming, planning, manipulating.

That's you cowering, disconsolate, seething.

Who is to blame for this endless melodrama, you ask? Look around. See that figure watching us as we talk?

That's you.

PITCHOVER

*A*pollo 18 (November 7-8, 1973) was an aborted mission originally intended as part of NASA's Apollo program. Its crew consisted of Commander Aiden Briggs, Lunar Module Pilot Donald "Don" Murrah, and Command Module Pilot Evan Fielding. Capsule Communicator at Johnson Space Center in Houston was Thomas Simms. After the events that transpired, the entire mission and associated transcripts have been classified. NASA and the U.S. government both deny the Apollo 18 mission ever happened.

***

Transcript of Apollo 18 crew members Murrah and Briggs in the lunar module making final preparations for the powered descent to the lunar surface. Fielding remained aboard the command module orbiting the moon.

112:47:50 Lunar Module Pilot Don Murrah: Okay. Coming up on 2 minutes to Powered Descent Initiation; I'm changing over here.

112:47:52 Commander Aiden Briggs: Okay.

112:47:54 Murrah: Master Arm, On. Two minutes to go until ignition.

112:47:58 Briggs: Okay, Houston. 2 minutes. Master Arm is On. I've got two green lights.

112:48:00 Capsule Communicator Thomas Simms, Houston: Roger that, Capsule.

112:48:01 Murrah: Mode Select is PGNS.

112:48:03 Briggs: Okay. Once again, in average G, I'll get the Engine

Arm switch. You confirm the fuel ullage, I'll get the Pro.

112:48:10 Murrah: Roger. (Clears throat)

112:48:20 Simms: Module, we're going to leave Battery 3 off...

112:48:22 Murrah: (Garbled) Auto, Auto.

112:48:22 Simms: ...until after ignition. We'll call you.

112:48:26 Murrah: (To Simms) Roger. (To Briggs) Evan will be sorry he missed this.

112:48:32 Briggs: (To Murrah) Someone has to hold down the fort and be there to take us home. Look, we're getting close.

112:48:34 Murrah: Looking out your window is strange.

(19-second pause.)

112:48:53 Murrah: Makes me feel giddy. Not in a good way.

112:48:56 Briggs: One minute, Houston, and we're standing by. We're Go for Powered Descent Initiation.

112:48:59 Simms: Roger. You're looking good here.

(18-second pause.)

112:49:19 Murrah: Okay, approaching 30 seconds. Blank DSKY.

112:49:22 Briggs: DSKY blank. (Pause) Average G.

112:49:30 Murrah: Got two lights.

112:49:31 Briggs: Okay, Engine Arm is Descent. I think the tapemeter drove. I'm not sure. (Pause) Confirm the ullage.

112:49:38 Murrah: Standing by for ullage. (Pause) Ten seconds. (Pause) Fuel ullage. We've got ullage. Goddamn...

112:49:51 Briggs: You okay? Proceed on 99. It took. 2, 1, 0...

112:49:56 Murrah: ...Ignition. Yeah, sorry.

112:49:57 Briggs: Ignition, Houston. Attitude looks good. Engine Override is On, Master Arm is Off. We got a Descent Quantity Light On at ignition, just prior to ignition.

112:50:04 Murrah: DPC tank's good. RCS is good at 15 seconds.

112:50:10 Simms: Roger.

112:50:11 Murrah: RCS is golden. Should be stable throttle up. (Pause) Stand by. There's...

112:50:20 Briggs: Throttle-up is on time, Houston.

112:50:20 Murrah: ...throttle up. (Coughs)

112:50:21 Briggs: And the computer likes it.

112:50:23 Simms: Roger.

112:50:24 Briggs: (To Houston) Still got the Quantity Light on. (Pause) Okay, attitude looks good, Don. But you don't...

112:50:29 Murrah: Belay that. At 30 seconds after ignition. Should have about 108 degrees of pitch.

112:50:37 Briggs: If you say so.

112:50:39 Murrah: AGS and PGNS are close.

112:50:43 Briggs: Okay, coming up on one minute.

112:50:47 Murrah: One minute. You ought to have 98 degrees of pitch. Okay, H-dot is high right now.

112:50:57 Briggs: Mark it, one minute.

112:50:58 Murrah: Altitude's high.

112:50:59 Simms: Module, Houston. I have a 169...

112:51:02 Briggs: (Garbled under Simms) looks good, Houston.

112:51:03 Simms: ...plus 3400, plus 3400 feet. Over.

112:51:11 Briggs: (To Simms) You're looking at it.

112:51:17 Murrah: Okay; 3400. I confirm. (Pause)

112:51:23 Simms: Module, you're Go for Enter.

112:51:27 Briggs: Roger. Go for Enter.

112:51:29 Briggs: 1:30. We're Go coming through 57K.

112:51:31 Murrah: Okay, the altitude's high and the H-dot is high. At least... (Pause) Okay, at two minutes, you ought to have 89 on the mark.

112:51:43 Murrah: We're still 30 feet per second high in H-dot. But we're about 7000 feet in altitude.

112:51:51 Simms: Module, we'd like you to cycle the PQGS switch Off and then back On.

112:51:52 Briggs: Okay, Houston. The switch is Off. And it's back On. Quantity Light is out.

112:52:06 Simms: Roger. That should be good now.

112:52:09 Briggs: Houston, we have Engine Thrust and Commanded Thrust, full-scale high.

112:52:18 Simms: Roger. (Pause) You all right, Murrah?

112:52:23 Murrah: Peachy. Briggs?

112:52:24 Briggs: I'm watching you...

112:52:25 Murrah: I'll be fine. Focus on your assignment.

112:52:30 Briggs: At 02:30, I'm about 89 degrees, coming through

51.5 thousand feet.

112:52:34 Murrah: 89 is great. We're catching up on our altitude. We should start dropping H-dot here a little bit. AGS and PGNS are together. AGS has us a little bit out of plane. And we're north; AGS has us north of track.

(12-second pause.)

112:52:53 Briggs: Okay, Tom; coming up on 3 minutes, we're Go and...

112:52:54 Simms: Module, you're Go at 3.

112:52:55 Briggs: ...we're out of 49K. (Hearing Simms) Roger. Understand we're Go.

112:53:03 Murrah: Okay. At 3 minutes. 82's your ball number. We're still coming down to the right altitude. So, H-dot is high.

112:53:13 Briggs: Okay. (Pause) The day of reckoning comes at 4 minutes, Don. (Pause) Thrust-to-weight ratio building up, looking good.

112:53:30 Murrah: Okay, at 03:30, you ought to have 79...

112:53:33 Briggs: Okay, it's right on.

112:53:35 Murrah: We're still a little high, by about 2500 feet. H-dot is still high.

(11-second pause.)

112:53:50 Briggs: Okay. The tapemeter moves in spurts and jerks, both on altitude and altitude rate in response to the first radar returns from the surface.

112:53:56 Murrah: (Coughs, clears throat)

112:53:58 Simms: Module, Houston. You're Go at 4 minutes.

112:53:59 Murrah: ED Batts are 37.2 volts.

112:54:02 Simms: Roger. ED Batts.

112:54:15 Briggs: And the radar lights are on.

112:54:19 Simms: Okay, sounds good. Both Nav systems are Go right on the line.

112:54:38 Murrah: Hey, Houston, is the AGS indication that we are out-of-plane, correct?

112:54:42 Simms: Stand by. (Pause)

112:54:47 Briggs: Okay, coming up on 5 minutes, Don. Let's take a check at it. About 74 degrees of pitch.

112:54:51 Murrah: That's good. 70 feet per second descent rate, so we're coming down. 36... We're still (garbled) thousand feet high...

112:54:56 Simms: Module, you're Go at 5 minutes...

112:54:57 Briggs: Okay, Houston; we're now out of thirty...

112:54:58 Simms: ...the AGS out-of-plane looks okay to us. (Pause)

112:55:04 Briggs: Okay. Go at 5. We're out of 36.5 thousand feet now. We've got the Earth right out the front window. (Pause)

112:55:13 Simms: Module, Houston. Battery 3, On, at your convenience.

112:55:22 Murrah: Battery 3...(garbled) is On. (Coughs)

112:55:25 Briggs: 05:30, Houston. We're Go. We're out of 34K.

112:55:28 Murrah: 73 degrees, 34 thousand feet. We're right on... altitude. The H-dot ought to... start dropping off.

112:55:38 Briggs: Except that we want to keep it high. Don, you're allowed two quick looks out the window. One now and one when we pitch over.

112:55:41 Murrah: I can't see a thing except Earth.

112:55:43 Briggs: That's what I'm telling you to look at.

112:55:45 Murrah: (Laughs dryly.) One last look at Earth?

112:55:48 Briggs: Okay, Houston, coming up on 6 minutes. (To Murrah) You feeling better?

112:55:51 Murrah: For the moment. At six minutes, you ought to have 72 on your ball.

112:55:56 Simms: Module, you're Go at 6 minutes.

112:55:57 Briggs: 72 is Go.

112:55:59 Murrah: 31 thousand feet. Altitude's great. H-dot's great. AGS and PGNS are awfully close, only a couple feet per second descent rate difference.

112:56:07 Briggs: Okay, Houston. As we went over the hump, Delta-H just jumped.

112:56:16 Simms: Roger that. Continue to monitor.

112:56:18 Briggs: And looks like it's back down.

112:56:21 Simms: Roger. Sounds good.

112:56:25 Murrah: 6:30, Briggs.

112:56:26 Briggs: It looks good.

112:56:29 Murrah: 72 degrees. Altitude is right on. H-dot is remarkably close.

112:56:33 Briggs: Okay, 30K, "windows-up" for the landing.

112:56:36 Simms: Throttle down time will be 7 plus 26.

112:56:43 Murrah: Roger...(Coughs)

112:56:46 Briggs: Okay, we got everything?

(11-second pause)

112:56:59 Murrah: At 7 minutes, 67's your angle. 27; that's great (garbled)...

112:56:59 Simms: Module, you're Go at 7.

112:57:00 Murrah: ...H-dot's slightly high, but okay.

112:57:03 Briggs: Okay, Houston. We're Go at 7, we're now out of 25,000 feet.

112:57:08 Murrah: We're quite a bit out of the Command Module plane.

112:57:14 Briggs: Okay, watch the throttle, now. Here it comes. (Pause)

112:57:21 Simms: LM Crew advises Throttle down.

112:57:22 Briggs: Roger that, Houston. It came at 7:27; computer likes it.

112:57:25 Murrah: (Garbled) feels like...

112:57:26 Simms: Roger, Briggs. Murrah, can you repeat? Over?

112:57:29 Murrah: (Unintelligible)

112:57:31 Briggs: Okay, 1:45 to pitchover, Don. Don? Jesus Christ!

112:57:33 Simms: What's going on up there?

112:57:35 Briggs: Murrah looks like hell. He's sick.

112:57:40 Murrah: I'm fine. Let's push through.

112:57:50 Briggs: 19K, Houston. We're Go coming up on 8 minutes. Standing by for the camera.

112:57:55 Murrah: Okay. The camera's on, Houston.

112:57:58 Simms: Roger that. You're Go at 8. Monitor fuel, 2. Murrah, you need medical attention?

112:58:03 Murrah: Fuel 2 is reading... 27. God... Goddammit.

112:58:09 Briggs: Don, what's wrong?

112:58:13 Murrah: Muscle cramps. Feels like my whole body... is rebelling.

112:58:17 Briggs: Hang in there, Don. I got the South Massif on the radar. Can you update the AGS, Houston?

112:58:26 Simms: That's affirmative; update the AGS. (Pause)

112:58:35 Briggs: Okay, Houston, I've got Nansen Crater on camera. Five miles out. Oh, man, we're level with the top of the Massifs, now.

112:58:45 Simms: Roger.

112:58:52 Briggs: Don, what are you doing? Hey!

112:58:53 Simms: Module, you're Go at 9 minutes.

112:58:55 Briggs: Acknowledged; Pitchover is at 9 minutes and 24 seconds into the burn; 24 on pitchover. Okay, Houston, we're out of 11,000 at 9. I think Murrah is having a seizure...

112:59:01 Simms: Stand by for pitchover.

112:59:04 Briggs: Oh, are we coming in fast!

112:59:11 Simms: Okay; through 9000.

112:59:12 Briggs: I need to get over to Don, Houston.

112:59:14 Simms: 8000. Medical emergency acknowledged. But you can't unstrap, nor can you divert from your landing. You don't have the fuel to...

112:59:15 Briggs: Fine, but I'll need the Proceed command.

112:59:16 Simms: In lieu of Murrah, I'll give it to you.

112:59:18 Briggs: Here we go. Pitchover!

112:59:19 Simms: Proceed command.

112:59:21 Briggs: Acknowledged. There it is, Houston. There's Camelot Crater.

112:59:22 Murrah: (Unintelligible)

112:59:23 Briggs: Don? Hey, you can't...

112:59:24 Simms: Module, you are *not* Go for landing at your present speed.

112:59:25 Briggs: Houston, we have a situation!

112:59:26 Simms: Module, readings indicate you are at 2500 feet, 52 degrees. Approaching too fast...

112:59:32 Briggs: Don't... (Screams)

112:59:34 Simms: 2000 feet, Module? Do you copy?

112:59:54 Briggs: Oh, God...

112:59:59 Simms: 1500 feet. Approaching a thousand feet; 57 degrees. Ease up!

113:00:28 Briggs: (Unintelligible)

113:00:32 Simms: You're through 800 feet already. Damn it, Aiden! H-dot's way too high. Acknowledge!

113:00:40 Briggs: Get off me! Oh, Christ! He changed after pitchover...

113:00:42 Murrah: (Unintelligible snarls)

113:00:51 Simms: Module, can you repeat?

113:00:55 Briggs: He was sick... fighting it off...

113:01:14 Simms: For God's sake, man! You're at 300 feet...

113:01:15 Briggs: But when we turned to face the moon's surface...

113:01:42 Murrah: (Howl)

113:01:43 Briggs: He tore my...

113:01:58 Simms: Module! Ease up!

113:02:03 Briggs: ...arm off.

113:02:11 Simms: 100 feet! Ease up!

113:02:15 Briggs: Would you look at that... staring out the window...

113:02:17 Simms: Fifty feet, Aiden!

113:02:23 Briggs: With his tongue lolling out like that... and all those teeth...

113:02:28 Simms: May God...

113:02:30 Briggs: ...looks like he's grinning.

113:02:33 Simms: ...have mercy on...

113:02:35 Murrah: (Howl—cut off)

113:02:39 Simms: ...your souls.

113:03:59 Simms: Module, do you copy?

(30-second pause)

113:04:30 Simms: Module, this is Houston. Do you copy?

(33-second pause)

113:05:05 Simms: Briggs? Murrah? Acknowledge.

(49-second pause)

113:05:55 Simms: Come on... Module, Acknowledge.

(45-second pause)

111:06:47 Simms: Did they both go insane? "He changed at pitchover;" what the hell does that even mean?

***

Command Module Pilot Evan Fielding returned to Earth after further attempts to reach any survivors aboard the lunar module proved unsuccessful.

NASA officially ended the Apollo program and cancelled any further missions, citing budget limitations and changes in technical direction.

To this day, humans have not returned to the surface of the moon.

HOLLOW

Mom never ate.

It was just the two of us. Mom doted on me and made sure I got enough affection, toys, and food. I never saw her eat, even at mealtimes. She didn't even bother setting out a plate for herself. "I'll grab something later," she would say. She didn't smoke, never drank. But she walked. Always tramping through the hallways of our apartment building at all hours. I accepted her restless roaming because whenever she returned, she seemed calmer and satisfied. Somehow.

We lived in a nice apartment—until we didn't. I came home from school one day to find that mom had packed up most of our belongings. "I lost my job at the laundromat," she explained. "We'll have to find somewhere else to live for a while."

It seemed like an adventure. I noticed the underlying worry in my mother's eyes, but I had childlike faith in her. We'd make it through fine; she'd find a way to take care of us.

We moved into one of those "pay weekly" motels and left most of our belongings packed and stacked in a small trailer my mom had rented. I hated the motel because the guy that lived in the next room was always screaming at night. I think he was a veteran and he had nightmares about the war. There was an old woman who lived alone on the other side of us, and she seemed incredibly sad all the time. Everyone that lived there seemed kind of depressed. Except mom. She ate it up. I think it made her feel better to know that her life wasn't as bad as these other folks.

I started to notice things about Mom. She became a snoop. She liked to gossip. She still roamed and still didn't eat. Then, one night, something weird happened.

Mom always wore her hair in what she called a "pageboy" haircut, and her hair always covered her ears. I remember a full moon shining that night. When mom came in, it was so bright outside that I could see her. I didn't say anything because I knew I should have been sleeping by then. Before she closed the door she reached up and scratched her ear. It looked very strange to me. Her ear didn't look like mine—or anyone else's. It was larger than normal, and flat. It looked like a series of flaps of skin that started on the outer edge and then swirled inward. Like a pinwheel, except there were many flaps, not just a few. I never asked her about it, though.

We lived at the motel for a while and mom continued her walks past all our neighbors' doors. She would get fast food or takeout for me since the motel room didn't have a kitchen. She seemed content, so I was too. I don't think I've ever seen her as happy as she was then. I even said something about it one time. "Mom, you always manage to look on the bright side. When other people are sad, you're still happy."

"I guess I'm just the product of my surroundings," she replied. Then, seeing the confused look that must have been on my face, she added, "What I mean is, I always try to make the best of things."

Mom got a new job cashiering at a busy grocery store. She worked days and weekends. At the end of the school year, she told me we were moving to a large apartment complex across town. There were four apartment buildings and each building had four floors. It was much larger than the motel. It felt like living in a big city; there was such an amazing cross-section of people. Young, old, families, singles, different races. I was thrilled with the swimming pool and for things to do with other kids in the common area and on the grass between buildings.

Then things started to go bad. I didn't know what was wrong at first, but I saw the set of Mom's shoulders, the frown on her face, and the constant furrow between her brows, and I knew something was wrong. At night, she walked more frequently, but came home unhappy, and out of sorts.

I didn't know it then, but she was rapidly losing her hearing. She could still carry on a conversation with me. She could talk to her customers without issues. But her ability to pick up sounds from far away had diminished. To make things worse, she started losing weight.

I never connected the two until she got fired from her job at the grocery store. Her boss accused her of starting arguments with the customers. I couldn't understand this change in her personality. She'd always been a gossip, but never mean about it. Now she seemed to be going out of her way to instigate ugly scenes with people.

Her situation gradually worsened. She was changing for the worse. Then, one day upon returning home from school, I walked in the front door and found her seated on the sofa. Her face was drawn and gray. Her clothes hung on her as if she'd shrunk. She looked at me and lifted a tremulous hand, "Come here, kiddo."

"Mom, what's wrong?"

"I'm dying."

Something inside me shattered. I felt shards of pain, yet strangely empty. "Do you have cancer?"

She shook her head. "I'm starving."

I knew we had plenty of food. I just shook my head, not comprehending.

She lifted her hair and I saw again her strangely structured ears. The many folds seemed very organic to me, like blades of grass or flower petals weaved into a perfect swirl.

She beckoned me closer. "I'm going deaf." I peered closer at the swirls. They looked oily and shriveled.

"Mama, are you going deaf or are you starving?"

"I'm starving *because* I'm going deaf."

And that's when everything fell into place. I understood the constant walks. The snooping, the listening. I fell into her arms and hugged her, and we cried together.

Once her hearing failed completely, she went downhill fast. I came home from school one day and found her, just an empty shell curled up on the living room floor like a dead insect.

I live with my aunt and uncle now. They both have normal ears; that's something I checked right away. Sometimes they fight. I lie in bed, eavesdropping. I guess I'm hoping I'll feel stronger somehow, that I'll gain some type of nourishment from the unhappiness of others. I'd like to have that in common with my mother. It would be a special bond between us, something to keep her memory alive.

Listening to other people argue doesn't make me feel closer to Mom; it just makes me hurt and feel sad that she's gone. I've started eating smaller portions. Sometimes I lock myself in the bathroom and throw it back up.

I've been thinking about puncturing my eardrums. Supposedly, it's not that painful. The idea gives me comfort. Maybe deafened and starving, I'll feel closer to Mom.

Maybe then I won't feel so hollow.

TIME TO SAY GOODBYE

Carol felt as if someone had submerged her head under water. The muffled radio news report oozed from the SUV's speakers. She yawned, trying to make her ears pop, without success. Her hands clenched the steering wheel as they continued their sharp ascent. They crossed a cattle guard and the SUV's tires rattled over each metallic bar. She navigated the narrow gravel road that led them higher into the mountains. SILVER MOUNTAIN, the sign said, and Carol recalled a sludgy rock song of the late 70s with a similar name. She tried to hum it, but the tune would not come. *Why*, she wondered, *are all my memories of Darla so vivid, while everything else seems so damned vague?*

Carol followed the winding gravel road while Penny dozed in the passenger seat. As they ascended, her mind drifted back to Darla. They had been together seven years, but stage 4 liver cancer had stolen her partner away six months prior.

Tall coniferous trees hemmed them in on either side of the road, making Carol feel trapped with her unhappy thoughts. She longed to break free of this constant bittersweet oppression. The reason she had wanted to take this trip was to get away from the memories, the daily stabbing reminders of Darla's death. Out here in the wild, Carol hoped to achieve some closure, and to say a respectful, if symbolic, farewell.

They finally arrived at their intended destination: little more than a muddy pull-off on the side of the road that some hikers at the Park's Game Lodge had recommended. Carol steered the SUV onto the shoulder, parked, and turned off the ignition. She turned to Penny, who had roused.

"This is something I have to do by myself." Carol reached out and squeezed her new girlfriend's hand. "You'll be okay here for a couple hours?"

Penny nodded and gave her a sleepy smile. "I bought some books at that thrift store yesterday."

Outside, Carol shrugged into a jacket and looked around her. A large tree stood nearby. The wind had recently snapped off a massive branch. Someone had hauled the branch away, but the fresh gash in the tree arrested her attention. *A wound, too fresh to have healed.* Carol looked at the ground and frowned. *No sawdust, even though the branch must have been enormous. Who could have carried it away?* Behind her, the SUV's engine ticked as it cooled.

A stand of trees to her left stood like sullen and silent townsfolk. *Birch? Aspen?* She wasn't sure, but decided on aspen. The sight of the skinny black and white trunks made her feel uneasy, as if alien life forms had gathered to witness her arrival. To her right, the gnarled branches of scattered bur oaks pointed accusatory fingers in every direction. Several of the upper branches had snapped off in high wind or under heavy snow but had never reached the ground; their brethren clung to them as if unwilling to let them go.

Carol wondered if she was like the bur oaks, also unwilling to let go, but quickly cast the notion aside. *Darla's memory is* not *dead wood.* Tears unexpectedly pricked her eyes. Carol pressed her lips together and willed herself not to cry.

Higher up the incline, Carol saw Black Hills spruce and Ponderosa pine trees in abundance. She took a deep breath, squared her shoulders, and started her journey.

Darla's memory weighed heavy upon her mind and heart, but Carol vowed to bid farewell from the mountain's peak.

The sun furtively hid behind scudding gray clouds. She passed a flat square stone. It reminded her of a grave marker. Darla had requested cremation. Her urn lay buried, hundreds of miles away, beneath a stone of similar color and shape. Carol quickly looked away.

She came to a fast-moving, icy stream and managed to make her way across despite the wobbly, awkwardly spaced rocks. On her left hunched a tangle of brush, impassable for the likes of her. She wondered how often small animals cowered within, hiding in vain from lurking predators.

The ascent suddenly became steep. Carol realized she was breathing hard, almost gasping in the thinner air of this higher elevation. The spruce and pines had edged in closer, like pushy salesmen hawking questionable goods at a flea market.

At the periphery of her vision Carol noticed burn piles, well off the trail but still visible. She imagined them as poorly designed shelters meant to house a long-forgotten race. Twisted oak trees lurked between the statelier evergreens. Some curving branches beckoned like gnarled hands; others snatched at her clothing as she passed.

The sound of faraway howling seized her attention. Carol could not decide which direction the echoing cry originated from. It sounded like a hound lamenting an injured leg. She had cried that way herself, grieving the loss of her love. Penny was fun, and maybe there would be love between them someday, but she and Darla had loved unconditionally, had held nothing back. The dog—if that's what it was—loosed another mournful cry. Carol bit her lip and pressed onward.

The skies shone sleet gray. An unseen bird cackled overhead. Carol felt eyes upon her back and shivered. *Are you scared of birds now?* Ahead, a row of lichen-covered granite outcroppings formed teeth; pointed incisors rose next to worn and rotted molars. The outcroppings slid to her right as she followed the faint trail. All around her were jagged tree trunks, the bulk of each tree having tipped and shattered. She found himself wondering how long ago the burn piles had been gathered. *They ought to come back and do more thinning; this forest is a definite fire hazard.*

Inky darkness approximating a pair of eyes and a yawning mouth startled her into immobility. She saw three caves within the wall of granite, formed by collapsing rock. Literal tons of stone in vertical and horizontal formations created ample space for beady-eyed creatures to peer out at her, ready to lunge and defend their territory with tooth and claw. The biggest of the three caves, she noted, was large enough to conceal a human.

Carol hurried on, puffing her way up the mountain trail. Several fallen trees were gray and eroded with age, reminding her of bones. She stumbled when a tree root that crossed the faint footpath snagged her boot. Another unseen bird cackled at her misstep. *If I twist my ankle, I'm in trouble.* Carol realized she had forgotten her cellphone and pushed on with grim determination.

Her foot found something spongy, and she looked down. She first thought they were balls of hair or fur, and then realized she'd stepped on regurgitated owl pellets. How did it feel to be a hapless rodent swept up in the talons of a ruthless night predator? Physically, she couldn't say. *But emotionally...*

The wind hissed warnings through the trees. Carol was far more comfortable in the cacophony of the city. The unfamiliar sounds around her now set her teeth on edge.

Several yards off the trail, the hollow sockets of a sun-bleached deer skull glared at her. She squinted and realized that something had gnawed part of the skull away. Darla was like that deer, Carol decided. She'd been an innocent in a brutal, merciless world. She deserved much better than what life had given her.

Was that a cough? Maybe not some*one*, but some*thing* had made a sound somewhere behind her. Carol threw a self-conscious glance over her shoulder and picked up her pace, despite the burning in her quad muscles.

The earthen switchback now had her walking over the top of the stones that formed the small caves she had noticed earlier. She shivered, thinking of fairytale trolls. Trolls of a different sort seemed as plentiful as cockroaches—and just as pleasant—on social media these days. She'd put together an online fundraiser for her ailing partner, and the snide comments about their lifestyle had shocked and infuriated her.

Carol took another hairpin turn and emerged into a clearing. She saw a second enormous row of granite teeth to her left. The first grouping of outcroppings was still to her right but now slightly below her, owing to the twists in the trail. Carol imagined a snoring giant buried in the earth. The area she was walking through now would be swallowed up when the giant awoke. She allowed herself a wry smile. She understood her mind was creating these flights of fancy as a means of coping with her lingering grief.

She climbed higher up the mountainside. At this elevation, stringy strands of green moss hung from the pine branches. She'd read that some called it Old Man's Beard and that it tasted exceedingly bitter but was edible in a pinch. They'd tried several herbal teas and other supposedly healthy concoctions to improve Darla's liver soon after her diagnosis, but nothing had helped. Neither had been much surprised.

At the next switchback, she stepped off the trail and climbed onto a shale outcropping. Carol peered over the edge to judge the drop. If she fell from here, she would surely break a limb. She decided to climb higher. A squirrel scolded her from a tree, as if warning her to turn back, but she continued her ascent. She felt her blood pounding through her body. Ahead, the jagged rocks narrowed on either side of the trail, creating a constricted passageway. She let her fingertips explore the rough surface as she walked, but pulled her hand away at the touch of unknown wetness.

Time continued its inexorable passage. Carol made her melancholy ascent, sweating and panting. At times, she felt as if she was dragging Darla herself up the mountain with her.

Then suddenly, she crested the peak. Cold wind surged up from the other side of the mountain and buffeted her, rocking her back on her heels. She looked around and spotted an outcropping of granite. Though she had finally stepped off the path and the constant carpet of pine needles, the ground beneath her feet felt spongy. Her movements were unsteady. A twig snapped behind her and she flinched, fearful of plunging over the precipice.

The sun cast a baleful red eye at her from between the wiry, wind-twisted pines. Shadows darkened the evergreen trees that dominated the sides of the nearby mountains. She turned her back on the sun and looked out over the expanse below.

It was a dizzying drop; here one would not survive the fall. She inched out farther, careful of where she stepped. *I could break my leg if I stepped into one of these small crevices.*

The gravel road—and all civilization—seemed very remote.

Far below her, Carol saw six aspen and her breath caught in her throat. Their trunks were snapped and shattered. An enormous chunk of granite, loosened by recent rains, stood nearby. Carol realized it had rolled down the mountainside and flattened the trees like bowling pins. She felt sure more stones would fall with the next rain. The outcropping seemed treacherous, and the imminent danger of another rockslide, perhaps beginning directly underfoot, made her skin prickle.

This is the moment, she decided. It was time to say goodbye.

***

"When I go, don't make a big deal about it." Darla spoke quietly, her face composed.

"Don't talk like that." A painful lump grew in Carol's throat. "Losing you is going to break my heart and you know it."

"I don't want you feeling all maudlin and sentimental." Darla reached for Carol's hand. "I know grief is part of the healing process, but don't wallow in it."

"I don't want to talk about this now."

"We're talking about it anyway. Tomorrow isn't promised to any of us."

Carol broke down and sobbed. Afterward, she would feel guilty, wishing she had been strong enough to comfort Darla instead of vice versa.

"You'll know," Darla said at last, after Carol exhausted her supply of tears.

"Know what?"

"When it's time to let go. Grief is a heavy burden. You can't carry it around with you forever."

***

On the precipice of the mountain peak, Carol knelt and closed her eyes. She clasped her hands together in front of her chest and visualized her late partner. Darla came to life again in her mind's eye.

I'm glad you aren't suffering anymore. I want you to know I'm keeping your memory and throwing only my grief away. I will always love you.

Fully invested in the ritual, Carol rose with arms outthrust and imagined the weight of her grief and sadness as a physical burden. Some force seemed to resist her for a moment, and she let loose a primal howl of sorrow.

The burden fell away.

Carol staggered and fell. She curled up on the granite and sobbed.

After a period of silent reflection, Carol opened her eyes. The beauty of the scenic overlook left her breathless. She rose and, feeling the tremendous burden gone, began her descent.

From far away, echoing through the mountains, she heard the *pop-pop-pop* of what might have been a hunter's gun. To her it sounded like celebratory fireworks.

Birds chirped happily in the trees. Their trilling songs filled the air. A bright-eyed squirrel paused on a limb as if to offer a friendly greeting.

The carpet of pine needles cushioned her steps. The brisk breeze tousled her hair and made her feel happy to be alive. Gravity aided her descent. The sunshine reemerged and rekindled their friendship. Branches waved gently at her as she passed.

Penny. The girl was beautiful, certainly. And she'd surprised Carol with her intelligence, her wit, and her astute observations about life, society, and the human condition. A long-term relationship might be in the cards after all.

Carol sauntered over to a pine branch, tore off a bit of Old Man's Beard, and shoved it between her cheek and gums. It wasn't as bitter as she'd feared. *More of an herbal taste*, she decided.

Small, bright yellow flowers bloomed beside the trail in clusters. Delicate purple blossoms dotted the landscape. She gently chided herself for letting them escape her notice during the ascent.

The breeze hummed a gentle lullaby through the trees and a tiny chipmunk darted daintily from stone to stone, its tail raised in the air.

She felt so giddy and lighthearted that she almost skipped.

Farther down the mountain, she noticed the burn piles again. *Symbols of rebirth*, she realized. Controlled burns kept the plant life healthy for enjoyment by future generations.

Her symbolic physical gesture at the mountaintop had allowed her to let go of her grief. She truly felt as if the burden had lifted. *No, not lifted; I dropped it over the edge.* Now she could move on and enjoy the beauty of life's journey.

She passed the caves again and realized she could see inside. The back of the largest was clearly visible, only three feet deep and obviously empty. It looked like it would be cool and welcoming on a hot day, and warm and dry on a rainy one.

Gazing at the splendor of the trees overhead, she wondered how different her perspective would be atop one, and then realized her outlook had markedly changed now that her burden of sorrow had been lifted. She laughed and the bubbling stream laughed with her. She stopped just to listen for a while. A smile illuminated her face. She crossed the stream on sturdy flat stones that showed her the safest, shortest way.

A common robin hopped from branch to branch on an oak above, as if sorry to see her go. She reached the SUV, grabbed the driver side door handle, and thought about what had happened atop the mountain.

"I've said goodbye to my grief," Carol announced as she climbed up behind the wheel. "And I think I'm finally ready to give the two of us a real chance."

She turned to look at Penny but found only an empty passenger seat.

Her blood turned to slush in her veins. Her mind raced back up to the peak and the resistance to her outthrust hands. Carol's vision grayed as a horrific realization overtook her. Her new lover, overcome by curiosity, had followed at a discrete distance all the way to the top.

Why hadn't Penny said anything? Carol's despair overwhelmed her. Her entire body shook. *And why—oh, god why—did I close my eyes?*

Carol slumped against the steering wheel. Tears burned her eyes. She needed to scream but could not. She wanted to sob, pound the dash, and lean on the horn but could not.

Like the aspen trees shattered by the falling granite at the mountain's peak, Carol's redoubled grief overwhelmed and obliterated her. Her battered psyche provided the dry kindling for the burn pile, and this new tragedy was the lightning strike that sparked the fire.

Numbly, she left the SUV behind and began to retrace her steps. Once again, she would haul her heavy burden to the top.

This time, however, she did not intend to hike back down.

***

Penny zipped up her shorts and made her way back to Carol's vehicle.

"Carol? You back, hon?" She looked around, frowning. She could have sworn she heard her girlfriend's voice and the slam of a car door as she'd crouched in the trees, emptying her bladder.

Penny chewed on her lip as she climbed back into the SUV. She thought Carol would've returned by now. If she followed the trail, would her girlfriend think she was snooping? Would she come across as impatient, or even controlling? She glanced at her flip-flops, certainly not ideal footwear for a rugged hike, and that decided her.

I'll finish this chapter. If she's not back by them, I'll try the trail. Probably meet her on her way back. Penny relaxed in the passenger seat. *Okay, two chapters. Three, if they're short.*

THE TRUNK IN THE JUNK ROOM

I'm not sure my grandmother ever existed. I have childhood memories, but sometimes memories can lie.

I can't prove my younger brother existed either.

Let me explain.

My grandparents lived out in the country, near the banks of the Missouri River. The trips there always made me carsick. The gravel roads curved and dipped with the hilly terrain. My stomach lurched; my head swam.

My grandparents' house was so old it had faded to mouse gray. You went in the door straight into the kitchen. The living room was behind the kitchen. It was empty except for a sofa and a television that only got three channels. There were two little rooms behind the living room. One was their bedroom, and the other was the bathroom. There was one other room, running alongside the house, and behind a door halfway between the kitchen and living room. This long, narrow room was filled floor to ceiling with junk.

My grandparents had emigrated from Romania. They never threw anything away. They kept stacks of newspapers and phone books, boxes of broken dishes, chairs with missing legs, empty mason jars, torn garments, and more.

Every kid knows a room like that is where treasures are found. But I wasn't allowed in, ever. My mother warned me each time we visited, "Don't go in there. There's *mice*."

When Grandma died, we kids were considered too little to attend the funeral.

One evening, months later, my folks had to attend a special dinner. Mom couldn't find a babysitter, so Dad drove my brother and me all the way out to Grandpa's place.

After a supper of tomato soup and crackers, Grandpa went into his bedroom and closed the door. He left the TV on, but the show bored us.

Reggie slid off the sofa and went over to the door to the junk room. He stretched his hand to the knob and twisted it. The door opened. I ran over to cuss him out and remind him about the mice.

"Come in, my lambs," a muffled voice said, "and I will tell you a silly story."

The voice sounded like Grandma's, but all I could see was a padlocked trunk on the floor near the door.

"This is a true story, not make believe."

We couldn't reach the light switch, but the TV flickered and glowed, so that helped some. We could see the trunk, but darkness hid everything else. Reggie sat cross-legged on the floor. I sat beside him, feeling dizzy.

"Many years ago, when I was a young girl, I saw one of Rasputin's bastard sons."

Grandma's voice seemed so natural and so familiar I didn't feel scared. Not then.

"He put on a performance in the village square. He had a large doll and pretended to make the doll speak. Do you understand, my lambs?"

We nodded.

"Someone in the crowd threw a rotten tomato. It hit Rasputin's son in the face. He was so small it knocked him down. The doll just sat there for a moment. Then it toppled over too. It hit the wood planks of the stage and its head smashed into pieces like a broken vase."

Reggie gasped and I shivered, delighted at the creepy scene conjured in my mind.

"Men shouted and women screamed. They had all thought the little man was the doll and the big man was Rasputin's son. Just the opposite was true!" Grandma squawked laughter, then said proudly, "But I saw through the trick!"

"What the hell's going on in here?" Grandpa's angry voice made us jump. He stood in the doorway wearing only pee-stained boxers and a dirty undershirt. It was hard to see, but it looked like he had Grandma's Sunday makeup smeared all over his face.

"Can't you never be silent, woman?" he shouted. "I'll finish the story. You always botch the punchline!"

Grandpa scooped Reggie up from the floor and set him on the trunk's lid. My brother just stood there, as if frozen. Grandpa sat beside him and said, "Rasputin's son rose to his feet and wiped tomato pulp from his face. He looked at the ruined doll, and his features filled with such rage that the crowd fell silent. He grabbed the doll, dragged it to the edge of the stage, and hurled it into the crowd—like this!"

Grandpa lifted Reggie to the ceiling and then dashed him against the floor.

I watched my brother shatter into pieces, just like doll in the story. I stared at a broken fragment that skittered close to my knee. A blue eye within the jagged shape stared back at me. It blinked, and the room spun. Then everything went black.

I woke up in our car. My parents sat in the front seat, silent. Reggie wasn't with us. I started to ask about him, but my mother turned around with a look so forbidding that my words died. I had never seen anyone look so angry yet so scared at the same time. I still haven't, after all these years.

My folks never brought him up again. His toys became mine. At the end of the school year, we moved across the state and carried on as if Reggie had never existed.

Maybe he hadn't. Maybe I'm misremembering.

We never went to Grandpa's ever again.

That all happened three decades ago. Grandpa died last week. I found out thanks to the Internet. Someone had written an article about him. Grandpa was exactly one hundred years and one hundred days old the day he died.

I wonder if I could find that ancient farmhouse.

I think about Reggie, and that room filled with junk. I'd like to explore it. Maybe I'd find an old trunk holding something remarkable within. Maybe I'd even discover the fragments of my broken younger brother.

After all, my grandfather never could bear to throw anything away.

THE RUNNER, STRANDED

Sam crouched near the center of The Kiddie Korn Maze, his heart thudding. The stalks loomed over him, leaning in from every direction, as if conspiring to never let him leave. Sam's breaths came in labored gasps. He fought the urge to run. *This is lunacy*, he thought. *It would be comical if it weren't so horrifying.*

Then, behind him, Sam heard the creature that had terrorized him all day approaching through the corn.

***

Sam Walters returned his key card at the lobby's front desk and shuffled across the motel parking lot. Already he dreaded the long, dull journey ahead of him. And when he arrived home this evening, he'd be greeted only by Adina's disapproving, unhappy frown and the kids' shrill entreaties for his attention. The rising sun's rays forced him to squint. That was why he didn't notice the man in the sleeveless white muscle shirt and red jogger pants until he spoke.

"I am stranded. Can you provide transportation?"

Sam looked up, startled. "No. Sorry."

The other man did not reply. Sam appraised him: tall, dark-skinned, shaved head. The stranger could have been his stunt double—if Sam ever did anything besides sit behind a desk all day. The man had, Sam noted, one milky eye. *Cataracts*, he decided. The man might've been a weathered thirty-five or a well-preserved sixty. He had one of those faces.

Sam expected the guy to harangue him all the way to his car, but he didn't. The stranger just stood in the middle of the parking lot, arms hanging loose at his sides, watching him in silence.

Keenly aware of the other man's gaze needling his back, Sam unlocked his car and slid behind the wheel. He jammed the key into the ignition, put the car in reverse, and backed out of the parking spot. As Sam accelerated past the tall man, they made eye contact. The stranger's gaze was inscrutable.

Sam breathed a relieved sigh as he left the motel—and the disquieting stranger—behind him.

***

Sam had told his wife the trip across the state was work-related. "Recertification training," he'd said. The vague yet plausible lie opened the door for his temporary escape.

In truth, Sam wanted time away from Adina and the kids, and away from the responsibilities of his home life. He saw no harm in this. In fact, he sometimes felt entitled to it.

He took advantage of a three-day weekend and traveled across the state. Every truck stop and small town gas station offered him the same mild vices. He gorged himself on the candy bars and salty snacks Adina frowned upon. He wasted money on scratch tickets and video lottery machines. He drank more than he should have, usually in squalid truck stop bars, but once or twice while behind the wheel. Sam bought cheap cigars he never got around to smoking. He purchased a couple dirty magazines that he sneaked into his motel room with as much guilt as if he'd hired a living female escort.

By Sunday, Sam had resigned himself to returning home. He'd rebelled in his own way, scratched the itch, and had resigned himself to the monotonous grind of his daily life.

***

An hour passed on the road. The sun inched higher in the sky.

Sam's stomach rumbled. The seat belt pressed against his expanding bladder. At last, he gave in and tapped the brake pedal. He slowed and steered his car onto the road's grassy shoulder.

He'd chosen a disused state highway rather than the interstate and hadn't seen another vehicle in at least twenty minutes, so he felt confident he could do his business without fear of discovery.

Sam exited the sedan and found his joints had stiffened, so he paced along the shoulder for a few yards to give his legs a stretch. He strolled into the ditch, unzipped, and studied the rusted strands of barbed wire fencing. *Never pee on an electrified fence.* Sam wondered where he had heard that country-fried witticism. Sam aimed away from the barbed wire—just in case—and visualized the tension draining from his body as his bladder emptied.

A casual glance backward cut short the draining of Sam's tension—and his bladder. The strange man in the red joggers stood near the hood of Sam's car, gazing down at him. Sam paused long enough for a couple cursory shakes and then zipped up his fly. The roadway remained empty. The man's presence was impossible. Sam imagined him running alongside of and keeping pace with his car. The image stuck in his brain. He hurried up the side of the ditch and headed around the trunk of his car. Sam gazed at him as he sidled toward his car door.

"I am stranded. Can you—"

"I already told you no," Sam shouted. "You shouldn't even be here, anyway!" His anger surprised him. *He can't be real.* Sam sorted through the facts as he reached for the door handle. Yes, he had encountered someone asking him for a ride back at the motel. But was the same man here now, asking for a ride? *Impossible.*

Standing beside his open car door, he studied the stranger. They bore a passing resemblance to each other. Sam could see how his mind had recreated the image of the man in the parking lot. *And the red jogging pants?* The color matched that of a sporty convertible that had caught his eye at one of the car dealerships back home. Sam realized that detail made more sense than anything else. He found it easy to explain the significance of the milky eye as well. *It's a representation of the murkiness of the future.*

Pleased with his self-analysis, Sam slid behind the wheel. He felt so confident he didn't even lock his door. He stared through the windshield at his imaginary stalker. The Runner's face remained without expression.

Sam raised his hand and flipped his mental breakdown the bird. He took his foot off the brake and stomped on the gas pedal.

He had not expected the astonished look on The Runner's face as he struck the fender and slid beneath Sam's vehicle. Nor had he expected the front wheel to crunch over something substantial. Most of all, Sam had not expected the piercing, anguished scream that rose and abruptly ceased after a second bump from the back tire.

Sam looked in the rearview mirror at his own ashen, sweating reflection. *That sure as hell* felt *real.* He drove forward until he saw The Runner lying crumpled in the center of the lane. The man bore no outward appearance of injury. Sam accelerated and sped away.

Twenty minutes later, a sun-faded billboard promised "Home Cooking." Sam read that much but missed the name of the business and how far down the road it waited. The familiar figure standing beside the billboard had distracted him. This time, instead of just standing there, The Runner flipped him the bird.

***

Sam sped west, intent on finding the business advertised on the billboard. He wondered if he could enlist help against the strange figure shadowing his every move. White lines and fence posts passed in a blur. The speedometer needle hovered twenty miles per hour over the speed limit. Sam didn't care. He hadn't seen another vehicle in nearly an hour. Besides, if a cop pulled him over now, Sam thought he'd welcome the company.

The sedan crested a rise and Sam glimpsed a small building hunched on the side of the road about a half-mile ahead. He took his foot off the gas. He had to plan and prioritize his stop.

Hitting the bathroom had to take top priority; his guts were in turmoil. He glanced at the gas gauge and saw the car only had about an eighth of a tank. He'd have to fill gas there too. Sam doubted he had time for a meal. The Runner could show up at any moment. What then? Ignore him? Run him over again?

He hit the turning lane too fast and careened into the parking lot of the roadside diner. A pair of gas pumps looked to Sam like weary soldiers standing at attention. He steered into the lot and hit the brakes. The sedan fishtailed on the gravel. Sam managed to pull alongside the gas pumps and put the car in park. He threw open his door and jogged to the entrance. The sign above the door read MARIE'S COUNTRY COOKING.

Sam saw two vehicles parked in front of the structure: a green and white Buick Skylark spotted with rust and a dust-coated pickup truck with a Confederate flag sticker on the back window. Sam took a breath and pulled open the door.

The floor creaked as he entered. Sam scanned his surroundings. The interior of the combined gas station and diner appeared to be deserted. Fluorescent lights flickered and buzzed overhead. Otherwise, silence reigned. A wall cooler filled with beer and soda stood against the far wall. A rack containing bags of chips, and a shelf unit stacked with candy bars on one side and automotive supplies on the other, stood near the cashier's counter. Tables and chairs occupied the rest of the modest room. A faint clatter came from what Sam assumed was the kitchen. He rattled the bathroom doorknob but found it locked. Not knowing what else to do, he paced back to the cashier's counter.

Sam noticed a service bell sitting on the counter beside the register. A hand-written note taped to the side of the bell read: *I'm either cooking in back or I finally kicked the bucket. Ring the bell to find out which!*

Smiling—mostly because he heard reassuring sounds coming from the diner's kitchen—Sam slapped the top of the bell with his palm. Tufts of curly white hair became visible through the serving window. The head bobbed as a sandpapery voice called out a greeting.

A diminutive, elderly woman emerged from the kitchen. She

wore horn-rimmed glasses and a faded floral print housedress beneath a white apron tied around her waist. Her wrinkled face spoke of a lifetime of joys and sorrows, equally measured. She was the most grandmotherly-looking old woman Sam had ever seen outside of a children's picture book.

"Sorry if I kept you waiting. I was making sandwiches for tomorrow's lunch rush." The old woman wiped her liver-spotted hands on her apron. "Now, how can I help?"

"I need to prepay for gas," Sam said. "And I'd like to use your restroom, but the door is locked. Do I need a key to—?"

Behind him, the bathroom door opened. A bearded man of about forty emerged, smoothing a checked flannel shirt over a generous expanse of beer gut. He glanced at Sam, sneered, and said, "You're a long way from the 'hood. You get lost?"

Sam said nothing. Part of him wanted to twist the loudmouth's arm behind his back until he apologized, but he knew that would only bring more trouble.

The old woman frowned and spoke to Sam. "Don't mind him. Rodney's mother, bless her heart, dropped him on his head when he was just a baby. He ain't been right since."

Rodney scowled at her and dropped into a chair at one of the dining area's tables.

Sam gave the old woman a thin-lipped smile. "Maybe I better just pay for the gas and be on my way."

"Nonsense. I'm the owner of this establishment, not him."

Rodney, idly toying with a pair of salt and pepper shakers, snorted. "Lord, Marie, he's stinkin' up the place! Can't you get him out of here?"

"Rodney Lee Yates, if you don't shut your mouth, I'll never give you a sandwich on the house again."

Remembering he had another reason to be on his way, Sam hurried into the tiny restroom and emptied his bladder. At the basin, he ran cool water and washed his hands and face. When he emerged, Sam noted that Rodney now held a bottle of soda and stood staring out the dust-grimed front window.

"Christ on a crutch; here comes another one!"

Sam exchanged a glance with Marie and strode to the diner's front door. His pounding blood rang in his ears.

Halfway between the diner's entrance and Sam's car stood The Runner.

"Why's he just standing there?" Rodney asked. He turned on Sam, his eyes filled with accusation. "Is he waitin' for you to give him the signal? You two plannin' to rob the place?"

Sam shook his head. "I don't know him," he said. "He's been following me and harassing me all day."

Marie frowned. "Should I phone the sheriff?"

"That old fart'll take hours to get here," Rodney said. "I got my Weatherby in the truck."

"We'll all be safer if your hunting rifle stays right where it is," Marie said. She turned to Sam. "You say he's been harassing you?"

Sam looked again at the strange man who kept materializing along his journey. He stood immobile, staring at the building. What did he want? He didn't need a ride, as Sam had first assumed. The man's motives puzzled Sam, just as his strange abilities confounded him.

Another figure came into view, and Sam realized much to his chagrin that Marie had slipped out the door unnoticed. She'd apparently taken it upon herself to speak to the stranger. Her earlier words echoed in his mind. *I'm the owner of this establishment.*

"What's she doin'?" Rodney asked. Sam recognized the question's rhetorical nature and kept silent.

In the parking lot, Marie said something to the strange man. He stared at her, his features blank. The old woman indicated the road, and then gestured behind her, toward the diner. Sam wondered if he could slip out the back, circle the building, and be ready to make his escape. *But what good would it do?* Sam wondered. *This guy shows up everywhere I go.*

The Runner spoke. Sam didn't need to be a proficient lip reader to make out his words. It seemed the stranger's entire vocabulary consisted of that single statement, always followed by the same request.

Marie put her hands on her narrow hips. The stranger, still

facing her, lifted one hand and gave her the finger.

"You son of a bitch!" Rodney balled his hands into fists and bounded for the door.

"Wait!" Sam warned. *The middle finger again; something I showed him first.* He pictured The Runner, his face impassive, flipping him the bird from beside the billboard.

Rodney shoved him roughly into the counter's edge. "I'll deal with you in a minute," he snarled.

Sam's thoughts raced. *Mimicry.* What had Sam done after giving the stranger the finger? He'd run him over with his car.

Rodney reached the pair and stepped between them. He put his hand in the center of the stranger's chest and shoved. The man tottered backward but showed no outward dismay at getting pushed. He righted himself, reached out, and took hold of Rodney's arm just above the elbow.

Even through the dust-grimed glass, the vibrancy of the subsequent burst of blood shocked Sam.

Rodney seemed to collapse in upon himself, like an open can of soda crushed by someone's hand. The redneck convulsed and sagged, gushing blood. He would have fallen but the stranger held onto him, staring at his face as if expecting a different response. Rodney's head lolled and Sam endured the horror of seeing brains burst from the big man's misshapen skull, like someone had stepped on a baked potato. The Runner let go of Rodney's arm. The dead man toppled, and a light of recognition illuminated Sam's brain. Lying on the ground, Rodney looked like someone had run him over with an automobile.

I did that, Sam realized. *This* thing *is learning. It tried to communicate but took a life instead. It can't differentiate.*

Marie stood facing the stranger. Sam knew he needed to act fast. Rodney had said he had a rifle in his truck. If he made a run for it, Sam felt sure he'd find the door unlocked. But then what? If he shot the stranger, it would only incapacitate him for a few moments. And he now understood the bald man could pass the physical effect of whatever damage Sam inflicted on to the next person he encountered.

Sam knew he had to consider Marie's safety and, if he could, her emotional well-being. In his mind's eye, he saw himself sprinting from the door and heroically scooping her up around her waist but dismissed the idea. *I'll distract him*, he decided. *Give her the chance to get back inside the store. It's me he wants.*

Sam slipped out the door. "Marie," he called. "Come back inside, lock all the doors, and phone the sheriff."

"What about you?" she asked, not moving. Sam realized she treated the stranger as one would a rattlesnake. Movement could be perceived as an attack. Better to stand still.

"I'm going to distract him." Sam circled the pair on their left, with Rodney's mutilated corpse between them. Sam kept his eyes on The Runner.

The blood-spattered stranger turned toward him, returning his gaze. "I am stranded. Can you provide transportation?"

"Where are you headed?" Sam had reached the bumper of his car. He paused to ensure the man was still watching him. Marie took a step backward.

The man with the milky eye only repeated the same words. Marie took measured steps toward the entrance. Sam kept his gaze fixed on the stranger. *What are you?* He wondered. *You're not a product of my imagination, but you're not an ordinary human either.* Sam had heard some crazy stories during his years in the Air Force, but nothing that could explain this. This was science fiction invading reality. Could it be an alien life form? Some type of advanced artificial intelligence? *Either way, there's something wrong with it. Something has corrupted its cognitive abilities.*

Marie had reached the door. He called to her.

"I'm sorry about all of this. I'm going to do my best to lure him away, so you'll be safe."

Marie, her face as white as her apron, said nothing. She disappeared into the building. In the silence, Sam heard the door close, and a deadbolt click into place.

The bald man recited his short speech again. Sam eased around the far corner of the sedan, closer now to the driver's side door.

Without warning, the strange man plunged toward him.

What if it's not me he wants? His car was the only other common aspect in all this. The man had rounded the front of the sedan. Sam turned and ran for Rodney's dusty truck. He found it locked, and spun back around, relieved to see The Runner still standing beside his car. Sam knew what he had to do but dreaded it. He kept his eye on the bald man and approached Rodney's corpse.

Sam slid his fingertips over the battered body until he located a promising hunk of metal in the dead man's pocket. Getting his fingers into the pocket proved a challenge; Rodney's twisted position thwarted his attempts. Sam wondered if the keys might be as bent and broken as their mangled owner. At last, he tugged a ring of bloodied keys from the pocket. They looked intact. Relief washed over him. He ran back to the truck, unlocked the door, and reached for the rifle hanging on the gun rack. He lifted it, thumbed the safety off, and chambered a round of ammunition. *Bless him for being crazy enough to drive around with a loaded rifle hanging behind his head.*

The Runner had crossed the gravel lot and now stood within arm's reach. Sam's skin prickled in revulsion. He pressed the end of the rifle barrel against the strange man's chest and pulled the trigger. The Runner jerked and sprawled to the gravel. Other than a small ring of burned cloth on his chest, he seemed to bear no physical injury. He lay in the grit and dust, staring up into the afternoon sky, as if contemplating the clouds.

Sam jumped behind the wheel and keyed the ignition.

He backed up and then drove up alongside the building until the passenger door drew parallel to the diner's entrance. Sam yanked out his wallet, removed all his remaining cash, and slid across the seat. He leaned the Weatherby against the wall next to the diner's entrance and folded the cash under the butt of the gun. Having done what he could for Marie and counting on the stranger to continue his single-minded pursuit, Sam slid back behind the wheel and put the truck in gear. Tires sprayed dust and gravel as Sam roared out of the lot. He turned at the first crossroad he encountered and aimed the pickup toward the interstate with the gas pedal mashed to the floor.

***

Sam reached the main highway in record time, but the increase in traffic made him feel uneasy rather than safer. He wondered what would happen if he got pulled over driving a truck that didn't belong to him. Chewing on his lip, he slowed, and steered onto the shoulder. Using the tail of his shirt, he wiped the steering wheel and anything else he thought he might have touched. He left the keys in the ignition and slid out the passenger door onto the grassy ditch.

Sam jogged along the shoulder away from the truck. The sun had settled beneath the horizon and the headlight beams of the oncoming vehicles made Sam feel hunted. His road trip had gone horribly awry. The lies he'd told haunted him. Sam tried to banish all thought except the desire to get home to see his family. He regretted not phoning Adina before leaving the motel. Although, if he found a payphone and called her now, what would he say? *Sorry I bailed on my responsibilities as a husband and a father this weekend. I guess I'm my own worst enemy. Funny story, though; I met a man who's worse. In fact, he might be the death of me.*

An idea came to him. If he hitchhiked and found a ride the rest of the way home, maybe—just maybe—that would shake The Runner's pursuit. Perhaps he could even fall asleep; that might break their connection as well and allow Sam to escape.

He moved from the ditch onto the shoulder and put out his thumb. Cars and trucks roared past him. After five minutes of walking, doubts began to crowd his thoughts. *Nobody in their right mind would pick up someone walking alongside the highway at nightfall.*

Misgiving slowed Sam's steps. What if he was alone and without a means of escape the next time his milky-eyed stalker appeared?

Sam stopped walking. He considered returning to the pickup. He'd turn on the flashers and beg a ride to the next town. One car passed him traveling slower than the others. He had started to turn, intending to retrace his steps, when he saw the vehicle's brake lights illuminate. The driver steered onto the shoulder and waited.

Surprise and hope intermingled inside him. Sam jogged toward the waiting vehicle. As he approached, Sam saw the car in detail. It was a classic: green, with a white hardtop. The taillights illuminated the silver letters on the back of the car. It was a Buick Skylark. Sam saw rust spots on the side panels around the wheel wells. *I've seen this car before*. He reached the passenger door and stooped to look in at the driver.

The old woman behind the wheel wore a faded floral print dress. An old-fashioned headscarf covered her white curls. A black purse roughly the size and shape of a concrete block sat on the seat beside her. She looked like someone heading to a church basement supper.

Sam opened the car door. Marie gazed at him from the driver's seat.

"You going to stand there staring, or are you going to get in and tell an old lady what in the world this is about?"

***

"So, you don't know who this fella is, but he's been chasing you all day?"

Sam sat in the passenger seat, his hands lying flat on his thighs. He hadn't realized how badly they ached from clutching steering wheels until now. Sam had told Marie everything, even admitting he'd lied to his wife just to get away for a few days. "Yes, ma'am, that's about the gist of it."

"And he just shows up out of thin air."

"Sure seems that way," Sam said. "Though I can't explain how he does it. At first, I thought I was imagining him."

"'There are more things in heaven and earth than are dreamt of in our philosophy.'"

Marie's words sent a shiver down Sam's spine. He glanced at her, sitting primly behind the wheel as they sped down the interstate. "Shakespeare, right?"

The old woman nodded. "I paraphrased. Read it years ago in *Reader's Digest*."

Sam smiled and let his mind drift. He recalled a pair of magnets he played with as a child whenever he visited his grandparents. They were a matched pair of Scottish terriers, one black and one originally white but yellowed with age. He still remembered the delighted thrill he felt when the magnets snapped together for the first time. He played endless games, repelling one terrier across the table with the other, and then turning the magnet around so they'd snap together nose to nose. One by itself just sat there, but if you moved the other magnet close enough...

"He'll keep coming for you, won't he?" Marie's question drew Sam from his reverie.

"I think so."

"How can you get rid of him?"

He shifted in his seat and sighed. "I just don't know. He sticks with me no matter where I go."

"Can you carry a conversation with him? Does he respond, I mean?"

"I've spoken to him, but all he ever says is the same thing about being stranded."

"He does have a bee in his bonnet about needing a ride, doesn't he?"

"I just can't decide if he's fixated on it, or if that's all he is able to say."

"Like he's lost his wits?"

"Something like that."

They sped past another mile marker. Sam saw a sign for a tiny roadside town.

"Yet he keeps coming," Marie said, barely audible above the hum of the tires on the road. "What if, instead of running away from him, you walked right up to him and told him to leave you alone?"

Sam didn't respond right away. Part of what she'd said resonated in his mind. *Instead of running away.* Sam had run away from his responsibilities as a husband and father. He'd lied to Adina. The moment before he'd embarked on his journey home, the stranger had appeared. Sam thought back to the motel parking lot and tried to remember what he'd been thinking. Had something in his thoughts drawn the stranger to him?

And ever since their first encounter, he'd been running from the other man. *I nicknamed him "The Runner," but I'm the one who ran away from my family this weekend.*

"Maybe you're right," Sam said at last. "I'll try to talk to him face to face one more time."

Marie glanced at him but didn't speak. Sam appreciated her presence and her patience.

"I think maybe *he thinks* I want to trade places with him. But he—or it—doesn't know how to communicate that." Sam felt a rush of excitement, as if a crucial puzzle piece had fallen into place. "What he keeps saying isn't a plea, it's an offer."

Marie's wrinkled face glowed in the dashboard light. "So you need to reject his offer."

"I have, though!" Sam said. "I've told him no several times."

"Maybe you're not speaking in a language he understands."

"How else would I—"

Marie cut him off. "You told me earlier you visited the city just to get away from your family."

Sam felt a twinge of guilt. "Yes, ma'am."

"Do you still feel like running away from them?"

"No!" Sam said. "I want to see my family again more than anything else. If I was supposed to learn a lesson, I damn sure learned it. I'm a changed man. No more running away from my responsibilities."

Marie tapped the brake pedal, and the old Buick began to slow.

"What are you doing?" Sam asked.

"Taking this exit so we can pull over, of course." Marie said. "You've had a change of heart. You know it, and I know it, but does 'The Runner,' as you call him, know it? I think it's time you two had a heart to heart, and the sooner the better, in my opinion."

Sam's skin broke out in goosebumps at the idea of The Runner materializing, specter-like, from the darkness as soon as Marie stopped the car.

At the crossroads she paused, considered, and turned left. Sam grew more nervous. He felt too warm and rolled his window down to let the night air cool his skin. A cluster of lights appeared in the distance and Sam realized they had left the highway near the tiny town advertised on the highway sign.

The Buick's headlamps revealed a cornfield to their right. Sam spotted a hand-painted sign and read it aloud. "Happy Halloween! Welcome to the Kiddie Korn Maze. Admission five dollars."

"Should I stop here?" Marie asked.

Sam nodded. "Seems appropriate. I feel like I've been going in circles all day."

Marie put her car in park and turned off the engine. "Remember what's in your heart," she said. "Good luck, Sam."

"Thank you," Sam felt a lump in his throat. "For everything, I mean. You're a diamond in a world of dirt."

"That's sweet of you to say." Marie reached out and gave his forearm a reassuring squeeze. "Now go out there and show him—or it—you've had a change of heart."

Sam stood beside the old Buick listening to the ticking of the cooling engine and the shrill drone of competing cricket choirs. The cool night breeze danced across his skin. He made his way toward the entrance to the corn maze.

Clouds scudded across the dark sky. Just as Sam reached the entrance to the maze, a cloudbank hid the moon from view. He could no longer see the lights of the town. Sam stood peering into the recessed darkness, waiting for his eyes to adjust. The cornstalk leaves rustled and hissed.

Shrouded within the darkness of the maze, a familiar voice spoke.

"I am stranded. Can you provide transportation?"

Sam visualized The Runner, standing somewhere ahead of him. In his mind's eye, the moon's glow reflected on the tall man's bald scalp and on his cataract-laden eye. Sam knew he had to find The Runner, had to end this face to face, but he also dreaded meeting him in the rows.

He began walking. After only two turns, he felt as if he'd lost his bearings. He kept up his flagging courage by telling himself that when the strange being read his true feelings, he'd give up his pursuit and leave him alone. He hurried along, making right and left turns in frantic, haphazard fashion. *Why did I walk in here? In the daytime, with people around, it's probably a whole different experience. How can I find him if I am lost myself?*

Sam considered stopping. He'd wait for The Runner to find him. After all, the being seemed to have an uncanny ability to do just that. Sam crouched near the center of the Kiddie Korn Maze. The stalks loomed over him, seeming to lean in from every direction, as if conspiring to never let him leave. Claustrophobia, coupled with a panicky sense of desolation and abandonment, seized him. Sam's breaths came in labored gasps. He fought the urge to run, to bust through the cornstalks until he reached the road and Marie's car. *This is lunacy. It would be hilarious if it weren't so horrifying. It's a damn cornfield,* he told himself. *You'll be able to leave here soon.*

But his mind and spirit were at odds, like two magnets repelling each other. He'd never wanted to get away from a place or a situation so badly.

The Runner heard his renewed plea.

Sam felt fingers touch his shoulder. He experienced a gentle buzzing current and heard a short crackle. Sam tried to spin around but sprawled in the dirt. He caught only a fleeting glimpse as a figure disappeared into the adjacent rows and surrounding darkness.

He realized he itched where he'd felt the strange touch. He scratched his shoulder, and then his neck, where the itch now felt more pronounced. He looked skyward and saw the moon. Using it as his guide, he bulldozed his way through the stalks of corn.

After a minute's headlong flight, he emerged from the cornfield and stepped into short grass. Beside him, he saw a narrow ditch. Above him, he saw a sky filled with stars. Ahead of him, he saw a car. The itch had moved to the back of his skull. It kept crawling around inside him as he shuffled to the parked vehicle.

An elderly woman sat behind the wheel, watching him. He walked up to the passenger window, bent, and peered inside. The old woman recoiled. Her features betrayed her apprehension.

"Sam? What—" Her voice broke. "What's happened to your eye?"

He didn't know who Sam was. He sensed, however, that the woman wanted to leave. That was good. He needed transportation. He opened his host's mouth and communicated his request.

ABOUT THE AUTHOR

Adrian Ludens is a full-time library associate at a community library and the PA announcer for a pair of semi-pro hockey teams. He enjoys reading and writing horror fiction, listening to all types of music, watching hockey, hiking, and exploring abandoned buildings. He lives with his family in the Black Hills of South Dakota.

Visit him online via Adrian Wayne Ludens – Author on Linktree and Adrian Ludens Author on Facebook.

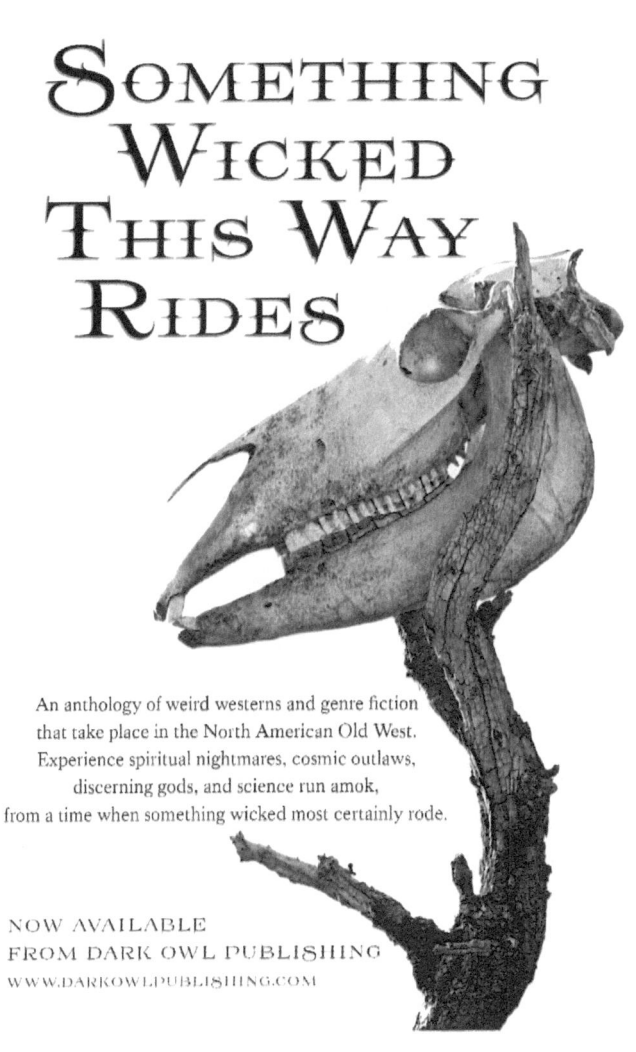

SOMETHING
WICKED
THIS WAY
RIDES

An anthology of weird westerns and genre fiction
that take place in the North American Old West.
Experience spiritual nightmares, cosmic outlaws,
discerning gods, and science run amok,
from a time when something wicked most certainly rode.

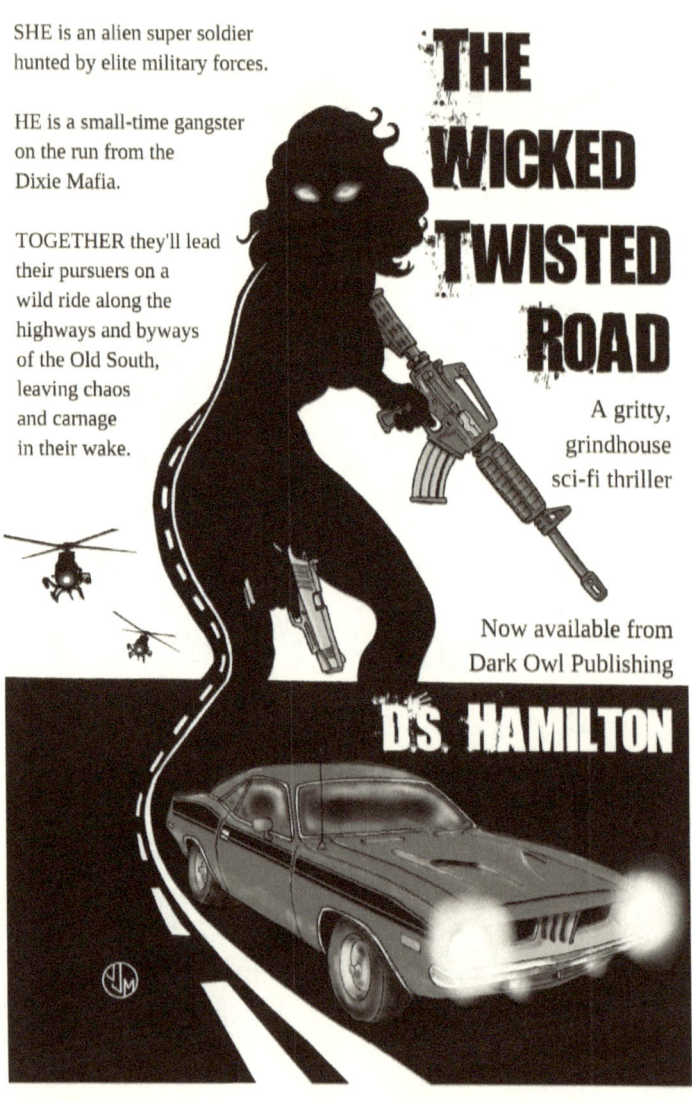

THE DARK

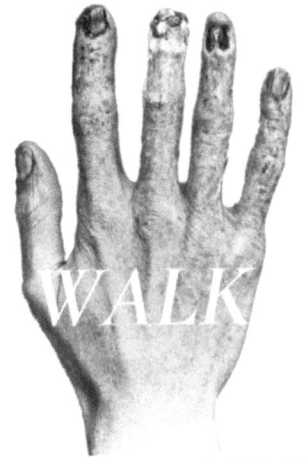

WALK

FORWARD

A HARROWING COLLECTION BY
JOHN S. MCFARLAND

Available in paperback and on Kindle from
DARK OWL PUBLISHING, LLC
www.darkowlpublishing.com